THE FISHERMAN

By
Mark D. DiRienzo

Copyright © 2011 Mark D. DiRienzo
All rights reserved.
ISBN: 0615503373
ISBN-13: 978-0615503370

DEDICATION

This first book is dedicated to the best parents a guy could ever hope to have, Larry & Gayle DiRienzo. I won the 'Parent Lottery' with both of you. You are truly the best. Thank you for everything…

Forward

When I graduated high school, I was like many of the kids you might see today: young, untested, innocent. An idealist, I was awkwardly shy, a romantic, a poet and a natural believer that good things happen to good people. I was healthy, athletic, internally I was smart enough to know that the world was a huge place and there was a lot about life I did not yet understand. I may not have been knowledgeable but I was hungry for those experiences and willing to travel to find them. Like many people my age, I wanted, no needed, adventure and felt myself invincible. In my naïveté, I unfortunately found that not all of the experiences I selfishly sought out would be good ones. Some would hurt me, some would expose me and others would ultimately break me.

Nearly fifteen years have passed since then...no longer am I untested, new or innocent. I am the sum total of my days and nights, my memories; the ones I fight to remember and the ones I need to forget. Deep in my haunted eyes, behind my face is a scarred, lined map of those adventures, of lessons learned and of deep layered unbearable loss. This reflection stares at me, reminds me of the coldness of an empty soul rich in experiences that were never longed for. I am what I have become; traveling hate. I used to be a fisher of men, now all I do is kill them.

PART ONE

CHAPTER #1

Buffalo New York in February is a total mess. With the temperature hovering around 1 degree and everything covered in snow the sky stayed completely grey with total darkness arriving about 4:30 in the afternoon. Every day seemed the same, just a mess.

Right now looking outside I could see it was at least not snowing which is a plus. In another life, I had spent a few years in a small suburb of Buffalo, so this dreary weather pattern, even as cold as it was, was only a reminder of what I know I left behind. The weather today would actually help me with my current job. It would aid in concealing my identity as I had to kill a man, especially if the weather blessed me with fresh falling snow, after the job was complete.

Richard Lazlo was the owner of a small bar and night club ironically called "The Office". Everyone on this little stretch of heaven on West Chippewa Street refers to him as 'Fat Ritchie". Even though he didn't know it or believe it, Fat Ritchie was not a major player in the local crime scene. He completely believed he was a big time hustler heartily ruling his small crew of wannabe fraudsters with a heavy hand and a flippant referral to them as his "family". Personally I think he spent too much time watching old Tony Soprano reruns.

Drugs and hookers ran in and out of his club. He had even started pretending to be a bookie in his spare time, more than likely he thought he was a real bookie though. In his ego filled mind, it clearly only made sense to start big or go home. This meant booking all sorts of sporting events. For the major guys in Buffalo, Fat Ritchie wasn't even a blip on the mobster radar screen. His operation was so small time it was nearly cute, like he was playing a game and the real players never let him know that at the end of the game he wasn't moving pawns, he was the pawn. Fat Ritchie was not even minutely a threat to their organizations.

I was hired to kill him because Fat Ritchie was blatantly stealing. He started out in the book making business by booking bets he couldn't cover and lost. Ultimately the little fat man had to borrow money from one of the major guys in Buffalo, Salvatore DiFlippo. Twenty thousand dollars was his first lend and Fat had managed to pay back only eight thousand minus the vig. Up until a month ago, Ritchie was current on his payments and the arrangement was working out well, but that was a month ago.

For whatever reason; be it his inflated ego that matched his ridiculously mobster-esque midsection that made his arms look reminiscent of a tyrannosaurus as they flailed around waving people in or away from him like they held real power, or his visions of grandeur and misunderstanding of his real place in the world that I now lived in, Fat Ritchie decided he was done paying back DiFlippo. The fact he was bleeding cash trying to open a second bar down on Chippewa Street could also have been a motivator, but when DiFlippo's collectors called to take their payment, Fat Ritchie didn't answer. Salvatore DiFlippo is a very patient man which is why the disrespect Fat Ritchie was showing towards DiFlippo by not conducting himself according to the rules of the game he thought he was playing, couldn't go unanswered. And even the burgeoning of New York organizations were watching…closely.

I considered Salvatore DiFlippo a friend. Very nearly the only one I had left. He had helped me walk through a very dark time in my life. Most of the work I did was through him, either hiring me out personally, or people he knew called on me through his personal and powerful referral. Occasionally, I got requests from someone new, just hearing about me word of mouth, but that was not the norm. When I first met Sal I knew I was in a safe place for my profession. Sal was always honest with me and didn't try to bullshit me. As a bonus he never argued about my going rate. $25,000: that is my going rate to kill. Of course that is just a basic, flat-rate job. I scout the person, learn their habits, and kill them in a way, and at a time, as I see fit. No extras. I am not a sick person; I don't take personal pleasure in killing people, or get off on it. It's just my job; I'm good at it too. My only personal rules are that I don't torture people and I don't kill children, ever.

Now of course with Sal's jobs and every one of my jobs have a personal touch if needed. If a contract requires a person to die and appear like it was an accident or natural causes, the charge is $35,000. If you want someone to disappear completely, I charge a flat rate of $50,000. My prices are all inclusive and non-negotiable. My reputation is my portfolio, I am not a show off, I am just good, fast, and precise.

I once did a job for two brothers that lived in Los Angeles. They hired me because they wanted a guy to disappear in Reno, Nevada. I told them my fee was $50,000. I should have known it was a bad idea the minute they started hemming and hawing, but I went along with it when they eventually agreed.

For all of my clients, I require half of my money up front, and the other half to be paid immediately upon completion of the job. I received $25,000 as our agreement stated, then drove from Las Vegas to Reno, found the target and made him disappear. That's when the trouble started.

First, neither brother bothered to answer my calls. I tried for what I felt like was a fair amount of time to allow them to make things right with me. However, when I finally made contact with them, I was told to "piss off" quoting them directly. They openly and blatantly refused to pay me the other $25,000 owed to me and said if I had a problem with that, I could go to the police. Funny guys, right?

I did what I had to do; I purchased a prepaid cell phone in Las Vegas and drove to LA. I stalked the brothers and was not surprised to see that they each now had a matching set of full time body-guards. I waited until they were in a rundown strip club in East LA just hanging out watching the second rate strippers sway gracelessly, it was almost like these guys had no concern in the world, like they thought they beat me and I would just go away. I was able to easily convince one of the girls to get one of the brother's personal cell phone numbers with a $50.00 bill.

Obviously, the last thing the brothers were thinking was that I was standing virtually right behind them breathing in the same cheap cherry scented smoke filled air, watching. I waited an hour or so, when they were good and drunk and then made the call. My 702 area code from my prepaid Vegas cell made them stupidly think I was still at a safe distance. The "brothers' brave" I think of them today, frivolously blurted out their rant and spite for me over the phone even foolishly threatened to "take me out" if I kept harassing them for their agreed upon payment.

I smiled confidently as I stepped into the private room they audaciously rented in the back of club. I didn't feel anything: mercy, sympathy or remorse for what I was about to do, even when one brother pissed in his pants and the other one started to cry. Clearly they didn't believe my portfolio was all it was hyped to be.

It was nice of them to offer me anything I wanted: money, drugs, and women, even themselves sexually. This was a last ditch effort for anything and everything I could ever want and I was pretty sure they didn't even have my $25,000.

After killing their body guards I killed both of them. Strip clubs are a great place to kill people because they are loud; everybody minds their own business, no one wants to be seen and DNA is everywhere. I quietly left the VIP room, tipped the girl on the bar, and went home. I didn't get my money but I did get a sense of satisfaction that my reputation was still intact.

In this business, reputation is everything. Perception is reality. If one guy gets over on you, everyone else will think you're weak and will try to get over on you until one day, you're the chump staring down the barrel of a loaded gun. Then it's game over, lights out, thanks for playing. I leaned that from Sal.

Rounding the corner onto Chippewa I was thinking of how this would probably need to go down. Fat Ritchie is a big guy, at six feet four inches tall, and at least three hundred fifty pounds of shear selfish fulfillment. Not only a drug abuser of all things recreational, he also dabbles in steroids. While overweight, he is also very muscular and strong that would at least give this job a tinge of uncertainty. Fat Ritchie's right hand man a guy named Vincent "Jumbo" Caranza makes Fat Ritchie look like a small child when they stand next to each other.

I knew when taking this job I would probably have to take out Jumbo as well. That didn't bother me. From what I learned about Jumbo, I probably wouldn't have liked him anyway, not like we were going to be buddies. Usually if I have to eliminate more than one person, I charge an extra five thousand dollars, but Sal was a friend I would throw Jumbo in for nothing, I get a lot of business from him anyway, why charge him extra? The payoff would come later in more business and safety.

Down the block from Fat Ritchie's bar, The Office, I waited for him to saunter into my view. Ten days of following him I know his routine well. Tonight was optimal to get this job over with because I knew he would show up for his weekly poker game. This needed to be public, personal even. In Sal's honor I wanted Fat Ritchie to die in the place he felt most comfortable and most secure; his very own pride and joy, his baby, his own bar. This night would send a message to the public and any other organizations watching not to cross my friend and employer, Salvatore DiFlippo.

10:30 pm Fat Ritchie pulled up in front of The Office with the iconic Jumbo. Stepping down out of Jumbo's Escalade they confidently walked into the bar. The poker game would start as usual, in about 30 minutes. Thinking about my duties, I planned on taking out Ritchie and probably Jumbo too, right in the middle of the poker game.

I wasn't worried about the other guys he was playing with. They were small time guys, complete bottom feeders. They hung around Fat Ritchie for free handouts and left over business, girls, deals, and dough. This is what made them feel important and tough; too bad it didn't actually make them important and tough. When push came to shove, I was sure these people would run like hell, and if I was lucky piss their pants too just like those brothers in LA.

I was not worried about being identified in this pathetic crowd tonight, but it is fun to spice it up from time to time. Though a clear athletic stand out in high school, I turned out to be just plain' Joe Average. I stand at six feet two inches tall, weigh around 200 pounds, and am fairly physically fit. My hair is black and I keep it short and neat, nothing fancy or too cutting edge, nothing remotely memorable. I have boring brown eyes that I have been told a time or two are deep and penetrating. I know they are really just eyes that have seen far too much. For added intrigue, this evening I decided to acquire a full dark brown beard and eye glasses. Normally, I am clean shaven and thankfully do not require glasses or contacts. Dark blue jeans, black boots and a long black trench coat completed my ensemble with a black, winter watchman's cap to top it all off.

Of course like a thousand other guys milling around on Chippewa Street tonight I also have on my favorite skin tight, black leather gloves. 10:50 pm blinks onto the dash clock making a mental check list of where I parked, how to get out of town and what is around me, it's time to go. I get out of my falsely registered rent-a-car and head toward The Office.

I have many false identities I use around the country. I keep one in Buffalo, Orlando, Dallas, Chicago, Vegas and one in Los Angeles. Every identity comes with a vehicle, a place to live, and a real job, at least on paper. In Buffalo and Orlando, I own my own consulting firm. In Chicago I own two different coin operated car washes. I just hire people to run them. In Vegas, I own a coin operated laundry mat. Again, I only need to hire people to run these places; I don't even care about the profits and losses.

I usually have one of Sal's guys do the hiring for me as well. In Los Angeles, my profession is an easy fit: "Actor" just like millions of other wanna-be's. In each city, I make a modest living and pay my taxes in full and on time every year. My rent and utilities automatically draft out of a bank account in the name on the apartment of whatever city I am needed in. I visit these places once in a while, I try to make sure I am around once or twice every other month, or so

There are many aspects to the dimensional properties of being in the line of work I am. When doing a job, it is important that I use a different identity from one of my "permanent reflections". I think of them as reflections because I know when I look in the mirror I am today going to be whomever stares back in my reflection. During a job, I have different "throw away" identities I use. I keep the permanent identities and the ones I use on jobs completely separate. I will only use an identity one time, so it is usual for me to react to any name I am called as if it is my own. I know exactly how to find several ID's, employee pass cards, high balance credit cards, and even local discount shopping cards to back up both my "permanent" and "throw away" identities. Once I have used an identity in direct association with a job, I burn everything relevant to that "person who committed the job" and move on to a different one. Costly, yes, but when that is why I charge the rates that I do. I don't put a price on my personal safety.

Unnoticed, I walk into the bar knowing the only security cameras are over the register tills and the walk-in alcohol storage cooler. Simply, enough the club is set up in a giant rectangle. Through the front doors standing looking toward the back of the building, the bar is on the left hand side and several tables are on the right hand side. Walking past the bar, I come to an open area that has a haphazardly purchased and placed old pool table and a dart board to make the place look legit. Like last time, and every other time I had been in this dump, the bar was crowded and the music is way too loud, but then that will just make my life a lot easier. After the cheap pool table, a hallway with three cutely labeled doors, "Smooth" I thought to myself. The left door says "PIMPS", the right "HO'S" and the one in the middle says "PRIVATE". I figured in this case I would take door number two, Private. The only other door in the place is the one behind the bar and that leads to the walk-in cooler, a smaller office, and the receiving dock for beer and liquor shipments. This just had to be a fire hazard and I almost wish I would have thought of that sooner.

I pushed through the door marked "PRIVATE", stupidly unlocked as it was on past occasions I was here, and stood in the small vestibule. In front of me is the emergency exit with the sign that was broken, unlit, and disgusting from years of tobacco abuse that led outside to the back alley where I would soon emerge ready to move on to the next job.

Previous visits to the bar allowed me to disabled the alarm on the door, which I really didn't have to waste my time doing since clearly Ritchie had paid off the fire inspector as it wasn't even working in the first place. I cut the wires just in case but I chuckled to myself at the complete idiot this guy was. To my left is another door with faded yellow glass with wire through it that was I am sure "safety" or in this case just old and pathetic that will lead right into Fat Ritchie's ego filled man cave or private office as it said on the door.

Having been in that office on a previous visit while the day bartender was busy receiving beer on the back dock, smoking a cigar and feeling safe and high on life with his aspiring criminal colleagues all the while Fat Ritchie was getting his rocks off back at his apartment with one of his two-dollar hookers who were more than likely not even qualified to go into the room marked "HO's", I scouted the office made sure the alarm was disabled on the back door, and plotted Sal's revenge. Thank God for stupid self-assured people, otherwise I would have had to break in after hours and scout it then. That's the least He could provide for me anyway.

I walked through the door to Fat Ritchie's office acting as if I was lost. In the back corner, an oversized mahogany desk with a tall black leather hobnail and wood accented chair behind it and a upscale computer that screamed money as the triple flat screen synced the screen saver through each other like it was one giant screen showing pictures of islands and sexy women, well that was what was on it when I cased the place anyway. On a side table, he had an aged dusty looking DVR that recorded his security cameras showing nine squares available for viewing, only two had video though, the other seven were black because clearly he didn't think he needed video and only had the two cameras. All good for me though since he never saw me coming.

In the center of the room was a top of the line poker table like the ones you find in high stakes rooms in top floors of Vegas casinos. Racks of poker chips lined the side wall with a safe and a gun. I thought to myself, "shouldn't someone be holding the gun, oh well." Immediately to my right was the ridiculous lounge area with a 65" plasma TV floor to ceiling speaker bars, stand-alone ashtrays that looked antique and a rich deep seated burgundy leather couch and two matching reclining chairs. Sure Fat Ritchie was a drug dealing low life scum bag, but he did have nice taste…in his personal office at least.

There they all were, sitting at the poker table smoke swirls hovering above their gleaming foreheads like smog on a high ozone day in Los Angeles. Fat Ritchie at the head of the table nearest the dummy safe which only had the money put out for chips and stayed empty the rest of its life. Predictable Jumbo and four other people I did not know sat all around him. I thought I recognized two of the guys as being on Fat Ritchie's crew, but I did not recognize the other two. Jumbo was the first to notice my presence and before he could say anything, I said hastily, "I'm sorry; I thought this was the restroom."

Fat Ritchie looked annoyed and as if he had just heard the punch line to a sort-of funny joke and Jumbo authoritatively said, "The bathroom is back the way you came. Now get out."

"Actually, I don't have to use the restroom. I just need a minute of Fat Ritchie's time…"

"Make an appointment; he's busy, right Ritchie? You're busy?" Jumbo replied with a quippy laugh and a halfcocked smile.

"Like the man said, I'm busy. Make an appointment and walk out now. While you still can." He said with laughter still dripping off his lit Cuban, he played another stack of chips on the table.

Empty threats, sad, I wasn't even scared, I felt like I had done this so many times that I was practically able to say their lines before they did, like on a Broadway play or as if I was watching a movie I had seen ten thousand times before. So I brushed off Fat Ritchie's remarks and said "Nope, this can't wait. I've come to settle a debt you have with Salvatore DiFlippo."

With this, Fat Ritchie's eyes got hard, the room stopped moving, and even the smoke quit swirling in the air, frozen. Jumbo put his cards down and put his hand below the table.

This was my favorite part, the part where I could extend grace. I could let them all out of the deal, if they were smart, likely they wouldn't be, but it was always worth a try. Before Jumbo could reach his gun, I had mine out a clear three seconds before he did and it was already pointing at him. I was trained by the best and I was an "A" student. The act was like magic. One second my hand was empty, the next there was a gun in it.

"Jumbo, I wouldn't do that if I were you. You're too fat and slow. My business here this evening is with Fat Ritchie. Everyone else is free to go if you so choose."

It appeared that everyone else at the table, including Jumbo, wanted to leave as they all stood to scamper off to safety at my request and open invitation for life. Before any of them could react, Fat Ritchie said "Nobodies fucking going anywhere. I can't believe this bull-shit. I am really insulted here. You come here, into my club, point a gun at me, insult me, threaten me, and call me a fucking dead beat in front of my friends. You want the money? Fine. I'll pay him the damn money. I worked out the final payment already with Dominick, but if that's not fast enough for Mr. big time DiFlippo, I'll give you the cash right now. Jumbo, get him the priss' money." He said as he took another draw off his cigar and threw yet another chip onto the table like he didn't care I was standing there with a gun to his head.

The Dominick Fat Ritchie was referring to was Sal's under-boss, or #1 guy, Dominick Mazzio. Either Fat Ritchie was lying, or Mazzio was running something behind Sal's back. I couldn't worry about it right now; I would deal with him later.

"Jumbo, sit! Everybody else, keep your hands flat on the table. Anyone moves and all bets are off. Ritchie, get your fat ass up and get me Sal's money yourself"

I could see hatred in Fat Ritchie's eyes. I knew if I didn't kill him here tonight, he would use all of his extremely limited resources to hunt me all the way to the city line where his money and interest would run out. Without a word, Ritchie got up, showed his hands in some kind of pathetic old west movie fashion as to tell me he surrenders, chuckled, and went to the wall safe hidden behind the audacious painting of himself in a king's robe and throne with money scattered all around him on the floor across the room.

I knew the order in which I would shoot. I also knew Fat Ritchie had a pistol in his safe since the combination was painted on one of the bills as a serial number nearest the bottom of the painting and eye level to the person swinging open the picture to expose the "hidden" safe.

When I found the combination I laughed to myself thinking Ritchie must have been proud of himself for as he commissioned this great piece of faux art thinking that bill serial number was a sneaky place to hide his safe combination.

He should have at least put serial numbers on the other bills scattered around his royal highness. In any event once that safe was open I knew the next scene in the play, Ritchie would grab his piece and make a move to shoot me.

I figured, while he was moving for his pistol, his crew at the table would move for theirs. If I let that happen, it would be close as to who walked away, and I didn't like things to be close. I decided not to let that happen.

The first shot hit Jumbo right in his forehead. Then I swung left and pulled the trigger two more times, striking the two I recognized as belonging in Fat Ritchie's crew. I didn't know about the other two at the table, so I shot two more times and eliminated them quickly. Five shots, less than five seconds, five people dead. Fat Ritchie didn't have time to react, and did what any man in his situation would do: He dropped to the floor and begged for mercy. Too bad my call for grace had run out three minutes earlier and their dear friend Ritchie had made them stay.

I was using a Beretta 90-TWO Type F, .40 caliber. The gun was very nice and I would regret having to dump it in the Niagara River later. It was no louder than any other gun, but with the loud music out front, and the office being in the back, I wasn't worried that anyone heard. I shrugged my shoulders back to let out the tension of the recoil from my shoulders.

"Ritchie, you're going to do exactly as I say. If you deviate from anything I say, no matter how small it is, I will kill you immediately. Get up off the floor, unlock your safe, open the door and step away. If you think you can reach that piece in your safe before I kill you, you're sadly mistaken. Nothing would make me happier than killing you, but as much as I have fantasized about it all day, I am not allowed to unless you provoke it"

Well, it was a little lie. I wanted him to believe he was walking out of here alive. I knew he would follow my instructions to the letter. Fat Ritchie opened the safe, and stepped back and kept his hands up this time with real surrender in his body language.

"Listen, I have $27,000 in that safe. I owe Mr. DiFlippo $12,000 plus $7,500 more for vig. Take it you fucking prick. If you take any more money out of that safe, I will hunt you down and find you, you sick fuck. You didn't have to kill everybody. I would have paid."

"Ritchie, I lied to you. I was sent here to kill you because you reneged on a deal with Salvatore DiFlippo. You're a classless piece of shit, and the world will be a better place without you."

One more shot and the world was a better place. I would count the money later, but I could tell it was at least what was owed to Sal.

If it was more, well if I am on a job and come across a victim's money over and above the debt owed, I keep it. I think of it as a bonus for a job well done, like a delivery driver tip. What the hell, the victim no longer has any use for it, right? I also took his pistol, noticing the serial number had been burned off with acid, I thought to myself that this was cheap, a gun a bottom-feeder would have. Ritchie couldn't even get weapons without serial numbers. He had to burn them off himself. That just showed how low caliber a boss he was, and I was almost embarrassed for him.

There was also a gallon sized clear plastic bag filled with a white powdery substance. Assuming it was cocaine, I threw it gingerly onto the poker table. Maybe the police would think this was a drug deal of some sort that went south. I thought myself generous to give some rookie cop a great mob story to tell his grandkids. I was getting so old at this job that I could almost read the headlines in the morning, if they found these guys by then. Later I would find out that Fat Ritchie lied, there was only $25,000. The fat looser even in death lightened my tip! What a joke.

I pocketed everything I needed leaving behind the crummy gaudy jewelry and drugs and took off out the back door. I walked up the street to my rental car knowing I needed to return it back to the airport. On the way there, I broke the Berretta down and tossed the pieces in the Niagara River. It made me a little sad because it was a great gun, amazing craftsmanship. After that, I stopped at a 7-11 off a side street. In the back of the building, there were two homeless men nearby warming themselves next to a barrel fire. I knew they would be here, as I had scouted this out as well. I gave each man $100 and a bottle of whiskey I bought them earlier in the day, they took their money and booze and left. I burned all of my identification and credit cards in their fire deleting from the universe the name I was using.

After that, I went and drove around finding a different convenience store and purchased a bag of potato chips, a blue slush, and a pack of condoms. I drove about a mile from the airport, stopped on the side of a bridge underpass, crushed the chips and dumped part of them on the back seat and then I wiped the entire car down with my shirt. By leaving the car messy, my straw on the floor and cup open and partly empty in the cup holder would ensure the rental people cleaned and vacuumed the car out before renting it again, eliminating any and all trace evidence of me. It was an unnecessary step, probably, but I am nothing if not meticulous about my privacy and safety.

Buffalo International Airport is small by most airport standards. I returned the rental car to the tired worn out looking Asian lady at the counter and took the shuttle to the airport. I walked around the terminal for 20 minutes checking out the magazines and listening intently to the national news to make sure I was not being followed. I went into the restroom and changed out of the clothes I was wearing and into a different outfit.

Luckily, everything I had taken out of Fat Ritchie's safe fit nicely inside my soft sided carry-on bag. The jeans and shirt I had on went into the garbage can. I left the overcoat hanging in the stall I had used. It would make a nice gift for some poor custodian. I used a pay phone at the airport and left a message for Sal with a prearranged answering service. My message was short and also prearranged.

"Hello this message is for Mr. Jones. Mr. Jones, this is Doctor Reeves, please call me at your convenience. I have your test results and everything is fine. Thank you."

If things had of ended negatively, my message would have been different, or non-existent had I not made it at all, but that theory was untested as I was still clearly the winner in all my jobs. Instead the test results would have come back inconclusive. I left the airport and hailed a cab. "Buffalo Hyatt Regency" I said throwing him a hundred. I was tired, hated to talk to cabbies, and wanted him to have a good story to tell his co-workers when he got off shift.

After checking in under my newest alias, I shaved off my beard, took a long skin scorching shower and went to sleep. My last thought before I fell asleep was not of the people I had taken from this world, but of the people that were taken away from me.

CHAPTER #2

Even with the most comfortable bed in Buffalo holding my frame in a heavenly embrace, with pillows, cool fresh sheets and my relaxing shower, I was groaning after a restless night of sleep. So I chose to keep the heavy curtains drawn and order room service. One piping hot ham & cheese omelet, crispy hash browns, a side of whole wheat toast with a pat of ice cold butter I melted between the two hot triangles of bread and a pot of searing hot black coffee. As I ate I creased open the local daily paper.

Fat Ritchie was the headline story on the chipper sunrise show. The blonde with a rock hard body and too tight shirt that appeared to be attacking her in a most unflattering way, almost looked pleased she was breaking the news and not the popular five 'o clockers like usual. Her near smile at the news Ritchie and his accompanying brood had been murdered was almost funny to me, so I smiled back. The news said the deaths "appeared" to be a drug deal or robbery gone wrong that "left six people horribly murdered in the heart of downtown". The Buffalo Police were investigating, but there were not any witnesses and they didn't have any "leads".

Immediately following Ritchie's untimely demise slash drug story aired, a small drop kick like ugly dog parade filed onto the sunrise set to announce a greet and bark play day at the local pound. Annoyed I clicked off the TV. The murder of a local "businessman" and five of his "associates" made the front page, above the fold in the local paper. The paper didn't have any more details than the straight-jacketed blonde on the TV so I didn't bother to finish the story. I actually thought she had read her lines directly from the paper, pathetic.

I ate the last piece of omelet, used the bottom piece of now butter soggy toast to wipe up any left-over food from the plate, and got dressed. After wiping down the room one final time, I checked out of the hotel and walked three blocks to an internet café. I ordered an overpriced cup of coffee that was worse than the hotel coffee and sat down at a computer in the back row that was from what I could see to be the most private location in the joint. There were only three other people in the café two looked like they had already been out running or exercising and one was circling jobs in the paper.

I went to a secure website that an associate of mine had made specifically for me and downloaded a program onto the computer I was using. This program would check the computer I was using assuring me that it was free of viruses and spy ware. It would also act as an eraser, eliminating everywhere I went on the internet. The best part about it was that once I logged off the computer, the program would terminate itself and disappear, like I was never there. Once I was sure the computer was clean, I signed into one of my encrypted e-mail accounts and checked my mail. Very few people had my address, and luckily I didn't even get spam at this address, however today there was an urgent message from Sal. I was instructed to use a secure phone and call his private line immediately. Preferably, before I left Buffalo and if I was still in Buffalo, he would like to meet with me. He said he would even send a car if I needed.

I must have read the message fourteen times due to the bizarre nature of the body of the text. Sal had never asked to see me like this before. I have to admit, I was a little nervous. I had known Sal for a lot of years and he was the only person left in this world that I actually trusted, the thought that I might not be able to made my omelet churn in my stomach. I signed off the computer and casually walked several blocks to use a payphone outside McDonalds. I called Sal's private number as instructed. He answered on the first ring.

"Good morning" He said

"Hello Sal. How are you this morning?" I said confidently and as if we talked daily.

"Very good my friend. Very good. Thanks for calling me so quickly. I would like to meet with you. As soon as you can. Are you still in the city?" He said abruptly and with a quickness that made me feel even sicker.

"Yes I am still here but I am booked on a flight that leaves in 30 minutes, can this wait?" I said confidently and with a little irritation to make it seem like I wasn't starting to sweat.

"That's no good. You can't leave yet. Please, as a favor to me, cancel your flight and come to my house. It is very important, I am sure you can afford to rebook later"

Sal had never asked me for a personal spur of the moment favor where I hoped at the end everyone lived, like this before. I was concerned and decided I would waste less energy just being intrigued instead.

I told Sal that yes; I would meet him in the afternoon at his house. I was still a tinge nervous though. I was meeting a person at a known time in their own home and I would not be able to scout the area before the meeting. In my business, this is what gets you killed.

Reasoning with myself as I walked around the city with no real destination, if Sal wanted to take me out, it would not be at his house, there was no way he would be so callous... I was hoping at least. I was tired of walking and seeing people with purpose and hope in their eyes, as they laughed together, talked on their phones, or ate at outdoor cafés and hailed a cab and took it to a small independent grocery store in a rundown neighborhood. I went into the store and purchased a quart of milk and a pack of gum. From there, I walked the neighborhood in a normal pace. I took it a bit slow at points, meandering around, checking for a tail. Nothing. I walked the streets in a small circle and then turned the circle upon itself and walked back. After about thirty minutes, I felt secure enough that I was not being followed, hoped my milk wasn't too warm, chomped on a fresh piece of gum and quickly walked to the small apartment I keep.

Knowing I was meeting with Sal directly, I wanted to be respectful and presentable. I took another shower figuring I smelled of the streets and the general outside, dressed in a sharp dark blue Ralph Lauren Purple Label Suit with a crisp white oxford unbuttoned only one time at the neck underneath.

It was one of the nicest suits I owned, if it was in fact my last day, I may as well look nice. I clamped on my big titanium Tag Huer watch on my wrist. I moved a heavy dresser that kept all my local clothes and some money taped to the top of the drawer holes and pried up a floor board underneath it. I keep most of my guns in safety deposit boxes in banks. I realize it is totally illegal to bring a firearm into a bank, but nobody ever frisks you, well I have never been frisked anyway.

I keep a few guns hidden at all my apartments. Today I decided on the .40 caliber GLOC 23. It's the compact model. I had two high capacity magazines that each held 15 rounds. You used to be able to purchase the high capacity magazines before the damned liberals had them banned. It's okay to have a magazine that holds ten rounds, but not one that holds fifteen. Go figure. I just used that as an opportunity to use those legal rounds to kill the same amount of people as the illegal ones.

Since Sal already knew my personal vehicle, I decided to drive it to his house as a sign of respect. I hoped he would be able to see I wasn't afraid of him, and I trusted him with my information. Honestly, I never know when I might be in Buffalo, so I own a ten year old four wheel drive Ford Bronco. It's the older model, the big truck, not the smaller Bronco II. I keep it in great condition. I rent a private garage five blocks from my apartment. Prior to starting the truck, I had to reattach the battery. The truck started right up.

I drove directly to Sal's house. Sal lives in an affluent neighborhood in Orchard Park, New York. Home of the Buffalo Bills football team. A gated community where every entrance and exit is monitored, not that anyone would care if I never left anyway, I was buzzed in and drove the winding confusing streets that I somehow just instinctively knew by heart and pulled in Sal's extravagant driveway. I had to look twice because his driveway was adorned with painstakingly and perfectly symmetrical multi colored and geometric stone that appeared to have depth and to be uneven to the eye. A new technology I had never seen before allowed the surface to be flat and lightly graded; almost like a clear coat of concrete was poured on top of the masterful work underneath. I shuddered to myself for a split second thinking of the reasons why a new driveway would have to be put in, more than likely it had little to do with looks, or keeping up with the Joneses.

Before I could ring the doorbell, it was opened proudly by a puffed out chested Mazzio. I know Mazzio is Sal's #1 guy, but I never liked him. Not even when I first met him, just never have. I don't worry about it because the feeling is clearly mutual. I have known Sal for close to 15 years. I have known Mazzio the same amount of time, way too long in my book. Even from our first meeting, we didn't like each other.

Sal was close to 70 years old, still in great shape and his mind was as sharp as ever. Mazzio was 62 years old. In organizations like Sal's, there are two types of people; muscle and brains. Sal was the brains and Mazzio was even now, still the muscle. Even though Mazzio was in the upper echelons of his life in age, you could tell through his suit he was still powerfully built and proud of it. I heard rumors that he still lifted weights for an hour a day, five days a week, incredible.

"Hey Dom, how are you?" I said like I cared or that we were friends.

"I am doing well. Come in already, you're letting all the warm air out of the house" he replied.

I went into the sprawling house. A long time ago, I spent a lot of time here with Sal. The house also had a huge backyard and an in ground swimming pool. There was also an authentic oyster shell bocce ball court and a winding garden along the outer edge of the yard filled with all kind of history and stories I am sure. The ornate driveway did a good job of alerting visitors to the immense beauty and care of the rest of the property. In the foyer standing next to Mazzio was another one of Sal's associates, Anthony Ragulli. He was about the same size as Jumbo. The difference being, where Jumbo was all fat, Ragulli was all muscle.

"You carrying anything kid?" Mazzio asked

Instead of responding, I looked at him like and he knew exactly that I was and who wouldn't be?

"Well, take it out and leave it with Anthony. We don't allow firearms in the house."

"Dom, you know that's not going to happen. I have never left my piece when I came in before and I am not going to leave it now" so I kept walking forward…Mazzio stopped me.

"Did I stutter?" Mazzio quipped in a serious hard tone.

I was shocked that Mazzio had asked me to surrender my weapon. This had never occurred before and was not normal. Anthony was starting to crowd my space and I was feeling really uncomfortable.

"Dom, you better tell your gorilla here to back off before I drop him. I am starting to get a bad feeling here."

"Woo, kid, relax. Anthony, take it easy. Everyone settle down. You really messed up last night kid. You were hired to do one job, and instead, you do six. It was a blood bath in there!"

"Look Dom, what do you want me to say? I did what I had to do to. Besides, when I take a job, I complete it the way I see fit. If that bothers you, tough shit."

"You got a smart mouth you disrespectful prick. If Mr. DiFlippo didn't like you so much, things would be different."

"Hey asshole, if you have a problem with me, we can solve it. Now." My voice turned cold and my eyes felt hard and full of rage. Even here in Sal's foyer I was planning on the five different ways I could end this situation for good and not get any blood spattered on his snow white carpet. Nothing would have made me happier than wiping the cultured marble floor with Mazzio and then doing the same to Ragulli. I'm sure the roses could use some fertilizer…

"Easy kid. I was just breaking your stones." Mazzio said, holding his hands out in a stopping gesture. "You did make a fucking mess last night, but the job got done I guess." He said acting like he wanted to give me a friendly pat on the back.

"Sal's in the library waiting for you." Mazzio said to me with a smile that accentuated his lip curl and made me hate him even more.

My eyes still rock hard waiting for the hammer to drop when I least expected it, "Dom, I need to see you after visiting Sal." I growled under my breath.

"Good, because there are a few things I want to talk to you about. I'll see you before you leave." He held his hands out in disgust like he had just shaken off at the urinal before washing them and walked away.

Ragulli escorted me to the library. Sal was sitting in a white leather chair under a reading lamp with a book in his lap. When he saw me enter, he got up gracefully as if his age was but a number and came over to me. After looking me up and down like an Italian mother in law, he hugged me with a genuine smile and real care. I thought he was going to tell me I was looking thin and offer me a meal. He ordered Ragulli out of the room with a flick of his Rolex adorned wrist like an annoying pet and directed me to sit in a matching deep luxurious white leather chair next to his. After we changed pleasantries and I was offered and received a cup of black coffee, soon after we got down to business. Sal started.

"What happened last night?" he asked me through a sip of scalding hot coffee that still had a swirl of hazelnut creamer on the top. As he lowered the cup I could see concern and confusion through the rising steam.

I explained to him what had happened in the bar, step by step. I didn't make anything up, didn't add or subtract a fact. I told him exactly how it happened, and why the outcome was so messy.

"It sounds like you did what you had to do. It might actually work out better the way you did it anyway. I doubt anyone left in his crew will want to step up and fill his role or try for revenge. I wired the other half of your money to the account. I added a little bit for a bonus."

"Sal, you didn't have to do that. Thank you. I appreciate that. What did you really need to see me about?"

"My friend, I have a favor to ask of you. I have a situation in Texas that needs your assistance. There are two people feuding, and one of them must go away. This man needs to disappear, completely. This is a job for a friend of a friend and I need it handled perfectly, and now."

"Sal, whatever I can do to help you. You need me in Texas and I will be there. Who will I be working for, you or someone else?"

"You will be working for a gentleman in Texas. He knows your pricing and he is expecting you to call him within 48 hours. I know the timeline is short. Can you do this for me?"

"Absolutely. I will take care of it".

"Good. Please my friend be extra careful on this one. These are dangerous times we live in."

"Sal, I am always careful. Is there something going on? Is there something you're not telling me?"

"No. I had a dream of my wife last night. We were walking through the Taste of Buffalo when it was our place back in the 90's. It was wonderful." He breathed in as if he could smell her signature Magnolia and Rose scented perfume and looked deep into the past as if he could hear the band still playing in the background. "I woke up feeling very old. Maybe I should retire, move to Florida and take up golf. What do you think?"

"Sal, guys like us, we don't retire. There's only one way we leave this business behind. Besides, you would hate Florida. It's too hot and humid, rains too much. You're right about being old, too old to take up golf my friend." He chuckled at that thought and shook his finger at me like a grandfather would at a dirty joke he knew the punch line was just outside his recollection.

I had actually met Sal and his wife at the same time about 15 years ago. She was the nicest lady you could ever hope to meet. She was sweet, charming and caring, always concerned with my eating habits, and invisible lint that she would wipe off my sleeves after hugging me, as if she didn't want to disturb whatever bold or crisp suit I was wearing that day. Sadly, I was also there when Sal had to say good bye to her for the last time. To this day I don't know what to say to an old man that still grieves the passing of his wife after 12 years as if it just happened yesterday? I was not one to offer advice as I was still having nightmares myself.

Setting down his now half empty cup of coffee Sal rose to say, "Be careful in Texas. If you need anything, don't hesitate to ask. Dom will give you the file on the way out."

"Thanks Sal. I'll take care of everything."

"I know you will." He hugged me again and the door to the room opened as if it knew I was coming toward it and closed quickly with Anthony's help leaving Sal alone to float in his memories, in his leather chair, next to the fire place.

Once the door shut, I saw Dom was waiting for me in the hallway. He had the file I needed as if he was hitting his place mark in a high school drama, but I knew it was more serious than that. Whenever I do a job for a client, I request a complete file on the person. Name, address, phone numbers, where they work, habits, what clubs or organizations they belong to, e-mail addresses, cars they drive, license plate numbers and pictures. After I get the file, I research them even more allowing me to fill in any holes that were left out. Then I will start to follow that person around to learn their schedule. This job would be no different.

As I was walking out of the house, Dom followed me to my truck. He started the conversation.

"What's on your mind kid? What do we have to talk about?"

"Last night, Fat Ritchie said he had already worked out a final payment through you and was more than a little surprised that I was there about the money he owed."

"Is there a question somewhere in that kid? What the fuck do I care what a low life scum bag like Ritchie says."

"I have to say Dom, he was pretty believable. Did you have some deal worked out with Ritchie?"

Dom turned around and waved me off as he did barking, "Piss off kid. I don't answer to you" He turned around, "Just so we're clear, no, I didn't have no deals with Fat Ritchie. He must have been yanking your crank when he said that, and you believed him. Amateur."

"I don't know who to believe Dom. I guess it doesn't matter now because I took care of the problem. I can only hope you didn't have something going on behind Sal's back. If you did and I find out about it, our next talk won't be so friendly."

"You know kid; the old man isn't going to be around forever." He said as if he knew something I didn't, "You want to keep working for *this* organization, you're going to have to show me some respect."

"Dom, cut the shit here. I don't respect you because I don't like you. And I know you feel the same way I do. Respect has nothing to do with our relationship. You hire me for a job and I do the job. If Sal retires, I might choose to not work for you anymore. And Dom, if you call Sal 'old man' again, I am going to come back here with a pair of vice grips and yank out all of your teeth."

CHAPTER #3

I returned to my Buffalo safe-house and reviewed the file. The next job was going to be in Dallas, Texas. This was great news to me. Not only could I leave the wind and snow behind, I was operating out of an area where I had another safe house and didn't have to start over from scratch. Besides, I could visit Reunion tower and remember a time when the big green lit building felt like safety. Almost like home. A faint memory came back to my ears like a whisper; "look daddy, the pickle building!" I shook it off and logged into my secure lap top to book my flight and hoped there was more than a jug of milk and peanut butter in my cabinets for a snack.

I have read books and actually met people that refuse to do jobs in cities they live in, which, to me, is ridiculous. Thinking about Dallas for instance where there are over a million people living just in the city alone. That does not even account for the surrounding suburbs like Addison, Garland, or Richardson. If you're good at your job, and careful, as I am, you don't have to worry about the local law enforcement or "bumping" into someone you might know. The odds of running into someone that knows you or can recognize you are astronomical to say the least.

My situation is a little different as I don't really spend enough time in Dallas to actually get to know people, but even if I did, I think the positives far outweigh the negatives. There is nothing more reassuring on a job than being comfortable with your surroundings. Dallas was a place I was very comfortable.

The file disclosed Jorge Gonzalez as the target. Gonzalez owns six dry cleaning businesses in Dallas, Texas. I was shocked to see the name of the man that wanted me to do this job, Michael O'Malley. O'Malley was a shrewd business man who also owned several dry cleaning businesses in Dallas. The problem occurred when another man, who was looking to retire by selling his five dry cleaning businesses, promised to sell to both O'Malley and Gonzalez. Apparently O'Malley didn't think that was fair and wanted all five.

According to court documents, O'Malley and Gonzalez were forced into a bidding war for the stores. O'Malley won the bidding war and signed a contract. Gonzalez got all American on O'Malley and pissed him off by getting a lawyer involved.

Now Gonzalez decided to sue both O'Malley and the seller for breach of contract and several other things even the court papers read as if the lawyer made each accusation up off an online form. While the chances of Gonzalez winning the case were slim to none, as there was no "real" contract ever signed; Gonzalez claimed a "verbal" contract and the delayed sale was not only pissing everyone off, but it costing all the sides a ton of money. Even Gonzalez knew he wasn't going to win his case, but he was enjoying the trouble he was causing for O'Malley, and kept adding continuances and interrogatories for the other sides to answer, gather witnesses, and creating sheer pandemonium for all.

I guess O'Malley did the math and figured it would be cheaper in the long run to hire me to make Gonzalez disappear. Without Gonzalez, the case would be closed and wrapped up within two months. I don't know how O'Malley knew Sal, but I never question it. Maybe I should have.

I changed clothes at my apartment, paid a few bills up and went to the airport. I used one of my aliases to get a direct flight from Buffalo to Dallas business class. Since I travel a lot, I always fly either business or first class. It's one of the few perks I feel the additional cost is well worth the money.

Another perk I allow my self is that I do not do any jobs in the month of July. What seems like a lifetime ago, July was a month that filled me with joy. It's not so anymore. Now I just use the month of July to spend a few days at each of my safe houses reviewing things. This is the month I register my vehicles, buy new identities, weapons, etc. I make sure I am stocked up for the entire year. I normally average 35 jobs a year. Some years I do a little more, some years I do a little less but it is always close to or right at 35. When I am tired or need a break, I will disappear to somewhere warm and tropical out of the country for a few days or a week. Make sure my eyes behold the beauty that Earth has to offer and when I am ready to return to work, I leave the white sands, crystal waters, deep tans and lack of clothing to do what I do. Sitting at 30,000 feet with my drink ordered I wondered why I didn't just stay out there, lounging on a hammock, and letting people live. It was as if the thought had never crossed my mind before. I just had always come back.

Could I still be angry all these years later? Was I still trying to make a point? This is why I did so many jobs a year. Too much time alone with my memories and thoughts was not good for me.

The majority of my work comes from Mafia type organizations. The majority of my work is through word of mouth and I could never know if that mouth would be one that saved my ass someday. These days, if someone wants to contact me, they can find me on several different on-line forums. One is a body building forum; one is a forum about dogs. People will leave me an innocent message and a way to contact them, I choose what I want to do, I don't take every offer, and I wasn't a "HO" as Fat Ritchie had so tastefully labeled his bathroom. People know I charge more than the average going rate, but they only contact me because they know I am one of the best at what I do.

The flight to Dallas was quiet and uneventful. My ice cold plastic cup of Jack Daniels Whiskey was handed to me by a friendly yet frumpy flight-attendant with a pillow and eye mask as I had requested and then I went to sleep. Of course, I dreamed...just not of pickle buildings or home, wherever that was.

CHAPTER #4

"Daddy, Daddy! Come help me get Scatters out of the tree!" the orange and white tabby had climbed up there again more than likely to get out of being dressed up like a doll again. A warm sunny day to get a cat out of a tree was better than no day at all. He climbed the ladder and retrieved the relaxing cat and scolded him in a playful way.

"Scatters don't scare my little girl that way again, you stay out of that tree or we will have you stand in the corner!" he said in a silly voice to the bored and reluctant looking cat fluttering his tail back and forth. The young girl of about four giggled back into the house ready for another day of tea and dress up as her mom called her in for lunch.

They were a happy family only longing for a simple life, helping others and creating a legacy of love. Mother floated around life, helping feed and take care of those in need no matter what. Being a pastor's wife gave her a sense of responsibility and pride that she had never imagined. Her blond hair flowed over her shoulders in a carefree way that was more beautiful than any magazine model. Her smile made goose bumps rise on his skin, and her tenacity made him red with frustration when he knew she was right.

Dad went back to the garage to finish his masterpiece of love for Scatter's mommy. This three story hand crafted doll house had a front door with a heart cut out and a real working doorbell. The house was reminiscent of some home style mansion that might just fit in to the working class town. A pastor he carved a cross on the top of the roof. When the house closed the top two pieces put together a cross, just like he always told her. When God joined two hearts they created God's perfect will and beauty. This was the story he couldn't wait to tell her when she unwrapped it on her birthday the next weekend.

"Lunch time!" Mom's sweet voice willowed out to the garage in a nice yet demanding way that meant "Come Now!" without sounding like it.

"Be right there..." he called up the garage steps. *Just let me finish this last hinge so I can stain it,* he thought to himself with a smile. He heard the phone ring and thought, "Whew! Saved by the bell!" as he wiped a bead of sweat off his brow. He was proud to be the pastor of a small church of about 50 parishioners on the inside of town just near the town hall. The smell of bacon, fresh cut tomatoes, and toast hit his nostrils just making him want to quit, listen to his wife, and go in for his favorite BLT on wheat.

Thinking of her standing there waiting to eat with him made him cringe, he hated to think he might be responsible for erasing a smile off her face. Putting down his screwdriver and determination, he remembered where it had all started. Purchasing his books in seminary school, he commented on her smile in an uncharacteristic move. It was one of the boldest things he had done in a while, maybe ever. He was even surprised he did it, and a little afraid of the outcome.

She was very excited that he had taken an interest in her, but didn't show it all at once. They chatted for a few minutes and he finally got the nerve up to ask for her phone number. She gave it to him. They both knew they were in love the moment their eyes met. It was for real and forever, they danced together when certain songs came on no matter the environment, loved their sweet daughter and someday would have even more children to fill up their house and hearts.

Standing at the sink washing his hands as instructed by his little girl, he turned to get a towel off the oven handle and saw her wiping the crumbs off the counter and thought of their first date, just two days after their first meeting. They met for coffee at a campus coffee house and talked for what seemed like days and got to know each other. They found they had a lot in common; they liked the same movies, the same authors, the same activities. Even from that first meeting, he carried her in his heart. Still to this day she sits in his chest a beautiful creature, never aging, never moving, always loving and dancing her way into his soul.

They continued to date all through college and graduated at the same time. Shortly after graduation, they were married in a simple but beautiful ceremony. Shortly after the wedding, he had two job offers waiting for him. A small rural church outside of Buffalo New York needed a pastor. The town had about 2,500 people, mostly farmers. The church didn't make a lot of money but housing was included. The second job offer was a bigger church of about 200 in Nashville Tennessee making a modest living with a parsonage.

At their favorite local diner they both discussed their future over BLT's and coffee cake. They knew from the beginning they wanted kids and thought raising them in a small town would be better than the big city. The couple spent many hours in prayer over this decision. After three days of deliberation and prayer, the decision was made; it felt clear that God was leading them to the small town.

Soon they were off on their new life in Buffalo. Not long after moving to their new home, they gave birth to a daughter. In an honor to God for all of the blessings He had bestowed upon them, they decided to name their daughter Faith. They longed for a simple, full life filled with love and happiness. They always thought if they gave, they would receive His blessings and live abundantly in their hearts if not always in their bank accounts or appearances. The simplicity of what was inside is what matters most and spurred them forward in their happiness.

Through all his memories, the one thing that pronounced itself better than any of the other memories was the ones that were being made now. Always full of love and laughter, at bed time, at movie time, at coloring time, at deep hard decision time, and just now at the table, together. After helping clear the table and do the dishes, she and Faith decided to take a nap. He kissed them on the foreheads and determined to finish the doll house, he returned to the garage.

A few hours flew by and Scatter's the cat wound himself in and out of his legs in the garage where time had otherwise stopped in his contentedness. He had just finished putting the first coat of stain on the doll house. Inside the kitchen, the telephone rang. While waiting for the stain to dry, he went in to see who was calling, but mother had just hung up the phone and told him she had an errand to run and would take Faith to play with her friend Skye at a church ladies' home. The lady was depressed and needed someone to talk to. She had called on the pastor's wife for direction and mother agreed to go and talk, maybe help fold laundry or do a load of dishes. Faith could keep her young friend Skye company and after tea and prayers she would be back to make supper.

The three walked to the family car and they kissed a sweet goodbye and told them he loved them both very much. They waved goodbye as Scatters jumped up on the work bench threatening a month's work as he hurriedly waved back then ran to scold and scare off the would be destroyer. As he turned around even the tail lights were gone.

Unlike those brief yet poignant moments in the campus bookstore, even their lives had grown a bit commonplace, though he appreciated her from the top of her head, her golden blonde hair, to her naturally soft pink lips that lightly gasped for air when he made love to her and even her concern over invisible age spots and lines he never saw, right down to her small, delicate feet.

Though he thought about her in a way no man ever could, the thought of their eternal separation never entered his mind as he considered a gloss coat of varnish, and whether he should have left that cat up in the tree. A paw mark appeared on the top edge of the roof like Scatters had considered stepping all the way on the building but chose wisely not to.

CHAPTER #5

As I exited the plane, the cracks for ventilation in the jet-way blew in hot Dallas air. The heat would be ok. At least here I could pretend to be a cowboy and no one would care. Everyone would just think I was blending. As soon as I walked out into DFW's expanse of an airport, I saw cowboy hats everywhere. So I walked over to a news stand and bought a cream colored hat that was just my style. I could never have too many hats anyway. $69.89 was the total on the receipt. As I tucked it into my pocket, pulled off the tag I saw my reflection in the too small mirror over the display near the exit.

What I saw threw me off for a minute. The cream colored still stiff hat didn't hide the truth. I hadn't always been a hit man. I didn't always work for corrupt people without morals and deal seamlessly with underworld organizations. I could almost see my dad a little in me, maybe it was my nose or maybe it was the glint of gold in my eyes…but when I was growing up, I never fantasized about murdering people for money. I even thought of the time when career planning was a big deal my junior year in high school. I had met with my guidance counselor in high school and he asked me with a positive tone and a smile filled with hope and almost white teeth what I wanted to do with my life, and I didn't say "Kill people".

I answered him with the truth though; I told him I didn't know what I wanted to do. I actually had an interest in law enforcement. I thought I would enjoy a job working in a jail or prison, maybe helping catch the bad guys like in a movie or comic book. I wanted to be a hero not a hired mob hit man. Sixteen years old, what did I know? I wasn't even a little concerned with the rest of my life. You're concerned with the football game on Friday and your date on Saturday at that age.

I know I was concerned with finding a way to escape my every day boredom and be on my own. I took the hat off, nearly seventy bucks and all it had done in three minutes or less was destroy my confidence and question my existence…I can't do this to myself again, I thought and held it to my side as I rode the moving sidewalks to the airports exit.

I remember my guidance counselor suggested I look into the military. He said it would be a perfect fit for someone like me. He said they would help me figure out what I wanted to do with my life. He said they would teach me a skill or a trade and train me. He said if I liked it enough, I could make a career out of it. If not, they would help me pay for college and it would look great to have that experience on a resume. When you're sixteen, and lost, the words of a knowledgeable adult can carry a lot of weight, I just wanted to get out of his office and make sure my beeper was out of my locker and on so my girlfriend could signal me when her parents were out and I could sneak over later.

He said if I was interested in law enforcement, I should talk to the Army about being a MP (Military Police) Officer or the Air Force about their Security Police. That was when I got interested in what he was saying. He said I could be a police officer in the Army or the Air Force and after four years when I got out, police departments around the country would be begging me to work for them. I was very excited when I left his office. I even left my beeper in my locker and never met up with my girlfriend, but I didn't remember until later that weekend. For the first time that I could remember, my life had purpose and direction. I stayed almost the whole night in the library looking up stories on the microfiche about the Army's Military Police and Air Force Security Police daydreaming about my future like kids do.

Two months after I graduated high school, I was shipping off to Fort Benning in Fort Benning Georgia. I told my recruiter I wanted to be an MP. He assured me that was a great job and I would have no problem getting it. My recruiter was dead wrong. They said according to the scores on the required ASFAB test, they knew the best thing for me to get into was Advanced Infantry Training. I didn't really know what it was at the time, but I was excited to be accepted in any division of the US Army.

The PBR group and the regular commuters that were on my plane had mostly gone to the baggage claim area and the rest of the people, who just had carry-on luggage like me, had taken cabs, shuttles and private cars back to their lives. After climbing in the cab and telling the cab driver where I wanted to go, I sat back in the seat and remembered the hardest two months of my young life.

Basic training was nine weeks long. I didn't suffer homesickness like some of the recruits did. I didn't have a family. My parents had died when I was 13 years old and I was allowed to live with a childless aunt and uncle who were not exactly thrilled to have me.

They treated me well and they never let me go hungry and provided me a generous place to live. They weren't really active in my upbringing. They had never wanted children and I always felt like I was imposing on them. When I started to get older, I felt like some boarder just renting a room instead of a family member.

We never ate together and they would go on vacation while I was still at school leaving just a note and a key under the mat when I got home. 'Gone to Florida, be back soon, food in the fridge should last you, hundred dollars in the junk drawer, bye.' So it seemed natural that we all three couldn't wait for me to graduate from high school to move out. I was an athlete in high school, but I was not prepared for the physical aspect of basic training. I had lettered in wrestling and also ranked #2 in the state in that sport. I learned everything I could from the people teaching me. The nine weeks seemed to slog by because I wanted to get into the training. I needed to be different, specialized, and purposeful. Using the Army as a surrogate family, I was able to move up quickly and when I graduated, I was the top of my class.

After basic training, I went to Advanced Individual Training (AIT). Once again, my ambition and drive to be number one made me rank at the top of my class. I felt a sense of pride for the accomplishments I had achieved. I was enjoying Army life and I bought into the whole package of the Army life. Worked hard all day, led men to the brink and congratulated them when we all made it through to the next level. It was something I believed in completely and was ready to give my life for my country.

Once AIT was complete I was exposed to the opportunity for attending Paratrooper training. I had never jumped out of an airplane, but I was excited by the thought of doing it. I found as time went by, I was kind of an adrenalin seeker and really enjoyed Paratrooper school. Once again, I graduated at the top of my class.

One of my commanding officers called me to his office to talk to me upon my graduation from Paratrooper school to tell me he thought I would make an excellent Army Ranger. He said the Army Rangers were the best of the best, the fiercest warriors to walk the earth, elite. He said if I applied for ranger school, he would personally endorse my application. Clearly I had made an impact on him in a very positive way.

I could smell rain on the dusty air as I rolled the window down in the back of the cab just to see if I was still human or not.

When I was on a job I sometimes forgot to remember the little things, like how cool satin sheets feel on a humid night slipping into bed just after a hot shower. I forgot that the Earth spins in five different ways and that gravity is my friend. I even sometimes forget that the temperature changes during the day and night.

I had applied for Ranger School, passed the Army physical fitness test with no problem, a corresponding combat water survival test and the grueling six day Ranger assessment phase. Once all three prerequisites were complete and passed, I was off to Ranger school.

Ranger school was one of the most difficult physical and mental challenges I had ever endured. It taught me the true meaning of loyalty, of my inner strength and I found how deeply I loved being a part of something special, something bigger, and something resembling family that made me better than what even I thought I could personally be. It was one of the finest, proudest moments of my life as I walked forward a graduate from Ranger School.

I was with the Rangers for four full busy and challenging years. During my time in, I experienced many amazing adventures I would never have had on my own, ever. We traveled to different countries helping to right wrongs and help desperate people. Although when I was with the Rangers, the US was never at war with any other country; my division was deployed and involved in several conflicts. We experienced firefights and anyone who got in the way of my brothers or attempted to kill me was eliminated. Killing people never got to me, I never spent time thinking about it, and it was trained out of me.

My team and I were suddenly deployed into Columbia, South America just when I had all but decided to make being Army Ranger as my career and resign for another four year stint. While we were there, our mission went badly and horrible things happened both on and off the record. Some I remembered and some that remembered me. Although we lost none of our own men during the mission, I did lose my urge to remain with the Armed Forces. I just moved on.

Returning to the United States, I first spoke with an Army Psychologist by order of my commanding officers. I chose to be honest with him about what I had seen, done, experienced, and where I thought I was going.

Leaving his care, I knew I was at least headed in the right direction, even if that was out of the Army and no other direction specifically. I spent the last four months of my Army career in Fort Bragg North Carolina training new Weapons Sergeants. When my time was up, I didn't have a family or a home or anywhere else to go so I basically threw a dart at the map and chose to land in Florida and spend some time on the dark sands of Coco Beach.

Thinking back on the sunrises and smell of the ocean flowing through tall sand grasses and palms made me wish the humidity in the air was from the ocean and not a Deep South heat wave.

CHAPTER #6

I had the cab driver drop me off at a restaurant within walking distance to my safe house. After paying the cab driver I took a seat in the restaurant where I could watch the front door and the street outside. Before going back to my house, I wanted to make sure I was not being followed or watched. I started to regret that the Jack Daniels I drank on the plane would be the last glass of alcohol I would drink until this job was over. I loved bourbon but never drank on a job.

After finishing my heavily salted Freedom Fries and a rich chocolate shake, I walked a circular route to my house. I walked down the street and window shopped a bit crossed the street and walked down a side alley to my complex. It took me almost an hour to feel comfortable no one was following me or even realized I existed.

Finally able to feel secure, I walked into my house; I dropped my bags in my third story condo, stood on a tall black dust covered kitchen chair to open my hidden ceiling safe and took out a weapon. As I stepped down I noticed my boot prints on the chair and silently wished I had hired a cleaning lady at this house. Texas was the worst for dust. I saw enough in my few moments of scanning the interior of my house to know that nothing had happened or had been disturbed while I was gone, just dust.

I had decided to carry a GLOC 23. The same model I carried with me into Sal's house only a few hours earlier. A little bit heavy for its size, but I am partial to a compact .40 caliber automatic. I liked knowing that I could feel it's weight. It was a very intentional piece of machinery. I would only need to grab my electric lock picking gun, pouch of pry tools, and tension bars to be ready for the next day's information gathering. With these tools and my innate ability to talk my way into or out of any situation, I can bypass just about any locked door encountered.

As I changed my hair color to a sandy brown I added custom deep blue contact lenses to my eyes. My goal is to not be remembered while I am looking for clues, facts, and data. Killing people is not the hard part. The hard part is not leaving any evidence before, during or after the crime has been committed. I fiddled with the many ways that I could comb my hair either straight back, or even better parted on the side. I even chose to add a pair of large window pane glasses to complete the look.

I clicked on the TV to check out the local news while the dye set in and checked out the forecast for the next day. The average temp in Dallas this time of year was a cool 67 degrees in the late day and starting at around 35 degrees. The temperature was luckily going to be hovering around 60 degrees for the next week or so, covering my stay with comfortable weather. In Dallas it was either going to be sweltering humid thick air like when I had landed at DFW or a beautiful freshly bloomed blue-bonnet kind of day.

One where people would pull over near a field or clump of the coveted state flower and photograph their children smiling and wishing they could pick just one of the forbidden trophy's. Instead they would post their pictures all over the web and enjoy the smell like early spring air and soft blonde hair for the rest of the day. Simple pleasures even I could still appreciate, even if I couldn't experience them.

Before bed, I completed my new look by setting out my clothes for my first mission of the week, so I could be looking normal and invisible as usual, wearing a pair of Chinos and a dark brown ribbed turtle neck with a lightly worn tweed blazer and I couldn't help but think I would more than likely look like a middle aged college professor and not the trained killer I truly was.

■■

"Look, I don't have to explain, this is what I need Bear. I have a delicate job that needs handling; you can do this and be set for life. Time is very important on this one and we're a day behind as it is. I need to see you today. Make it happen." The phone slammed down with one hand and an unlit cigar rested between Mazzio's thick index and ring fingers in the other. He looked at himself in the reflection of the sliding door glass and felt more than confident in Paul "Bear" Berrazino. Mazzio didn't care about what made Bear nervous, luckily Bear owed him a favor and like everyone else, when it was time to repay a favor, you couldn't refuse.

Dom's assistant came in and said a message had just been called in, "Come to the club in an hour."

"Get my car" Mazzio said to *his* right hand guy, Anthony "Tony" Ragulli as he grabbed his coat and stepped out into the cold Buffalo air.

Mazzio told Sal DiFlippo he had some business to attend to in town and left. While in the car, Ragulli said to Mazzio from the front seat;

"You know Dom; I could do this for you. I would gladly do this for you."

"I know Anthony, but I need you here, with me. This is only the first step. Things are going to get real ugly real fast and that's when I will need you. When we get there, wait in the car. You'll be involved with every step of this, just wait."

Silence was Ragulli's answer with a nod of his head and a full forward stare as if this mission to meet Bear was life or death for him. This meeting might be the glue that put Ragulli at the top of the food chain if and when a power change ever came to be after Sal finally moved on over for the next big guy in town. In Ragulli and Dom's mind there was only one man for that job, and Mazzio was the only one who could really take that job and do it any justice. The thought of justice and this job only brought a sly smile to Ragulli's face as he turned down the street to the freeway to take Dom to his all-important meeting.

■■

The first thing I did after my morning coffee was to lock up my safe house and walk down to the local bus stop. I rode the line until I arrived at the beautiful Magnolia Hotel in downtown Dallas. I checked in under my latest alias' name, accepted a tall flute of champagne with a slice of strawberry on the side and followed the bellman to my room overlooking the city. After pushing a twenty in his outstretched hand, I shut the door.

I phoned down to the concierge for the number of a rental car company and had a car delivered to a different hotel close to the one I was currently residing in. I walked to that hotel and picked up the rental then I drove across town to an internet café. After running my normal routine of security scans on the computer, I checked the bulletin boards for messages. None. I created a new encrypted e-mail account for use while I was in Dallas; DFWPBR was my new handle remembering the PBR group I had seen in the airport yesterday. I should go at least enjoy some bull riding while I was in Texas. Before or after the job was the question. I considered the thought, logged off the computer and left, deciding that before might be too risky.

Using a pay phone on the next street over from the café in a small parking garage, I pressed Michael O'Malley's cell phone digits into the sticky and clearly unsanitary phone dial. Germs...hate them, but I needed the competing DNA just to be safe.

This place looked like it got a lot of DNA traffic, so I would defiantly be sanitizing my hands soon after this call. As I considered where my nearest germ killing gel was in my bag a man answered on the third ring.

"Hello?"

"Michael please."

"This is. Who wants to know?"

"Ryan Bristow. We have a mutual friend in Buffalo, New York."

"Buffalo? Ah, yes, yes we do. Thank you for calling. I am glad to hear from you."

"Let's get down to business. I am here to consult on an issue you are having. Our friend stated you understood my rates."

"Rates, like there are different types of this genre of employment? I gotta hear this."

I started to hesitate, surely he was kidding, but decided to move on at his request to my fees, "The fee to resolve the issue and make it go away without a trace is $50,000. I require half up front and half when the issue is resolved. So what you will need to do-"

I was rudely interrupted. "WHAT! 50 G's? That's crazy! WAY too much! You're out of our mind."

I peaceably continued and thought about my strip club brothers, I wondered if O'Malley would be someone I knew or used to know ever quickly. "Sir, I was under the impression you were aware of the rates that I charge, is this not correct?"

"I know your rates. I was told it would be $25 G's and now you're telling me double? No. You're trying to screw me on the deal here, You-"

There was no way was I going to allow this guy to talk to me this way, so I didn't worry about being rude and interrupt him "Mr. O'Malley, there has obviously been a mistake. I apologize for wasting your time. Good luck solving your issue" and then I hung up on him.

I walked back to my car and drove it to a different hotel that was located near the hotel I was already checked into. After making sure I was not followed, I gave my car to the valet with a hefty tip and entered the hotel.

One of my favorite restaurants in Dallas, the Bistro At The Adolphus, is located here. I knew when I booked my trip to Dallas I would want to eat here. I just really do not like to eat in the restaurants of the hotel I am staying at or restaurants of hotels close to where I am staying.

It goes back to the basic rules of keeping a low profile and being invisible. I would make an exception in this case. It was a little early for dinner, but I was hungry and pissed off.

Once seated at my elegant table that would have been better for two than one, the hostess whisked away the extra silverware and delicate fabric napkins except for my own. I ordered the flash seared tuna loin served with jasmine rice, stir fried vegetables and a soy mustard sauce. I ordered a bottle of Pierre water with a sprig of mint. The wine list came and I seriously considered drinking a glass of chardonnay, but resisted. I chose to take my time enjoying every bite of the tender fish. The vegetables were crispy and flavorful, when the green snap beans popped open in my mouth I could feel the warm fresh flavor of spring time and it relaxed me.

After finishing my meal and treating myself to a decadent sliver of cherry cheesecake, I paid in cash, left a large tip for the staff that had waited on me and walked back through the hotel to the business center. Thankfully, as usual the business center was deserted. People who could afford the pricy Adolphus didn't need a business center; it was likely they had their own people and couriers to do their business errands.

I found a terminal toward the back that faced the front doorway and ran my normal security scan on the slightly dated PC and checked to see what messages I had. Like I expected, just one short message waiting for me from Sal. Completely to the point, "Call me, S." I signed off the computer and left the hotel lobby. My car was already waiting for me outside with a valet holding the door open. I tipped him with a nod as he quickly walked off to the next requested vehicle. On the way back to my hotel, I stopped at a different hotel and used an internal pay phone to call Sal.

"Sal." I said in one word, the sound of it was enough to ask a million questions. For starters, why did you send me here, do you even know about this guy, what is my next job, and why didn't you warn me to name a few.

"I am good." He said as if anticipating my thoughts. "Thank you for calling me back so quickly. I hear things are not well out there. What's the problem?"

"Price. Your client is trying to haggle about my fee. This is non-negotiable."

"Yes, I understand. I have spoken directly to him and he assures me he will pay the full fee, no questions ask. I will guarantee that he pays. If anything else goes wrong, I will cover the difference personally and double your fee."

I breathed out with a nod Sal couldn't see, said good-bye and hung up. Sal knew I would do it. I didn't like O'Malley. I didn't like his type. I decided I would call him back, but on my terms. I wanted to let him know who was in charge and I wanted him to sweat a little; Sal would know what I was doing and perpetuate it. I decided to go see a movie before going back to my hotel.

I had no idea that back in Buffalo, Mazzio was meeting with Paul Berrazino.

■■■

Berrazino owns a strip club outside of Rochester New York. Although working for a larger organization than Mazzio, Berrazino was not as high up on the food chain as Mazzio. After stopping at the bar to catch up and throw back a few drinks, Berrazino and Mazzio went to Berrazino's private office in the back.

"Ok Dom, I have a few things I need to get to today, so let's get right down to it."

"I probably need three or four guys to take care of a guy, just get me hooked up with a crew. They need to be top notch, this guy is a pro. There are a few stipulations though."

"Stipulations? What do you mean stipulations?" Berrazino asked

"Now's not the time Bear, I will let you know what you need to know when I need to tell you. For now just know I need some guys to be ready in a few hours. I have a leak in the company that needs to be filled…with lead." Bear sipped on his whiskey and glared back in a confusing uninterested way. Dom faltered and said, "Look I am going to make you a very powerful man when this shit goes down. I need this done right though. I am talking no traces here. Not a speck of suspicion on me or you. Nothing."

Bear flipped on the television in the corner to let Dom know he needed more info before he would be deeply interested. "It's gotta seem like this leak was just doing his job and then flaked out and disappeared in the wind." Dom got up in a silent transactional wisp of a single moment.

The deal was done, both men agreeing in nothing but body language and tone of voice. "Your crew? You? Nobody talks about this. Nothing. No whispers, no rumors, not even any thoughts. Or I will lose it, and you remember what happened to ol' Pitariu when he tried to screw me over, right?"

As he reached for the door knob Bear flipped off the television and sat back in his chair thinking of the aforementioned *accident*. "Not one thought, ever." And with that Dom shut the door on the conversation and any further knowledge of the target. Dom could hear the TV come back on in the office and the sports news cast pop on and be turned up loudly. Bear was already at work assembling his guys. 'Always keep a favor for a rainy day in your back pocket' Dom chuckled to himself. Rainy day, hell, this was going to be a shit storm.

CHAPTER #7

After the movie, I stopped in at a local big box retail store and purchased a pre-paid cell phone, and a miniature laptop with a dark colored neoprene sleeve to protect it. I paid for everything with a credit card. I drove a bit and found a little coffee shop with live music, a poetry slam on Thursdays and my favorite part, free Wi-Fi. Time to get my new laptop online. I unpacked in the rental car knowing the likelihood of cameras was very low at a location like this. Sitting in the parking lot of the big box retail store I would have been videotaped at every angle. I often wondered if the fitting rooms were really safe from prying eyes. Especially since even airports have the right to look through you more than your personal physician can these days.

I walked in with my neoprene sleeve snuggling close to my new navy blue miniature computer, ordered a black coffee and pretended to enjoy the gravelly voiced new age duet on the short stage.

I powered on, quickly set up my new network, ran my usual clearing sequence and quickly created a safe environment to send and receive messages. Instead of talking to Sal or Dom, I really needed my computer guy. I just punched out a quick note telling him I needed to speak with him and sent him my cell phone number. I am a pretty handy guy when it comes to computers, just not a hacker. When I sometimes require the services of one, I call on Geoff.

Several years ago, I needed someone to do a high profile job. Sal knew a great computer hacker named, Geoff. Sal said it wasn't cost effective enough to keep one on his payroll personally, but had used Geoff in the past with excellent results. He said the best hackers in the country lived on the West coast, and Geoff lived smack on the beach on the West Coast in a house that would make a person feel faint it was so large. He had an insane security system and from his terrace liked to watch the ladies of the beach and check the waves for an occasional surf diversion. More than anything though, Geoff liked to surf the electronic waves of the internet and hacked for some of the largest organizations in the nation. He never missed a meal and never would as long as he continued to be successful in his line of work. The sick part was Geoff was handsome like the Polo models in the magazine pages but rough enough around the edges enough to be a Tommy Hilfiger model.

Sal said Geoff was the best. He had been in the computer business since the beginning. He helped a former Harvard student get the largest computer company in the U.S. off the ground and running. Sal confessed that there wasn't a system in the world this guy couldn't get into. The only problem was this guy worked independent. He rarely sold his services, and when he did, the charges were exuberant, but nearly always worth it. Usually it wasn't economical to hire Geoff, but the results were always guaranteed. Independent or not like Sal always said; "Without loyalty, there is no accountability." Sal figured out a way to make Geoff loyal.

Sal met Geoff one summer when he was bored and started to gamble online. Like all gamblers, and all hackers, he didn't like to lose almost as much as he loved a good hack. So he used his specialized skills to break into an on-line poker site that was operating off shore based in the Bahamas. Geoff made himself a ghost administrator, doing this he was able to see every player's cards he was playing against. In just eleven days, he won close to eight million dollars. More than likely he would have won a lot more had he not played one night highly intoxicated. So inebriated in fact that he forgot to cover his tracks before signing off and passing out.

The people running the on-line poker site were just lying in wait for him to mess up and give out too much information. They were clearly not happy with losing that much money in such a short amount of time to one person. They hired a great computer guy of their own who waited like a lion watching his prey for the precise moment when Geoff forgot to cover his tracks. They were able to figure out what Geoff did. They were also able to track him back to his house in sunny California. They did what anyone in that situation would do and sent someone to kill him. Geoff contacted the website owner and offered to pay him double what he had illegally won from them, but the owner refused. He told Geoff the only payment he would receive was his luxuriously tan head in a bowling ball bag.

Sal heard about Geoff's situation and called the owner of the on-line poker site and set up a meeting in Las Vegas, Nevada. Over the course of a very expensive dinner, drinks, and penthouse suites for the weekend as well as high roller tabs and personal servants, Sal laid out his plan to the poker site owner. Sal told him he would be compensated, in full, for the eight million dollars he had lost immediately. Sal also said the public would never find out about the lack of security or what had occurred behind the scenes as long as Geoff was allowed to live.

Sal explained that he understood how the system worked and essentially, the online poker website didn't lose a dime. The administrators make their money by taking a "rake" (a percentage of the total amount) from each pot. So the money Geoff won was all from other players. If the public were to find out about the website's lack of security everyone whose money was lost when played would demand a refund. The online site wouldn't be required by any legal entity to refund anyone their money. However, by not refunding everyone's money within a few days, when word of what happened spread, no one would play their website anymore and the site would shut down losing all possibility of profit. Not to mention or even taking into account all the other hackers that would "attack" the site as well wanting to get their cut, just like Geoff had done.

The deal Sal offered was clearly in the owner's best interest to take. His website would continue making money, he would gain 8 million dollars, and no one would ever find out about what Geoff did. Sal felt like the deal was solid and flew back to Buffalo after their dinner meeting. A prideful man, the website's owner refused Sal's offer after using up the penthouse, the girls, and booze.

He boldly waited to tell Sal as his plane was being pushed from the gate. Sal was not shocked when the guy went as far as to say if Sal ever told anyone about their meeting or what Geoff did, he would send a "crew" to Sal's turf in Buffalo.

As the website owner looked out over the clouds hovering aloft of the Gulf of Mexico flying back to the Bahamas, he wasn't alone. I sat two rows behind him staring at his head eating my honey roasted peanuts and drinking ginger ale wondering how God had made people so dumb as to underestimate Sal. Sixteen hours after landing in Nassau, I was sitting on a remote beach lying in a hammock barefoot in a large light cream yellow linen button up shirt and chinos wondering why I might ever find reason to leave such a paradise. I read in the local newspaper, the Daily Garden, that the website owner was the victim of an apparent robbery. His body was found in the restroom of a night club.

Someone had stabbed him in the heart and left him in a locked stall. His wallet, jewelry and watch were missing. It was too bad I knew exactly who that someone was, but a free trip to the Bahamas was definitely worth the loss of my favorite Cole Haan driving shoes to his bloody pool of splatters that leaked into my socks from his pumping chest wound until his heart stopped beating the liquid out onto the floor.

An hour after the owner was killed, and two hours before the news found its way to the papers and news casts, Sal offered the same deal to the CFO, who was the website owner's right hand man and son-in-law. The son-in-law liked money a lot more than he liked his father-in-law and accepted Sal's offer.

Around the time that the body was being recovered from the restroom of the nightclub, the shooter that was ordered to kill Geoff was notified the contract was no longer valid because the person responsible for payment was dead. At the same time as I was finishing my lunch brought to my cabana by a beautifully bronzed sheet wrapped local servant the shooter was boarding a plane to head back to his home country. I had all the luck, besides, who needed shoes in paradise?

Sal contacted me via messenger after a few days and gave me my next assignment. Geoff was not told the owner was dead, any deals had taken place or that the ransom for his head had been paid. He still thought a man from the Bahamas was out to kill him. So I flew to Ontario California and from there drove out to Palm Springs.

Geoff had refused to leave his house for any reason. Sal had to track down his 95 year old mother and then had to convince her that he was the only person who could save her son's life. So Sal and Geoff's mother set up a lunch meeting with him for me. Sitting across from his mom, the three of us ate in relative peace at Bing Crosby's Restaurant and Piano Lounge. It was the oddest lunch I have ever eaten. What passes for casual conversation between a hired killer, a mother and her son when the son could be a perspective target?

Geoff was nervous about the meeting and didn't know what to expect. After our meal, and after promising Geoff's mother that I would return Geoff home safely to her, I had her escorted home and he and I went to a private room in the club. Before I could say anything he looked at me squarely in the eyes and said "I really don't want to die today." I told him not to worry because I was there to eat a good lunch and to offer him the job of a lifetime.

I said everything Sal told me to. I sold him on the thought that it was a shame that someone that had his skill decided to throw it all away gambling. I told him I would make him a deal. The organization I worked for would square his debt with the poker website. He would not have to repay us. Not one penny.

I never talked about Sal or said that Sal had anything to do with the deal. I wanted to keep Sal in the shadows, a man Geoff should fear, as if I was his friend, but in reality, at that moment, one wrong statement and I would have to go against my promise to Geoff's mother and kill him right here in the club.

Sal's organization wanted to employ Geoff's specialized computer skills from time to time. He was to provide us with everything we wanted, whenever we wanted, for as long as we wanted, eternally. He was also not allowed to gamble anymore, period. For his penance, he would go to work, free of charge for six months for the website he previously ripped off. During that time, he was supposed to upgrade their systems and make sure no one could ever do what he did to them. He thankfully readily agreed.

I hated to eliminate someone just after lunch with their mom. That just seemed wrong, even to me, though it would play into my reputation well. As soon as the six months were up, the company offered him four million dollars a year to be in charge of all their computer systems. He refused their initial offer and later when they offered him five and a half million a year, he accepted. Geoff has been forever grateful to me and the still unnamed benefactor Sal for not only saving his life, but for making him wealthy beyond his wildest dreams so he could to continue to run on the beach and get whatever he wanted whenever he wanted

A few minutes after sending my message to Geoff, I received a text message back. It was a file and I downloaded it into my cell phone. A few minutes later, my phone started to ring.

I answered, "Hello Allen! How have you been?" Allen was the character name I gave him and he answered to. I think it made him feel like an international spy or something. He once asked me for an alias and I had given him Allen. Cutely enough, the name of the website owner from the Bahamas was Allen. Call it a subtle reminder, but I didn't want to make any assumptions that Geoff knew exactly the right answer to all my questions, which was always yes.

"I am doing well. How are you?"

I knew we could talk openly because the file I downloaded into my cell phone was a file that encrypted my phone calls and text messages. As Geoff explained to me once, a cell phone is a miniature computer and it was easy to reprogram them adding the features you needed. I also knew the phone he was talking on was encrypted and probably cost more than the entire coffee shop I was sitting in.

"Good. I need some help. I am not even sure this can be done, but I want to give you a person's e-mail address. I was hoping you could somehow access his computer and tell me what is on it. I need it to appear that I was in his house and accessed his data personally. Can you do this?"

"For real? That's it? If I can access the computers at the Pentagon, and I can, then this will be no problem. If you want to speed things up, give me his home address. I can trace his internet provider through his address and use their info to access his computer." I could hear his dog yapping in the background for attention.

I gave Geoff all the information required and he said he would e-mail me everything he found. I told him I would check it when I could I didn't want to use the hotel's WI-FI system from my room for about one million obvious reasons.

"Are you still jumping around from libraries and internet cafes to get your messages? You know, it would be a lot easier to purchase a lap top computer and grab a wireless go anywhere card. You could use the computer while on the job and then when it is over, just ditch the computer. They are so cheap now that you can afford it man."

"Yeah, but if someone finds the computer can't they trace back all the data I looked at and all the websites I visited? Can you shut that dog up?"

"Dude, once you get the computer and the wireless card, check your e-mail. I will send you a file. Download the file to your computer but *do not* open it. Once your job is complete, just open the file and your computer will be completely useless. Make sure the computer has 32 gigs of free space to hold the program and only use the Evonica wireless network, if you use something else it will leave you open to views but someone would have to be trailing you. The code uses a 16 bit PSP that creates a wall of information blocking the real uses from being seen.

Even I wouldn't be able to see where you went or what you were looking at. That thing would totally be toast. And no, Corky is just expressing his dislike of the fact you never come see us. What's up with that, you sound like an old grump. You need to get laid man. Come on over and I will hook you up and then you won't be so jumpy." He said with a confident laugh and then talked in baby talk to Corky like he was a child and could understand. People and their pets.

"Okay, that sounds good. I'll do it. It will sure make things easier. I got one of these cheap $400 laptops today, it's navy blue, is that acceptable?" I laughed back at him knowing he didn't care about the color but his list of specifications was endless.

"Give me the ID you are using and I will set it all up in the system for you. I will activate your wireless card; get your billing and all that straight so you won't have to fuss with it."

"Ok, I will call you back after I buy the wireless card."

"Just go to Mike's Computer Repair on west seventh and ask for Caleb, he will give you the one I bought you just now. It will already be configured, just make sure the serial number ends in 9013. Ooh yeah, I gotta go on a walk, I mean take Corky on a walk, and I see a hot pink umbrella with my name on it..." and like that he was gone.

I am a creature of safety so after I found the store he was talking about I watched it for close to an hour to make sure I wasn't being set up. When I went in, I made sure my gun was close at hand and I knew where every person working in the store was. I went in and purchased the Wi-Fi box with the wireless card without incident. Now, not even the internet could hide from me. Geoff set up my billing using one of his aliases. Not that it mattered, because most of my credit cards come from Geoff and several of my aliases from him as well so who paid for what was irrelevant. I was pretty sure he owed me at least the $100 a year in wireless access he'd just bought me for pretty much ever and that was fine by me.

Geoff loved it when he needed to hack into Master Card to create an account in whatever name I wanted with whatever credit limit I needed. At the end of the billing cycle, Geoff would either hack back in and zero out my account balance, "It's no problem; I do it all the time for me. I got a house full of cool shit that hasn't cost me a penny." He would muse. The best was when he just let it go to collections. No amount of skip tracing even with some fancy high priced outsourced company could find me. With no real person attached to the account the card company would just write the loss off to fraud.

By the time I had the computer up and running, I had received two messages from Geoff. The first was titled the "Allen's Assassin File" that would destroy my computer after the job was done.

At least Geoff had a sense of humor, and I kind of liked that about him. It reminded me of me, before my world ended. The second was what I had asked for in the first place. Geoff supplied me with a giant list of Internet websites, bank account information, and all calls to and from O'Malley's cell, home, and business phone.

Geoff had also found a boat that O'Malley listed in a fake name and stupidly registered to his business. This was all great info to have even if I wasn't sure how to use it yet.

Over the next two days, I drove over to O'Malley's neighborhood and did a drive by on his house. Living in an affluent suburb of Dallas, Highland Park I cased his life for a good 30 hours coming back at all imaginable times. I was so quick to catalog automatic light patterns and sprinkler systems. I even borrowed a dog from a local homeowner who was at work and walked it around in the afternoon to see what kind of witnesses were around for daily life. I got a feeling for the area; pretty, white bread, and dull. Just a bunch of ell laid bricks and mortar full of fake yards and fake houses with fake rich people as I suspected. On Wednesday I felt like I had seen enough, left, but stayed close enough to be able to ask for a precise favor from Geoff.

■ ■

The day after meeting with Bear, Mazzio was wringing his hands knowing that Sal knew something was up with the latest drama to bestow itself on the organization. So he left for lunch and made a call to Bear.

"Bear, Dom. I need to give you the job, do you have the people?"

"I need to know the target. I don't care what this is about." Bear coughed back through the phone at Dom with insolence.

"Rick Stevens"

"Stevens? Holy shit! What the hell are you doing Dom? I don't know if I want to get involved in this. That guy is untouchable! You don't mess with a guy like that and live Dom. Besides, I don't have the rank to make this kind of call. You fucking know that dammit!"

"Listen I need this done. Now you know why it needs to be done right. I'm backed into a corner here. There are other things at play, things are set in motion and cannot be stopped. He needs to go away and you are going to do this, understood. You owe me, Bear, you owe me."

"I don't know. What's the old man going to say? Did he give his consent? I need to talk to him to feel confident on this one." Bear waivered.

"He has no idea about this and never will! That is why Stevens needs to disappear. Completely. No trace, no questions, nothing. It shouldn't be hard to make a man that doesn't exist disappear. Even you should be able to find a crew to handle this."

"Holy fuck Dom. You're keeping it from the old man? What in hell's angels are you doing here Dom? Are you wanting an early grave, 'cause I don't. Your secret is safe, with me, um I mean I am done with this conversation." Bear said in a near whisper with a slam behind it as if he had shut himself in a tornado shelter to hide from the ensuing storm.

Taking his tone lower to a more paternal stern voice, Dom started soothing him…"Bear, we've known each other most of our lives. You need to trust me on this. This guy is a headache that needs to go away. This is really important here. Help me out?"

"I am and already do regret this. Ok. I am going to send five guys. I will send a three man team and a two man cleaner team. I will need to know what job Stevens is working on. I will need to know the client and the target…" he trailed off…silence…then a scream, "Shit Dom, this is going to be expensive!!"

"Five guys is too many people knowing too many things. Have the hit team also clean up after themselves. Hell, am I going to have to send you a requisition with detailed instructions and shit? Have a van ready and transport the body to the van. After that, Texas is a big place. Find an empty field or something. I have the full file here; I am sending a copy over to you. Your guys can pick him up while he is working the target. There are recent pictures of Stevens as well. He loves the coffee shops for whatever reason, start there."

"With a pro like Stevens, I want at least three guys going. They will be the best I have, guys that are loyal to me. They realize if I move up, so do they. They're each going to want 10 grand, plus expenses and a royalty for his head."

"You insult me Bear…You know for this I will pay $125,000. You divvy it up as you see fit. I don't give a shit what your guys want. Just do it. I have the money in the white car outside your club with the file and photos."

"Shit Dom, I didn't even say yes yet. I mean, we can do this for that price, no problem. When do you want my guys to get going? What's the time table on this?"

"Sooner the better. He left for Dallas late yesterday or maybe even the day before. We're behind him. Can you get your team to Dallas now?"

"It won't be a problem. Now, if you'll excuse me, I have some calls to make. Promise me one thing Dom."

"What is it Bear?"

"When this is all over, explain to me why you are doing this"

"I won't need to explain it. You'll understand. I promise."

■■

2:30am Central Time, O'Malley's house phone rang. Geoff hacked into the phone companies system, and called O'Malley, linking me into the conversation. Geoff muted his end for entertainment and safety value, and I waited as it rang on O'Malley's side. The genius was that the call being rerouted through the phone company O'Malley could trace it a million times and would end up at the phone company every time.

After three rings, a very tired and croaky O'Malley picked up his house phone.

"Hello? Who is this?" he said through dry words as if he was a mouth breather at night.

"Good Morning Michael. I hope I didn't wake you." I said thinking I sounded as if I was that talking car from the 80's television show Knight Rider. Man I loved that show.

"What the hell? Hang on…"

I heard O'Malley talking to what I presumed was his wife in the background. He was laying down some bullshit story about an alarm company calling him about one of his businesses. He went to another room in his house.

"What the hell are you doing calling me at 2:30 in the morning? At my fucking house! Are you insane?"

"I am a little crazy and insane. I mean for fuck-sake, I kill people for a living. And you'd do well to not forget it. You need to understand one thing. Even though you are *going* to be paying me to resolve a situation, I do *not* work for you. Also, it might be a good thing to remember that I can reach out to you anywhere, anytime if you try to cheat me on this deal." I said with the confidence of a man that is used to getting exactly what he asked for. A confidence I heard thousands of times over the years from Sal.

"Listen asshole, I don't care who you think you are or what you do, but do not come around my house. I have connections you know?" He said trying to gain composure and sound scary.

"Too late Mike. I was at your house earlier today. I took a walk through it. Check your things. I actually took something from you, something small and insignificant. I bet you will never guess what it was…"

This was a lie but a believable lie after I provided him with a little more information. This little lie would drive him crazy for months. He would always be on the lookout for something missing. That is, assuming, I didn't have to kill him when this job was over. Oh well, it would be fun for me either way. Before he could interrupt me, I continued on.

"…And Michael, does your wife know about the fun you had alone the other night? You remember, the night you spent almost three hours on that filthy adult website that specialized in Korean school girls? Ooh I bet she has no idea about how you've been exploring *that* fetish. Maybe she needs a card to tell her about it. Clearly, she doesn't know, right? Oh, and before you interrupt me, I took a walk, not literally but figuratively, through your bank account records. Do you even *have* a spare $50,000 to pay my fee? If you do, I didn't see it in your accounts…."

"WHAT THE FUCK! YOU MOTHER …."

"Michael, lower your voice. I am not yelling at you so don't yell at me." I said like I was a half-witted bill collector for a cheap collection agency hoping to make a buck and be 'friendly' even soothing to him. "You know I did this for you. I do care about you Michael; I did this to prove a point. Do *not* fuck with me. Understand? If I think for one minute you have lied to me or are trying to manipulate me or you are not going to pay me my fee, I will decide you are the issue and will resolve you."

The other line was silent yet I could hear him using his inhaler, I almost chuckled but kept it inside. I hated for him to die before I had my chance to finish the job. "Now, by all your bullshit posturing, you have made me waste more than an entire day of my life that I can never get back that could have been better spent working on YOUR problem. You don't have to like me Michael; you just have to pay me, and now you owe me extra since I wasted so much time on you. You can rest easily knowing your situation will be resolved. That is, assuming, you do have the money, right Mikey?" I said egging him on.

"Yes I have the money. Don't worry. My dry cleaners are cash cows and I have a lot of 'gray income'."

"I'm sure you do. Is that like your 'gray boat' you keep at that private dock?"

"What the hell? How did you? Never mind. What do I have to do?"

"Very simple. All you have to do is check your e-mail address. There will be an account number. Wire $25,000 into that account within the next 60 minutes and let me do my job."

"I need more time. I don't have $25 g's laying around in an account to wire to you. You'll have to wait until the banks open tomorrow."

"Michael, Michael, may I call you Mike? What the hell, you should say yes because I'm going to anyways. We have already gotten off on the wrong foot. Why are you trying to mislead me here? I know your business checking account has $34,788 in it right now. Use that money and replace it later. Tick tock Michael. You now have 58 minutes…Oh and do tell your wife that pink is definitely her color. It brings out her bedroom eyes." And I hung up with a smile. Geoff would call back when the money hit my account. He just loved this stuff. I was glad he was listening, that way he would know how legit I was in the event he ever decided to be disloyal or gamble again.

Geoff was having so much fun that we sat listening to O'Malley's bugged phone and commenting on the rest of the conversation going on in O'Malley's house as if we were virtual flies on the wall. It was quite worth staying up late, wishing I had a glass of Pappy Van Winkles 18 year old Bourbon to toast the heavens with and I laughed as I heard him say. "So it's gone? Good, good. Ok, so he'll get the money in the next 30 minutes. Honey! Check the video's, was there a strange guy here during the last couple of days? Today maybe?"

I answered him like he could hear me, "You already know the answer to that."

Geoff answered for him in a female falsetto, "YES RICKY DEAREST!" We laughed and hung up.

I disconnected the call. Normally jobs aren't this complicated. I had a bad feeling about this job and I wanted to make sure O'Malley knew what was at stake and not to try anything. By the time I showered and brushed my teeth and slipped into my satin pajama pants that were perfect for this typical humid Dallas weather, Geoff had texted me to tell me the money was in my account. Little did I know though, the time spent screwing around with Michael O'Malley's head would prove very costly.

CHAPTER #8

The next morning, Dallas had welcomed three new faces. All three from New York. They all arrived in town separately to avoid suspicion. Giovanni Lima flew in on a direct flight from Buffalo New York to Dallas Ft. Worth. Angelo Ferro flew in on a flight that had two stops from Rochester New York to Dallas Ft. Worth. Angelo's brother Max, flew from Buffalo New York to Austin Texas. While in Austin, he rented a car and drove three hours to meet up with the rest of Bear's team in Dallas.

They timed their trip well. All three of them had a room on the same floor of the Crown Plaza Suites. They were also arriving right at the beginning of CONDFW Convention. CONDFW was being billed as one of the biggest Science Fiction & Fantasy events in the country. Since they all flew in from other places, they needed to spend half a day gathering the supplies they would need for their job.

The Ferro brothers first went to a moving place and rented the smallest moving truck they had. They used a fake id to do the rental and paid for it with a stolen credit card. They were not quite sophisticated enough to have fake credit cards and told the rental clerk they were driving across country and needed the van for 21 days.

After driving off in their van, the Ferro's went shopping at a home improvement store purchasing several large plastic storage bins, two axes, a chain saw, two hack saws, several plastic tarps; three full sets of painters pull over clothing, three pairs of goggles, three 50 pound bags of hydrated lime, several rolls of duct tape, several boxes of latex gloves and four gallons of bleach. All of this looked suspicious so they added 10 flower bushes, some seeds, soil, and miscellaneous bulbs for planting. Two gallons of tan colored paint and brushes with grout cleaner just to make it look legit. They separated the items as best they could making it look like one brother was being more generous than the other and told the story of one of the brother's needing a home and yard renovation to the clerk who helped them figure it all out. They paid for it at separate registers to keep the story going.

While the two brothers were out shopping for the hardware, Giovanni Lima also went shopping. Through Berrazino, Lima met with a man in the back of a pool hall.

This man had all manner of weapons. Lima purchased three pistols pre equipped with silencers, one Heckler & Koch PSG1 sniper rifle, a cut down 12 gauge pistol grip Mossberg shot gun, one Intratec Tec-DC9 (Tech 9) sub-machine gun pistol, a fifty count bag of flex-cuffs, three switch blade knives, and ammunition for everything. Lima was told to purchase whatever he wanted and to spare no expense. Lima was also told who their target was. Knowing Stevens only by reputation, Lima was very nervous about going up against him. Lima knew that if he was able to take out Stevens, he would then shoot to the top of the underworld and possibly even become a made man. He was not taking any chances, this was his big break and he was going to make sure those bumbling brothers didn't get any of his credit.

Making one more stop on his way back to the Crown Hotel Lima spoke with another man that Berrazino knew who provided Lima with several vials of chloroform and a police issue Taser. He then met up with the two brothers at the hotel and asked them about the flowers and other items they purchased that were not on their list. They started to explain and Lima rolled his eyes at their ineptitude and turned from them going into his room mid-sentence. Shutting the door forcibly muttering "Idiots" under his breath. Once again, Lima thought it was a great decision to not tell the two brothers who their target was.

Between the three man team, the next morning they had five different cars and the rental van. One person would always have to be in the rental van and that would need to be kept close at all times. The other two people would drive in one of the cars. They would switch out the cars frequently. Each of the cars trunks were lined with plastic tarps and everything sealed tightly with duct tape over night. If a bloody body had to go into one of the trunks, they would leave behind no blood or DNA evidence, or at least that was the hope anyway.

The back of the moving van was also set up to receive a body. The entire area in the back was covered with plastic and also sealed tightly with duct tape. The plastic storage bins were laid out and already lined with lime. Once the body was dismembered and placed in the storage bins, the rest of the lime would be poured over the pieces. The tarps would be pulled down and placed in the storage bins and everything would be sealed in duct tape, the wonder ingredient for any aspiring hit man.

Each man had one pistol, a switchblade knife, and two sets of flex-cuffs with a small vile of chloroform. Lima would keep the sniper rifle with him and was in charge of this operation and did not want to be involved in any "up close" work with Stevens. He was definitely the manager and would sit back and hope for an opportunity to get rid of the bumbling brothers along with Stevens. Angelo had the Tech 9 while the elder brother Max had the shot gun and the Taser.

They knew they were supposed to make Stevens disappear quietly and without witnesses. That's what they intended to do but if things didn't work out like they planned, then they were just going to do what they needed to do and then make the body disappear. Besides, no one would know who Stevens was and there would be no body for the police to identify even if there were witnesses. Once everyone was set, they set out to find and follow one Jorge Gonzalez.

■■■

Back in Buffalo, Mazzio received a phone call from Berrazino.

"Hey Dom, It's Bear. You free?"

"It will always cost you Bear, but sure, this is secure. Good news?"

"My guys are in place. They are equipped and ready to handle anything. So far, they have not seen your guy."

"Good, listen, I need to know the second they take care of this. Seriously, I don't care what time it is, the second this is done, call me. This is important."

"No problem. I told my guys the same thing. As soon as they have him, call me immediately."

"Great. Thanks again Bear. I won't forget this."

"No you won't" and the phone clicked dead. Ragulli walked into Dom's office to discuss the final preparations for the master plan.

■■■

I had located my target at his home address. He lived in a very nice neighborhood, so my upscale rental car wouldn't seem out of place. Jobs that required me to make people disappear were always the trickiest.

It would be so much easier to just break into someone's home and kill them, or follow them into the restroom of a restaurant or sporting event and put a few rounds into them. Making them disappear took a little skill, a little knowledge and a sprinkle of luck. I have been doing this for close to fifteen years and only one time has a body I made disappear came back. Well, sort of.

I once had to take care of a guy that lived in southern Florida, right outside The Everglades. My client paid me to make him disappear. I did the job with one very clean head shot and then took him into the glades. Filled with alligators and other predators, The Everglades would make the body disappear for good and I would have very little dirty work to do. I cut the hands, feet, and head off the body and then dumped it in the water. On my way out of the glades, I stopped a few times and threw the hands, feet and head into the water at different areas. My work was done, so I washed up and left Florida.

Three days later, I was reading a newspaper on-line and I came across a story about a headless, handless, footless body that was discovered in the glades. A few critters started to eat the corpse as per my hopes, so everyone thought a gator had gotten a hold of a person. They never found the head, hands or feet and assumed the gator or other predators ate those parts first. The last I heard, the cops were trying to match the body with their missing person reports, and even if they did, they would only find a grieving wife and a bunch of fake life insurance claims that would need to get paid back.

Oh the woes of being one of the women involved in this lifestyle. I found myself glad that when I was married, my wife and I were so in love with each other that neither one of us ever had anything to feel guilty about…my heart still panged like being stabbed by a tiny needle…just in one place, but every time it was deeper and deeper.

I followed O'Malley's guy from his home to one of his businesses where he stayed all morning. At around noon, he left and went to lunch meeting a very attractive and curvy young blonde lady in high heels and a swatch of fabric that was supposed to be a shirt dress.

After lunch, he visited her house for about an hour and then he went to the rest of his stores and by six pm, he was at home. The entire day was uneventful and a little boring, even predictable and common. I would continue to track his movements and eventually formulate a plan on how I wanted to take him.

I had another quiet dinner alone eating calamari and eggplant parmesan from a local Italian owned family joint on the West End and then returned to the hotel with a box of tiramisu for later.

After spending an hour in the hotel's pool doing laps and bullshitting with the neighbors in the hot tub, I scrubbed off the chlorine and shared frothy man germs from the community cappuccino slash hot tub in my waterfall shower and went to bed skin still hot, window cracked to get a soft breeze. I had no idea that I had been followed and watched.

While asleep, the dreams came again, they hurt my insides like a nail being driven into my skin…I awoke in a cold sweat to the soft innocent sound of a meow from my fire escape. Something was wrong… I could feel it.

■■■

The Ferro Brothers were each in one of the cars and Lima was in a plaza down the street from Gonzalez's house. All three of these guys were pretty good at what they did and knew that if they stayed on and completed this job, they would rise very quickly in the organization

There was a house on the street behind Gonzalez's house that was up for sale. It was down two houses and provided a good view from the master bedroom of Gonzalez's. This is where the Ferro brothers decided to set up so they could observe the situation. Earlier in the day they acted like one of them was the sales person and the two others were buying the house complete with pictures in front of a sold sign so they could occupy the house without suspicion. The night before, Lima took a screw driver and removed the outside door handle of the vacant house. He was then able to remove the realtors lock box. After the lock box was removed, Lima put the door handle back on to ensure no one surprised them while they were using the house.

They opened the box, got the remote code off the internet and could now gain access whenever they wanted without arising suspicion. If someone did come in the house while they were there, they would simply have to eliminate them and they were ok with that. They ate their dinner and kept a close watch on Gonzalez's house as they waited to hear back from Berrazino's contact for more information when it came in.

At about four ten in the morning, a rental car drove through the neighborhood. To anyone else looking, if they had been awake, this would have been a normal occurrence as the rental car never once slowed down or stopped. It just drove through the neighborhood and left. The Ferro brothers notified Lima who was able to skip trace the license plate number using the DMV website.

The car was traced back to We-Rent U-A-Car at the airport. Lima called a phone number Berrazino gave him and spoke to a computer hacker that their organization used. Using some internet website, the hacker was also able to access the rental company's computer system and found out which name and credit card was used to pay for the car rental.

With that information, Berrazino's contact started a computer search of all the hotels and motels in the Dallas area to see if they could find out what hotel their target was staying in.

After Gonzalez left for work, the same burgundy colored rental car appeared as if out of nowhere and followed Gonzalez. Neither the Ferro brothers nor Lima had any idea where their target was watching Gonzalez from. They decided not to follow their target at this time, figuring they would be able to find the hotel he was staying at from the rental car company. Each of the men split up and sat on one of Gonzalez's more prominent stores to see if their target showed up.

CHAPTER #9

The people in his congregation were "salt of the earth" people. They were honest, had very humble hearts and were fun to be around. For a person that spent a lot of his life without any family, he truly enjoyed having a large extended family to call his own. He loved being the pastor at the small church.

There was an older couple that came to church every single Sunday. Blizzard or an ice storm, dousing rains, no matter, they were in attendance. They even came during July that Sunday when the air conditioner for the church went out. That was actually the first day they started to become friends.

The old man asked him if he was going to have the air conditioner fixed. He said he was, but he was not sure when. The pastor had taken a look at the church's finances and there just wasn't enough money to have it fixed right now. The old man said he had a nephew that owned a small engine repair shop and he would be more than happy to send him out to take a look at it. The old man refused payment of any kind. He said he liked the church and was glad he could help out. The next day, the air conditioner was fixed.

To show his thanks, the pastor invited the old man and his wife over for dinner. Homemade meat loaf, fresh mashed potatoes, and corn on the cob from their garden. The older couple brought a bottle of red wine to go with the dinner.

The old man found out the pastor had spent some time in the Army but didn't like talking about that part of his life. The pastor found out the old man was a partial owner of Buffalo's minor league baseball team that had a ball park in downtown Buffalo. The old man said he had a lot of nieces and nephews that owned businesses around Buffalo and he spent a lot of his time helping them out where he could.

The evening started a lifelong friendship for the two men. Once a week the pastor would meet the old man for lunch. Once or twice a month, the old couple would have the pastor and his family over for dinner at their beautiful home. Despite their age difference, the two men truly enjoyed each other's company: one for being taught and one for teaching the wisdom God had given him.

One afternoon, the pastor received a call from the old man asking him if he could meet him at Roswell Park Cancer Institute in downtown Buffalo.

The pastor and his wife went right over. The old man's wife was diagnosed with cancer and was given three weeks to live. The old man was devastated. The doctor's thought it was best if the old woman didn't leave the hospital. She was admitted that day. During the next few weeks, the old husband never left her side and the pastor never left his.

Spending the majority of his time visiting the sick old lady and spending time with the old man were very trying for the young pastor. Even after spending many hours in prayer, the woman's condition hadn't improved. During this time, the pastor literally met hundreds of people that came in to visit the old man and his sick wife. The old man seemed to know everyone and was well respected in Buffalo. Even the majority of Buffalo's politicians stopped by to visit and pay their respects. At the time, the pastor didn't think anything of it. But later, it would all make sense.

When the old man's wife finally passed away, the pastor was there. They were the only two people in the room when she left this world and went on to the next. Both men openly wept at her passing. They held each other for support and the pastor prayed. He would always remember the question the old man asked him at the end of that very sad day.
"Does God punish us for our sins, by taking the people we love and care about most away from us? Would he do that?"

CHAPTER #10

Berrazino's contact got back to Lima early the next morning. Berrazino's contact ran the name and credit card number through his computer system to see if he could find what hotel Stevens was staying at. This proved to be a dead end. If Lima and the Ferro brothers wanted to know where Stevens was staying, they would just have to follow him.

Back in Gonzalez's neighborhood waiting for him to leave for work, I didn't plan on following him today. I only wanted to see if I could get into his house. A plan on how I wanted to complete this job was loosely starting to form in my mind and getting inside would be the best way to move forward with it.

At around the same time as the day before, Gonzalez left for work first opening the garage door and then coming out a few minutes later. With a jingle of his keys and a cup of coffee poured into a travel mug with a self-serving dry cleaner logo from his own company emblazoned on the side in his right hand he opened the door and got in.

While Gonzalez was backing out of his garage, I saw that there were no other cars inside. After doing a little research, I also knew Gonzalez was the only name on the loan for the house and all of the utilities were in his name. I wanted to make sure he didn't have a live in girlfriend. Though I wondered how someone like this would even get a girlfriend, he was pudgy and had huge black glasses and a greenish complexion that made him appear older than he was. I guessed that money can buy anything at all. For the moment, the neighborhood was quiet.

After about forty minutes it was time to go in. I called Geoff and told him what I wanted to do. He said he would call me back in five minutes. I got out of my car and walked towards Gonzalez's house. Using my cell phone, I called his home phone number. After six rings, an answering machine picked up. I hung up and called again. The same thing happened. I felt more than confident that the house was empty.

From my past observations, I knew Gonzalez was like most of the people that have house alarms. He would enter his house through his garage. Inside his garage, there would be a door leading into his house. The alarm would not be on the outside garage door but on the door leading into the house.

The best thieves never try to wear disguises or attempt to "sneak" up on a house. They simply walk down the sidewalk and right up the driveway like they own the house. So this is what I did. I went right to the front door. I leaned on the door bell and heard it chime in the house. After a minute, I did the same thing again. No one was home. So I acted like I was calling him, peeked in a window, checked my watch, turned, looked around the house for a key like I knew it was there and poked around to the back still looking like I was calling him.

I walked around the side of the house through the small gate and used my electric lock pick gun and had the man-size door to the garage open in less than 12 seconds. I closed the door behind me, but made it look like I had gotten the key from above the door frame just in case any nosy neighbors or neighborhood runners had seen me. The garage was what you would expect it to be: basic two and a half car garage, with shelves, a work bench, garbage cans, and a riding lawn mower. A minute after I was in the garage Geoff called me.

"I have the information you requested. Ready for it?"

I had asked him to hack into the alarm company's computer system to get the disarm code for Gonzalez's alarm system. Geoff was almost insulted with such an easy request. I learned a long time ago instead of asking Geoff to do things for me I would ask him if it were *possible* for him to do something. He would take it as a challenge or like I was questioning his skill and ability. He always pulled through, I suspected that he would do it whether possible or not. He wanted to please me so bad, he would always find a way to make what I needed happen.

. After disarming the system, I walked into Gonzalez's kitchen. He had one of those new coffee machines that just use a little cup of pre-measured and pre-packaged coffee grinds and water and viola coffee, a perfect cup in less than a minute.

I almost wanted to try a cup considering how much he clearly loved it. There was a wall of coffee cups, and individual coffee grinds in every imaginable flavor stacked under the counter and a spinning kiosk of them right next to the machine. Clearly not a female in this house, that coffee would have been much better organized and no way would country blue be the main color of the kitchen decor either.

The downstairs of Gonzalez's house consisted of a kitchen, dining room, sitting room, bathroom, and living room. There was a staircase leading to the second floor and French doors leading to the fenced in back yard.

The upstairs contained two more spare bed rooms, an office, another full bathroom and the master suite with attached walk in closet and master bath with only one toothbrush and the side of the sink it sat by was disgusting. A woman would have this place wiped down every night or morning, no way would it look like someone had shaved there every day for a year and never wiped out the sink. It was a very impressive house. For a brief moment, I contemplated buying it from the bank, renovating, cleaning that sink, and renting it out after Gonzalez was dead. I quickly dropped that idea and started to think more about how to kill him. For some reason, my mind kept wandering back to his messy sink.

It would be too easy for me to hide in his house or break in after he was in bed. Then I could quietly kill him and move him to the trunk of his car. Then, in the middle of the night, I could just drive off to…to where? How was I going to make him disappear completely? I had an idea but it would take a little prep work and timing would be the key.

I went back down through the kitchen and looked through Gonzalez's dated side by side refrigerator. Like many bachelors, there were not a lot of home cooked meals in there. It consisted largely of old condiments; take out containers and an open bottle of wine. I might get lucky here. I quickly went to the garage and searched through the garbage cans. Luckily I found what I was hoping to see.

I went back into the house and searched until I found where Gonzalez kept his alcohol. I was very happy with what I found. I had figured out how I was going to kill Gonzalez. As long as O'Malley paid me in full, this was going to be a quick, easy job I smiled to myself.

I left Gonzalez's house to make preparations to dispose of his body. I made sure to leave everything as I found it, even though I figured the coffee maker would be a fun trophy but I would just buy one with O'Malley's money to keep in Buffalo. I also remembered to set the house alarm before I left. I was feeling pretty good and looking forward to going to some place warm after this. I got back into my car and drove off. Like before, I did not know that I was being followed.

■■■

Max Ferro was watching a man named Gonzalez, a local dry cleaner franchise owner's, home when he saw a stranger walk right up the driveway as if he knew where he was going. He couldn't see what the stranger was doing, but assumed he was ringing the doorbell; he kind of looked like he was hoping the guy was home but he had just left.

Ferro huffed to himself as he drew in a slurp of hot mocha cappuccino thinking the dude would have to come back later. Two minutes later, the stranger, who Max could still not identify as anyone important, came around the side of the house to the walk-in garage door. Max had a perfect view of the target as he looked around for a key, slipped into the door and entered the home. Max slipped from where he was watching the house and popped on the other side of the gate. The door had a small scratch by the key hole that was similar to what was left when he had used a small lock picker on previous jobs.

Suddenly it hit him; this was the man he was looking for. Lima would be glad for his description, finally got one up on his brother. Stevens was in the house for eleven minutes and then he left as if disappointed not to find his "friend". By the time the maroon rental car passed by Ferro, Lima pulled in front of Ferro's car, put on his signals one at a time to show that he had put the tracking device on the car and that pursuit was imminent. Ferro followed Lima back to their two story watch house and followed the target via his lap-top.

■■

The heat was ridiculous outside today, the very concrete had to be sweating from the humidity hanging around being held down by the few clouds that did little to shade the sun from radiating painfully hot rays on the city. I figured all I needed to do was get a hold of some Rohypnol. Rohypnol, also known as the "date rape" drug is a little white tablet with "ROCHE" inscribed on one side and a 1 or a 2 inscribed on the other side, depending on the dosage in milligrams.

Rohypnol can be ground up and dissolved in a drink and it is very luckily for me, not so much for Mr. Gonzalez, undetectable by taste. It starts to work in approximately thirty minutes, long enough to make the process interesting but not dangerous.

Found in many college campuses around the country, Rohypnol would be no big deal to get a hold of before my plan unfolded. A bar owner in Dallas' West End, whom I dealt with before, almost always had some on hand.

While I was driving across the city to the Salty Kitty before it got too busy, my cell phone rang. I didn't recognize the number, but I still answered it, thinking maybe O'Malley wanted to pay up in full. That would make me respect him a little more I thought…maybe not.

"Hello?"

"You free to talk?"

Almost never had I gotten a call from Geoff without my requesting it via secure text. Most of our verbal transactions started or took place using encrypted e-mail or bulletin boards. Something must be wrong.

"Allen, I always have time for you." I joked using his pseudonym, "To what do I owe the pleasure of this call?"

"I guess you probably already know there are people tracking you. Just want to give you a heads up. Someone is trying to find you."

"What? What the hell are you talking about?"

"You know I am dialed in to everything, right? I keep tabs on certain things for safety reasons, and well some for fun. If you don't use it you lose it right?" he quipped like I wanted to keep joking at this point. "For example, I keep tabs on different credit card numbers I use, things like that. You get what I'm saying here?"

"Cut the shit kid, what's the point? No one needs to find me."

"OK, one of the services I provide you is like a free credit report service. All of the credit card numbers I give you; I have listed in a program on my hard drive. Any time one of these cards is used, a record is generated for it. I have alerts set up in the system-"

"Wait a minute Allen. Are you tracing me? Trying to follow me? Why would you want to know what I am doing?" This time I used his fake name to remind him who I was and what I know. I spoke very slow and low and added as much menace in my voice as I could muster. I did not like where this conversation was headed.

"Woo, buddy, just wait a minute dude. It's not like that. Not at all. Hell, every credit card number I get, I add to my program. I do it for you, for this reason even. Some of the numbers I keep, some of them I give to you when you ask. I am not tracking your movements, I don't give a damn what you do man. Geeze, I have set up alerts in the system to notify me if someone is researching the credit cards, their purchases, last uses and things like that."

"Allen, my patience is running out here. Get to the point. Now."

"Here's the point. I got on-line to check my e-mail and that son of a bitch was filled up with all sorts of alerts for one of the numbers I gave you. From what I can tell, you used this card to rent a car. Someone somewhere has gotten this card number and is running it all over Dallas. They are checking hotel and motel data bases, boarding houses, bed and breakfasts. It appears that someone is trying to figure out where you are staying or something."

What the hell! How could this happen? O'Malley? Who was trying to find me? Was I being followed right now? I glanced in the rear view mirror and took a hard left turn at the last second without using my blinker. I drove down the street and pulled over, but I didn't see anything suspicious.

"You still there? I thought you would like to know about this."

"Thanks for the heads up on this Geoff; sorry I just get all jittery when too many weird questions come up. How come you never told me you were doing this anyway?"

"It never came up before, never thought it would matter. I have gotten alerts a few times before, but it was always on credit cards I was using. Look if the Feds are ever after you, the person you want to know is me man. Geeze, I mean I have never gotten an alert on a card you have used like this, that is what made me react. When I got the alerts today, I had to research the card number to see if it was one I used. That's when I found out it was an old card I gave you over a year ago. Knowing the type of work you're involved in, I thought you might be in danger and I wanted to warn you."

"All right, consider me warned. Thanks. I have to figure out who is chasing me."

"If there is anything else I can do, you know how to reach me." I heard him say as I flipped the phone shut totally pissed off. Hot blood ran through my heart and I could feel the hairs on my arm standing up in anger.

I sat in my car for a few minutes thinking. What had I noticed, what had I seen? I didn't think O'Malley was smart enough to dig that deep. Why the hell would anyone be looking for me? Was there anything suspicious or out of the ordinary? I didn't see anything overt. I considered placing a call into Buffalo to see if there were any answers but now I trusted no one.

I reviewed what I knew. Someone had gotten a hold of my credit card number I had used to rent my car. One of the rental clerks? No, that didn't make sense. If they had stolen my number, they would have used it to make fraudulent purchases for televisions or game systems or cars, something big like that. Another customer at the counter? No one was even in the store when I got my car. Someone must have hacked into their system to get my number. But how did they know what credit card number I was using and what name?

The heat in my veins was overtaken by a deep cold ice feeling as time seemed to stop in an instant. I could almost smell the Magnolia trees as if de-ja vu was in full affect. I had to stop the racing in my head, panicking was only going to make me weak. 'Work backwards Rick' I said almost audibly but my mouth never moved, only my brain ran ahead of me full force. This feeling was sickening in the way I felt every July all over again.

Backward from the beginning, how would I track a false batch of information on a target? All the pieces fell into place. The only way someone would have known about the rental car would be if they saw me in the car and took the license plate number. Then, they would have had to hack the system and search the plate number. From the plate number they would have gotten my card number and the name I was using. That's what they searched the hotels with. Someone was looking for me, and they had already found me. I had to stop them from finding the rest of me. Gonzalez gets a pass today, but my job just got much more expensive, no way was this costing me my place on this planet, not now, not ever.

I pulled back on the road and headed towards the Northpark Center Fashion Mall. I wanted to be in a public place while I thought this through. I parked at the end of an isle next to two other cars. I breathed in deeply as I popped the hood to have a good story for why I was crawling around in the mall parking lot for a common car problem. I exited the maroon Mark V, pretended to check the oil, and knelt down and to check under the front of my car. I did not find anything. I proceeded to search the engine compartment as best I could. I still did not find anything. I checked under the back end of my car and found a small, square device that was crudely affixed to the underside of my bumper. Shocking handy work by I bet some ridiculous low life that thought he was better than me. Not this time I thought.

I was familiar with the device because I had used them in the past. As I yanked it off the frame of the car, I realized the model I was holding was guided by satellite technology, much the way a GPS device is. Someone could be following me from 1,000 miles away if they wanted to.

Whoever was looking for me was either very well-funded or a professional. Either way they could have hid this thing better. Maybe they didn't have a lot of time to put it on? All of these scenarios spelled bad news for me. I had a difficult decision to make. Get rid of the device by destroying it, then the people who were tracking me would know I was onto them.

Sure, it would buy me a little time, but eventually, they would pick me up again and I would not have the luxury of knowing when or how. I could keep the device on my car and pretend I didn't know it was there. I could drive the car someplace, a hotel or something, and leave it there. Whoever was looking for me would think I was staying at the hotel. That was a definite idea. At least eventually I would know who was tailing me. I also didn't want to put someone innocent in danger by affixing it to another random car, I knew how that felt….pain in my chest crept up my arms and into my neck, I chunked the box in the backseat and talked to the would be followers as if they could hear me.

"Fat chance asshole, you better look in your own mirror first!" and drove off.

The first store I found was another national big box retail outlet. I had to act fast; they could be watching me right now. I quickly purchased some deodorant, a tooth brush, and the rest of the toiletries a person would generally have while traveling. I also purchased a few shirts and a few pairs of pants, two random books, bottled water, snacks, a timer for a light, and a duffle bag. Then I drove across town to a motel near the interstate. I rented a room and parked the car directly in front of my room. Normally I would never do this…I had to make sure I wasn't panicking, I didn't want to miss a step, but if someone came looking for me; I wanted them to believe they had found me.

I unpacked my groceries and hung up the clothes. I opened the toiletries items and spread them around the bathroom counter. I wanted it to appear like I was really staying in this room. I even messed up the sheets on the bed and put the do not disturb sign out like I didn't want anyone in the room.

I attached a timer to the lamp and set it to automatically come on before dusk and shut off at 11:13pm. If someone was watching the room from outside, I wanted them to believe I was in there. Once I was satisfied the room looked the way I wanted it to, I left.

The next part of my plan was based on the belief that whoever was tracking me was doing it remotely and did not have a visual on me. I took a cab back to the airport and rented another car in a different name with a different credit card. Now I could move around again and not be worried about being followed and get into my own bed. I wasn't sure what I was angrier at; myself for having been followed and not knowing it, or the fact that someone was following me?

Was this maybe the government who had finally stumbled onto me and they were the ones tracking me? Maybe someone from one of the families got arrested and was trying to sell me out to the Feds for a lighter sentence? Maybe someone had hired out to have me killed? Who would have the juice to do so? Did they talk to Sal first? Was he ultimately behind this for the way I handled Fat Ritchie? No way, I thought…No way.

Usually, the simplest explanation is the right one, but, if this person was hired to kill me, when he had the opportunity to do so, why didn't he? I went back to my original thought. Maybe it was really just O'Malley keeping tabs on his investment? All I had were questions and I really needed some answers. I needed to quickly finish the job I was sent here to do so I could concentrate on these other problems. With my new, "clean" car, all I needed was some rohypnol, a pair of workman's coveralls, and a shovel.

I decided to drive to The Salty Kitty so I could get this job done quickly, knowing that my back could be lit up with a target on it at any moment. This pushed my strategy outside my comfort zone and made me double check all my motives and my whole plan. Although I appreciate the female body, I was definitely not there to spend money on strippers I would be shocked if at this moment I even noticed a naked woman.

No, I was there to see the clubs owner, Bramwell. I had never met him before, but I did do a job for him once, and he definitely owed me or at the very least Sal. He was a fairly high-level guy connected in Sal's organization. He was the eyes and ears for Sal's business dealings in Texas. I also knew he would have what I needed.

The club was busy and there was a bouncer working the door. After showing my id and paying the ridiculous $21.00 cover charge, I was admitted into the club. As far as strip clubs go, this was one of the nicer ones I had seen at least. Catering to an upscale clientele, the club was splashed in new age modern colors of dark grays, deep reds, and glossy black swirls. There was a main bar opposite the main stage and mini bars at the corners of the room. It didn't stink like cheap cherry scented smoke. There was a second floor, which I assumed had private VIP rooms. The club was very full and I walked directly to the bar.

I told the bartender I needed to speak with Bramwell. A few minutes later, a small rat looking guy and two huge bouncers came up to me.

"What can I do for you, champ?" Said the rat man.

"Bramwell?"

"No. I get to manage this 'fine' establishment. "

"Then you can't do shit for me. Tell Bramwell a friend from Buffalo needs to see him immediately." I probably should have been a little nicer but it had been a long day and I was not in the mood for games.

"You're in the wrong place buddy." He said as he turned away and yelled at me over his shoulder loud enough I heard him over the music, "You should leave now. Thanks for stopping in." One of his guards stayed to escort me out, and one left with him.

"I think you look like a rat. I also think you should get Bramwell before I have to remind him who is here to see him using your ugly face as a target." He stopped, turned around, looked at his bouncer with his hand held at mid belly on the bouncer to his side, walked up and touched the other on the back, both were immediately dismissed.

"We don't need to cause a scene here. Have a seat at the bar and I will see if he needs to see you. Enjoy the merchandise why don't you, I'd give you a private room but sounds like you need more than a blow-job to calm down." He got very, very close to my body, completely in my personal space bubble which today was larger than usual and said to me in a low threatening tone with a goofy half smile on his pointy face, "Make no mistake 'friend', if Bramwell gives me the ok, Mike and a few of his associates are going to take your ass apart."

"Fantastic. That sounds like fun." I said, reaching for where my gun was, just for reassurance.

After fifteen minutes of waiting, I decided to order a six dollar bottle of water from the bar. Gotta love strip club pricing. Everything is priced to generate single dollar bills that will be used for tipping. Bottled water is six dollars; alcohol eleven, cover charge was 21 dollars, all leaving me with a bunch of single dollar bills.

As I sat there thinking about why most tanning oils and sprays smelled like coconut and not something else, I felt a large man walk up beside me. I stood instinctively and he led me to the rodent man who personally escorted me through a door located near the bar with oil on velvet style painting of two women pleasuring each other in bright cartoon colors. Not quite art but it fit.

As we walked in, the big bouncer named Mike followed us. We were now in a narrow hallway with several doors. I was clearly off my game all tensed up and ready to strike. I wasn't sure if we were going to see Bramwell or they were taking me out of the public eye so they could "take me apart". The rat walked up to one of the doors and knocked then walked in as if he owned it. We walked directly into Bramwell's office.

"This is the piece of shit that I told you about, he demanded to see you and threatened everyone. Just give the word and I'll have Mike take care of things." He snickered.

I said nothing, just stood there and prepared myself to move if it came to that. I was already planning my escape. Luckily the fire exits were well lit in the narrow hall way, the Fire Marshall must be proud. If things went south, I knew I would push the rat into Mike, and then shoot Bramwell first, and then the rat and Mike. That's how it is in my line of work; always meeting new people and thinking of the easiest and fastest way to kill them.

Bramwell didn't say anything right away. He stood silently and observed the situation. Six feet five inches tall, shaved head, and a long, thick, dyed blond goatee, at well over 300 pounds with black skull tattoos on each of his large forearms, this guy would be a two shot kill, one to stun, one to end it. Surprisingly slick in appearance with a nice pair of black dress slacks, Gucci shoes, and a dark maroon short sleeve dress shirt with some sort of texture pattern on it made him look like an overweight biker. If a person wasn't careful, they would miss the intelligence in his light blue eyes as he soaked me in.

"A friend from Buffalo? Micky, did he tell you he was a friend from Buffalo?"

"Yeah Mr. B, he did but-"

"So he tells you he is a friend of mine from my home town, and you give him shit? What the FUCK is wrong with you Micky?"

"Mr. B, this ass, err, I mean, this guy threatened me and was fucking disrespectful."

"So, not only do you insult a friend of mine, in MY club, then you have to embarrass me in front of him and then you say he was disrespectful? This man asked to see me. You refused. Who is being disrespectful here? Not happy right now Micky. Get the fuck out of my office. And Big Mike, if you want to keep working here, or on Earth, you get the fuck out too. Leave me with my friend. Don't go home tonight Micky, until you talk to me."

After Mike and the rat left the office, Bramwell lit a cigarette and introduced himself as if we had always known each other and had planned a barbeque in the backyard or something.

"Langston Bramwell." He stuck out his hand, "I apologize about that. Some people, you know? Everyone just calls me Bramwell."

"Nice to meet you Bramwell. I apologize for causing a scene but I am on a tight timeline and I really need some help."

"What did you say your name was?"

"I didn't. I work with Salvatore DiFlippo."

"I work for Mr. DiFlippo too-"

"No, I don't work *for* him, I work *with* him. There's a difference."

"Ok, give me your name and I will call Buffalo and get you checked out. Once I get the ok, I will help you."

"Langston, can I call you Langston?" I said not waiting for an answer. This was getting ridiculous, I should have just stayed in Gonzalez's house and killed him in his sleep, "You're making the same mistake Micky did. I can assure you I am on legit business. If asked, I can also assure you Sal himself would want you to help me in any way you could. If you want a name, I'll give you a name. Richard Fanning."

Bramwell literally froze in time as if he had just been hit with a freeze ray from some comic movie. I knew that name would get his attention. Bramwell's ex-business partner used to own a nightclub with him and they were both laundering money through the business. As it so often happens, some small time player got arrested and was offering up Bramwell and Fanning to lighten his time.

The Feds started an investigation. They talked to Bramwell first. They leaned on him, threatened him and tried to scare him. Fortunately, or unfortunately, depending on who you were and how you looked at it, Bramwell didn't scare.

He told the Feds to go fuck themselves and arrest him if they wanted too. They released him. They moved on to Fanning. The Feds told Fanning that Bramwell was going to flip on him and sell him out. They said Fanning would be going away forever with big men that would like to get intimate with him. Fanning cracked and agreed telling the Feds everything.

Once Bramwell heard, he called Sal and asked for help with his problem. This was a special case and I was paid $75,000 to make Fanning disappear without the Feds thinking it was Bramwell, as he was the obvious first choice. I was on a tight timeline as Bramwell's arrest was imminent.

With the help of Geoff, I also set it up so Fanning would appear to be the dirty partner, while Bramwell was totally innocent and clean. When we were done, the Feds thought they had been played by Fanning who took all of his laundered money and disappeared, even apologizing for their bad decisions.

They also thought Fanning was framing Bramwell to take the fall for him. Bramwell was once again brought in and questioned. This time, the questions had a different theme and tone. They wanted Bramwell's help in trying to track down Fanning. Bramwell told them how much Fanning loved Europe and how disappointed that he was that he'd been lied to. When the questioning was over, Bramwell was cut loose with an apology and the Feds continue to look for Fanning as well as the missing money to this day.

They will never find him, because what's left of him is currently in two fifty-five gallon drums of acid in a storage facility in Albuquerque New Mexico. The storage fee is charged directly to a credit card they have on file every month. As far as Fanning's laundered money, I took all $346,780 of it and deposited into one of my off-shore bank accounts.

All he could bring himself to say was, "That scum bag can rot in hell. He took all of my money and disappeared. He tried to frame me for it too."

"Not exactly, you paid $75,000 to have him killed and never be found again. The frame part was Sal's idea because he thought you would be useful to his organization. Was Sal right? Are you going to be useful Langston?"

He tipped his smoke in the ashtray nervously and turned his eyes to the right hard as if he was slicing the air with his gaze, "I don't know what you're talking about."

"You had a code word to use with the person you hired in the event you needed to speak to him directly. That code word was never written down. It was told to you, in person, by Dominick Mazzio. He whispered it in your right ear at Campisi's Restaurant on Mocking Bird Lane. You remember that word, don't you?"

"What is it then smart ass?"

"King." I whispered into the empty space that sat around us as if no words had ever been spoken before. It was so quiet I could almost hear the tobacco burning inside his cigarette as the smoke formed swirling patterns above his bald head.

"Holy shit, you're the guy!"

"Yeah Bramwell, I'm the guy and I sure as hell could use your help."

"Anything: girls, sex, weapons, cars, a crew, what do you need?" He picked up the phone to call my favor in.

I told him I only needed six 2 milligram tablets of rohypnol. Bramwell opened a safe that was hidden under his desk and gave me what I asked for. I thanked Bramwell for his time and I left the club. As I was leaving, I heard him call Micky back into his office. I went to another big box retail store and purchased a very nice digging spade, a cheap pair of tennis shoes and a pair of painter's coveralls. Then I went back to my first hotel. I needed to get some rest because I knew the next day would be very long and I would need all of my skills to get through it alive.

CHAPTER #11

The last mission I was a part of with the Army changed me. It brought me to a cross roads in my life. I didn't know it at the time, nobody ever really does I imagine, but the choices I made then still have an effect on the things I do today.

On paper, it was a simple operation. I would be part of a ten man team that was tasked with gathering intelligence on an up and coming drug cartel based in South America and we were only going there to observe, record, and report.

We were dropped in the area of the cartel's operations without any problems; we had everything that we needed for the next eight days. We had our c-rations, jungle sleeping bags and a lot of insect repellant. Nothing else really mattered except that we stay hidden, and that we all knew where we were going to be picked up from in a few days. As far as operations went, this was supposed to be an easy one. This was something we had done numerous times in the past; business as usual.

Research showed that we would encounter several small villages along the way to the cartel's compound. All of our research indicated the villagers were poor farmers and not involved in the drug trade nor were they supposed to have any ties to the drug cartel. In all of the missions I went on with the Rangers, during all of the little conflicts and skirmishes I was involved in, our Intel had never been so wrong.

There are different degrees to darkness in jungles. Sometimes it was light enough at night that we could see everything we needed to. Other times, it was so dark; we couldn't see our hands in front of our faces. The one constant was the many different shades of blacks, and browns, and greens all in one place.

There is always a mist hanging in the air, making everything appear to be cloudy every moment that passed was different than the next. There are no hard lines; everything is soft, mushy under our feet, and subtle smells along the passages through the growth we traveled in. I wondered if it was flora or fauna or was it just animals and life that went along without violence or disturbances that weren't perfectly in order with the way life moved in the wild. It was always very hot and humid, and never quiet in a jungle, even at night the chirping and whirring of God's creations could drive a man insane with fear.

It was our seventh day there and everything was going along as planned. We had the compound staked out and were gathering great intelligence on what was happening there. People came and went, covered trucks came and left couriers on small rickshaws and bikes came with bags laden with materials and left empty handed but smiling, clearly having been well compensated. We also took in some of the activity going on at a nearby village located approximately a mile and a half from the cartel compound. To our surveillance reports and our previous Intel reports, the villagers were just that; villagers.

Cloudy, cold, and overcast day the sun never broke through the clouds. The air was so heavy we could feel the rain in the air. As dusk settled in the heavens unleashed their expected downpour. Hours of heavy laden blankets of rain poured on to our location. To this day, I never experienced rain like that. Having already been there for seven days, we were almost done closing down our operation to leave the next day. Cold, tired, filthy, soaking with mud from caked on dust, and grime, hunger was the least of our worries but complicated our escape. It was raining so hard that we couldn't even see the compound anymore.

I don't remember who said it in our group, but someone said they were tired of eating shitty c-rations and we should stop in the village and get some real food. It wasn't uncommon for us to do something like this, especially with all of the Intel and surveillance we had on this particular village. The sergeant made the call; we swept the village and didn't find anything suspicious. A village elder offered us the use of one of his large out buildings that reminded me of a barn. It was big and airy, and very dry inside, even with the rain pounding on the roof. There was one main room with nothing in it. There was a set of double doors on each end of the building. He explained the building was used as storage, but didn't have anything to store in it right now.

We made a small fire in the middle of the building where it was clear burning had occurred in the past, traded the rest of our c-rations away to the villagers for goat meat, milk, potatoes and homemade bread. As we were cooking the food, everyone started to relax a little bit. We were all just starting to eat and discussing who was going to take first watch for the evening when the shots rang out. I couldn't even hear the rain any more, the sound of blood pounding through my ears as I attempted to triangulate the sound's origination. I heard the realization of our set up as if it was an audible voice in the momentary silence of my group that seemed to click by in slow motion as if the seconds were hours.

We were all Army Rangers, warriors. We had all been battle tested and were unafraid to fight when we had to. We all knew instantly we had been suckered into the building and an ambush was being unleashed on us. It wasn't time to think or plan. It was time for action. Everyone on the team knew what to do without discussing it. We all got as flat to the ground as we could and someone put the fire out. I will always remember how in the midst of gunfire and a rain storm, how dry the ground smelled. It was a moment that I can't shake even to this day; anytime I walk into a dusty old used bookstore or barn, the smell takes me back to that time.

The shots that were piercing through the worn wood walls were coming from the front and right side of the building. The enemy was shooting at us with high powered automatic weapons; double barrel shot guns, and small arms. Our eyes quickly adjusted to the darkness and most of the shots were coming in high over our heads. No one was really panicking, yet.

I looked into the eyes of the men nearest me, the rest would fall in line, and we had to move, now. Four of our guys stayed in the building and started to lay down some suppressive fire from behind pillars and the one old tractor that was in the building. The other six of us, myself included, started making our way towards the other set of doors. We needed to get outside and flank the people that were firing on us. We had a plan and knew what we were going to do, just like in training. Once out the doors, three of us would go left, and three would go right.

When we got to the doors, we encountered harsh and quick resistance. There were at least six or seven people watching the back doors. They were armed and shooting, luckily they didn't have the training and experience that we did. We dropped them quickly and went out into the village. It was still raining and without any electricity in the village, it was horror movie scary dark. The kind of dark that as you enter it, your blood vessels sizzled with anticipation of death.

People were everywhere and most of them were armed. Every person we came across, we killed out of necessity. They had been told to eliminate us. It was systematic, fear based, and brutal. My remaining four team members were able to leave the building joining us in the fight. As we neared the edge of the village, the number of people shooting at us started to decline, they were hiding from us, and from their hideaways, some were still trying to kill us, when all we wanted to do was get out of their village. I hated this part of war.

We had choices; we could leave the village and head to our pick up zone or continue the fight. Once again the sergeant made the call. You don't start a fight with a bunch of cold, tired Rangers and then run away and hide before it's finished. So we went back...

Not only were we trained in jungle warfare, but we were also trained in urban warfare. Once we came back and reentered the village it became apparent to us that we were fighting both villagers and members of the cartel. You don't give it much thought when you are in the heat of battle. You are not thinking at all, just reacting. You fall back on your training and experience, shut down, and shoot. What these people didn't understand about us was we were trained killers. That is what OUR government trained us to be. Then they set us out into the world so we could perfect our skills. So even though we were in their village, outgunned, outmanned, and blindsided by their ambush, they didn't stand a chance against us. We destroyed them all. We killed every person in that village that night. We killed men, women...children. I killed men; I killed women and the children.

I tried to justify it by saying it was in the heat of battle. They were shooting at us so it was in self-defense. It doesn't matter. It doesn't help how raw you feel on the inside. We didn't have to kill everyone in the village. Near the end of the fight, some of the villagers were walking out into the open with their arms raised to surrender to us. We still killed them.

Does it make it right, even if I was following orders and protocol? Does it make it right that it was classified, that no one would know, that I could compartmentalize it, that I could use it to make a living, to breathe each day and not feel responsible for the lives snuffed out instantly without thought, the cries for mercy that I ignored, that I could have given my life for theirs, but they would have still died...was it right? No. Not even then. Not ever.

When we were finished we burned everything in the village. All of the buildings, the supplies, and the bodies. Everything was offered as a sacrifice to the earth and rain that evening. The sergeant called in a progress report to a LT somewhere else. The LT talked to a captain and someone, somewhere up the chain of command, decided that our best course of action was to provide ground support to the air strikes that would be taking place within the next few hours.

We were instructed to position ourselves around the compound so no one could get in or out. If we saw anyone trying to gain entry to the compound or attempting to leave, we were to kill them. We did.

Several hours later, the cartel and the compound were just haunting loud, screaming, memories. The air strikes killed any remaining people we didn't. Once the strike started, many people in the compound attempted to leave. A lot of them were women and domestic workers. Maids and cooks I thought to myself as I continued to fire. I'm killing maids and cooks. It didn't matter to the air strike team. We had our orders, and our orders were to kill. When we had confirmed a "successful" end to our mission, we were air lifted out of there.

As I sat in the chopper flying home, I felt disgusted, ashamed and embarrassed at the things that I had taken part in. It sickened me physically as I chose to swallow my own vomit so as to appear strong to my team and it all made me question my humanity. How can a person do such awful things to other people and then walk away and go on with his life? I was never a religious person. We didn't go to church in my family so I never really thought about God. For the first time in my life, I was thinking of Him.

It scared me to think that one day, I heard a Sunday School teacher tell me somewhere in the back of my head that I might have to stand before Him and answer for the things I did on this day. How do you tell God that you slaughtered some of his creations because it was your job? Can you even tell Him you were doing it for the good of your country? Would He even listen or care? Didn't he see it? Did he see me and the men on my team? No.

CHAPTER #12

Another night of painful dreams and I was up and awake before the sun was hoping it would quiet the screaming in my head. I quickly grabbed everything from my room and brought it to my car. I then returned to my hotel room and wiped everything down that I had touched and left enough of a mess to ensure everything would be cleaned thoroughly. I would not be returning to this room.

I drove across town to a plaza that was near the motel room that I had. I was hoping the person tracking me would think I had spent the night there. There was a convenience store in the plaza and I purchased a cup of coffee, a newspaper, and a bag of doughnuts. I walked from the plaza to my false motel room. I wanted it to appear to anyone watching that I had stepped out early in the morning to get some breakfast and the paper. I was hoping they would think they missed me leaving to get coffee.

It wasn't a long walk but with every step I took, I was waiting for a bullet to rip into me. The creepy feeling of knowing someone is stalking you waiting to kill you was making me question everyone who I ran in to: their intentions, glances, and words. If this was the end for me, I would gladly accept it. Sitting silent in the darkness of my mind, I used to fear my meeting with God, the alleged creator, but now I looked forward to it. Sure, I would have to answer for the horrible things I did, but He would also have to provide some answers for the horrible things that He did. Maybe He was the one doing the avoiding?

I made it to my fake room without any shots being fired. I had left a small discolored string on the bottom of the door frame and another one near the door handle. If anyone had attempted to gain access to my room, I would know about it. Both strings were still in place. I opened my door and out of habit, I cleared the small room and bathroom. It appeared to be in the same state I left it in.

I would need to drive around my car with the tracking device on it so the person following me would think I was still unaware of his presence. An outline of an idea was forming in my mind and with a little luck; I thought I could use the tracking device to my advantage. I took the car and started to drive around aimlessly. I was checking to see if I was being followed. I drove around for over an hour, but I did not see a tail or recognize anyone following me. Good. He was still tracking me electronically, perfect.

I stopped at a flower shop and picked up a few bouquets of flowers. Then I drove to a cemetery to scout it out. This was not an original idea, but I figured I would explore a few graveyards. I would look for graves that were being dug that day for funerals the next day. I would return after dark and dig them a little bit deeper with my shovel. Then, after I eliminated Gonzalez, I would transport him to the grave and dump him in. I would add the dirt over him and tomorrow, after the funeral, he would have "disappeared" completely. The trick is to make sure you dig a deep enough hole.

I found two great spots in the same cemetery. Both were out of the way and off the main access road. I walked to nearby gravestones and laid down some of the flowers I had purchased. A guy laying down flowers and spending a few minutes at a headstone is normal; a guy wandering around aimlessly in a graveyard with a shovel would cause some suspicion, so instead I kneeled at a little headstone. Jenna Linder, I put all the rest of my flowers on her grave noticing her parents hadn't been there in a while. I dusted off the cobwebs in the granite vase to the side of her stone where I put the flowers. I noticed as I stood two unmarked graves, one on either side of her. Only a small plastic white marker with an initial and last name that looked several years old marked the spaces. The names matched up, Jenna's mom and dad. The peace that came from that moment of knowing they were with her, not suffering every day, hating themselves for letting her go, took my breath away for a moment. I would be back after dark to do some digging and Jenna I would not soon forget.

My next stop was to head back to Gonzalez's house and spike his wine with the drugs I got from Bramwell. I parked my car in a plaza parking lot two blocks from Gonzalez's and started walking towards his house. I took a casual stroll around his neighborhood looking for anything suspicious. There were several houses for sale in his neighborhood. I walked by one house looking at the information packet in the weather proof plastic roll container above the for sale sign and noticed there were five rental cars parked in the street in front of and near his house. Huh. Maybe it was nothing, or maybe it was something. It seemed a bit odd to me. I filed the thought away in my memory and continued on. I didn't see anything else remotely suspicious. Maybe brokers or potential buyers had just come in from out of state to see this rather regular house? I kept walking.

I slowed my pace as Gonzalez's house came into view. Once again I used my cell phone to repeatedly call his house. Once again, I didn't get an answer. I rang the doorbell a few times and waited. I casually checked my watch and looked like we were supposed to meet. I scanned the neighborhood and didn't see anyone so I walked around to the same door I had picked last time. I got in the garage, closed the door and then walked into the house. I used the same alarm code to deactivate the alarm. I was so fast I was afraid in my haste I had forgotten something.

I opened the refrigerator and found an open bottle of wine. It was newly uncorked, and still had a little over two thirds of the wine left in it. I crushed up all of the tablets I had into a fine powder on his counter and added all of them into the bottle. Once I was sure they were all dissolved, I put the bottle back in the fridge. There was no turning back now. Tonight was the night. If Gonzalez showed up with company, I would have to kill everyone and make them all disappear. I was hoping it wouldn't come to that. I didn't dig enough graves for that.

I wish I had the luxury of more time to follow and scout Gonzalez to better learn his movements and habits. I just couldn't take that time with someone doing the same to me and trying to learn my habits.

I left Gonzalez's house and again walked slowly through his neighborhood back to the plaza where my car was. I noticed a moving van parked in the plaza. It had been there earlier, but something about it bothered me. Had I seen it before? I tried to remember but I just couldn't place it. I tried to shake the feeling off as being paranoid, but I had learned over the years that paranoia keeps you focused and alive. I committed everything about it to memory and jumped back in my car. I would go grab lunch and then sit on one of Gonzalez's stores. Hopefully his day was hard enough to warrant a nice glass of chardonnay.

■ ■

Back at the house for sale, Lima was also up early. He was watching the tracking device over the net. So far, there had been no movement.

Late last evening, Angelo Ferro took a ride to see where the car was parked. It was in the lot of a small roach motel off the interstate. Ferro sat on the car until around 11:30pm. There wasn't a lot of activity at the motel, but in room #117, the light went out at approximately 11:15 pm. Ferro paid the older man working the front desk of the motel for information.

Although he did not find the name he was looking for, he discovered the person staying in room #117 was a lone male that fit the description of their target. Ferro was confident that they had found where the target was staying and drove back to the house.

Their target was on the move, finally. Lima wasn't sure if he should have left one of the Ferro brothers on the motel all night and was nervous about not doing it. He was happy to see their target on the move. After a few stops, it appeared the target was on the way back to Gonzalez's house.

"I think he is going to get into that house again. He's on his way here"

Angelo asked "Why can't we take him now? We could do it quietly while he is in the house and then wait until Gonzalez comes home and do him too. We clean it all up and we're out of here tonight."

"I don't know why, but we have our instructions. If I had to guess, this is a non-sanctioned hit and our target is breaking the rules. Once he officially breaks the rules, we are allowed to take him." Lima replied

"But who would know? There wouldn't be any witnesses to our story"

"Listen Angelo, we do it like we're supposed to. Neither one of us is high enough to make decisions or change decisions, so just shut up and listen. We do this thing like we were hired to and we'll move up."

Like before, their target went into the house. He was only in there for four minutes this time and then he was out. He walked around the neighborhood and then simply vanished.

"Damn, this guy is good. If we would have been tailing him, he would have spotted us. Where the hell did he go?"

"No clue but he is on the move right now. I gotta call Bear and give him an update. I think this thing is going to go down tonight."

∎∎

Back in Buffalo, DiFlippo was meeting with Mazzio.

"Dom, is there an update from this Texas thing?"

"Nothing yet. As soon as I hear something, I will let you know. It seems like an easy job, so I don't expect it to drag out much longer."

"Ok. Good. The people in NY will be pleased when this is over. Are we current on everything else?"

Every meeting with the old man was the same. Mazzio was really getting tired of it. Are we current on this? What's going on with that? Blah, blah, blah, blah, blah. Hopefully, this would be the last meeting with the old man. Once Stevens was eliminated, Ragulli would eliminate the old man, and together they would make it all appear that Stevens did the Dallas job and then came back here and had a falling out with DiFlippo. Mazzio would say Stevens killed DiFlippo and went into hiding.

Mazzio would step up, a broken hearted hero ready to fill Sal's shoes and offer a three million dollar reward on whoever killed Stevens that would never have to be paid. It would be perfect. The only people that would know the truth would be Berrazino, Ragulli and maybe the team that took Stevens out.

Ragulli wouldn't say anything because he would be promoted to Mazzio's position now and Berrazino wouldn't say anything because he would be afraid of being named in a conspiracy to kill a mafia boss. If word got out that he was involved, no one would trust him and he would be dead within hours. Plus, Mazzio planned on offering Berrazino a garbage bag full of cash. Mazzio wasn't sure if he would eliminate Berrazino's team or not. If they did a good job, he might just "buy" them from Berrazino and put them to work for him. The old man's ramblings snapped Mazzio out of his plans.

"Listen Dom, I think I am starting to catch a cold or something. I am not feeling very well. I am going to go back to my room and lie down. I don't want to be disturbed the rest of the day or evening, unless we have confirmation on the Texas thing."

"No problem Mr. DiFlippo. Get some rest and I hope you feel better. If you need anything, soup, hot tea, anything at all, let me know." Mazzio said as if he cared.

"Thanks Dom. We have been together a lot of years and I know I can always count on you."

After the old man went to his room, Mazzio had a meeting with Ragulli.

"Anthony, I spoke with Bear today. It appears this thing is going to happen tonight. I need you to be ready."

"Just say the word. I can take him out right now if you want."

"No, let's make sure Stevens is out of the picture first. Let's stick to the plan. The old man isn't feeling too well today. He said he was going to spend the rest of the day in his room. With a little luck, this whole thing will be over before the sun rises tomorrow."

■■

Dusk was settling in on Dallas. After I followed Gonzalez home, I spent the rest of the day driving around. I stopped at a mall and killed a few hours there. I cruised the motel on the interstate but didn't stop. I drove to another one of my favorite Dallas restaurants, Sonny Bryans Smokehouse. If this was to be my last meal, I wanted it to be good. I ordered the dinner plate with ribs, brisket, and pulled pork. I also got a side of onion rings and they were the best rings I have ever had! I finished my meal with a nice fresh baked cobbler. When I was finished eating, it was nighttime.

I left the restaurant and drove to the cemetery. Time to work off some of my extra calories I consumed at dinner. The gates were closed and locked. I pulled my car over to the curb, popped the trunk and I tossed my shovel over the fence. After that, I jumped in the car and parked it in a restaurant's parking lot a few blocks away and walked back to the cemetery. When there were no cars or people, I picked the lock on the fence and slipped through the gate. I closed the gate and relocked the fence behind me. I grabbed my shovel and went to the graves I had scouted out earlier.

In the old days, most of the graves in this country were dug six feet deep. Speculation is they were dug six feet deep to discourage grave robbers or animals from digging them up. In recent times, graves are nowhere near six feet deep. Some states have a minimum depth that graves need to be dug. In California, most graves rest comfortably two feet below the surface of the grass. It's the same for Texas.

The grave I was looking at appeared to be dug about five feet deep. This would account for the coffin and the concrete bunker it was sealed in. I slipped the painter's coveralls on over my clothes and dug another three feet down into the ground. When I was finished, I went over to the second grave I scouted earlier in the day and dug that one down three feet as well. I probably wouldn't need it and it was more than likely going to be a waste of time and energy, but I liked to leave nothing to chance.

I hid my shovel in some bushes with the painter's coveralls at the gravesite and returned to my car. As I was walking to my car, the hairs on the back of my neck started to prickle and stand up. I stopped walking and bent down as if to tie my shoe scanning the area but did not see an immediate threat. I had been in this business a long time to know and understand that my subconscious had picked up on something that my conscious mind had missed. My gut was almost always right, except once. I stood up and cautiously continued walking to my car.

In the restaurant's parking lot where I parked my car, I recognized a blue car. The car looked a lot like one of the rental cars that were parked near Gonzalez's house. I wasn't sure if it was the same but I needed to get closer to see the plate number. The restaurant was in a plaza and the blue car was parked in front of a movie rental kiosk outside a gas station.

I walked to my car and got in. I pulled out my cell phone and acted like I was using it to call someone. I scanned the front of the convenience store that had a few booths set up for eating from the ready-made fried menu. Through the glass, I saw a lone male keeping watch of the parking lot.

"Gotcha!" I said allowed in a loud whisper to myself. I quickly closed my phone and drove out of the parking lot. With the tracking device, my pursuer wouldn't be in a rush to follow me. I was hoping I would have enough time to put some distance between us so I could dump the car and lose him. Now that I knew what he looked like, I would be able to handle him after I completed my job. It was a good thing I had taken the time to finish both graves after all.

I drove through the city and jumped on the interstate. I needed to find a place to ditch the car where there were a lot of people. I needed to lose my pursuer in a crowd long enough to finish my job and bury the body. If it had been earlier, I would have gone to a mall. But since it was after 10:00pm, everything was closed. I decided to drive to Historic downtown Dallas near the West End. Bars, clubs, dance halls, and restaurants all within walking distance of each other was perfect. I could park my car in a pay lot and get lost with all the other club goers. When I was sure I wasn't being followed, I could slip away. That's just what I did, ditching the keys in a nearby trash can and calling a cab in a fake drunk voice to meet me by the 5 and 9 club Nuevo.

I walked around a bit across the street from the club and bounced between a few different clubs waiting on the hit man and my cab, wondering who would show up first. I didn't see my pursuer and was sure I was not being followed. The cab finally showed up and I staggered across the street with my clothes looking a little disheveled to add to my shtick and slumped over like a drunk would saying meaningless strings of words that sounded like I thought I was going to get laid when I got back to my hotel by a girl I thought was following me. I kept asking the cabbie to look and see was she following us. She was supposed to be. The cabbie would laugh, call me a dumb ass drunk and tell me no, no one was following us. A story he could tell his wife when he got home, some drunken entertainment for him made me happy. He left me at a hotel just a block from my second car just where I left it. I told him thank you and to keep the change from a hundred dollar bill. The fare was only $27.00. I was sure his night was made; I know using him as an informant was priceless. When I was done staggering into the hotel lobby, and I was sure I wasn't being followed, I went into the men's room, cleaned myself up, and when I was sure I had not been followed, I ran out to my car and drove back towards Gonzalez's house.

■■

Max Ferraro was responsible for following their target. Angelo Ferraro was responsible for following Gonzalez and Lima stayed at the vacant house to keep watch on Gonzalez's house. Max had a laptop in the car with him so he could follow the tracking device. Lima also had a laptop at the vacant house so he could keep an eye on their target as well.

Lima had given the update to Berrazino earlier in the day. Berrazino told Lima to wrap this up as soon as now, other business was waiting for him back in NY. Lima told him he should finish his task before the sun came up and would be on the first plane back to Rochester.

Their target had bounced around a bit today after going into Gonzalez's house. He showed up at one of Gonzalez's stores and followed him around for a while. Then the prick went to a mall and had a fancy dinner while the men sat on sandwiches from a local shop and Max ate a pizza pocket and eggroll with a huge 44oz soda watching Steven's car at a local restaurant near the cemetery.

Max said he was probably digging a grave to drop Gonzalez in. Lima thought if they could find the grave their target dug, maybe they could just drop *him* in there and not have to cut him up. It was good to have options, the cleaner the better; it was nice to have this guy doing their work for them.

The target was on the move again. He got on the interstate and was really moving. Lima told Max to relax and just follow him with the tracking device. Angelo was just walking in the front door as Lima was hanging up the phone with Max. Gonzalez was home for the night.

There was nothing to do now but watch and wait. When their target showed up later tonight, they would be ready to eliminate him. Lima was surprised at how easy it had been so far. He knew of Steven's reputation and couldn't believe the assassin had been so careless.

Maybe a lot of his reputation was bullshit. Lima had seen it before. A lot of mafia guys did it. They inflated their own reputations to look better and more needed to their bosses. Maybe he was just getting sloppy in his old age. Lima would have to remember what happened to Steven's so when he was the top hitter, it wouldn't happen to him.

■■

Max didn't want to look suspicious sitting in his car so he walked to a pay phone in the plaza. He pretended to use the phone for 15 minutes and still didn't see his target. He was getting antsy. He hung up from his pretend phone call and went into the convenience store and grabbed a few fried delights off the local menu, grabbed a job guide and a huge soda then settled in by the front windows so he could spot the target and see where he came from. A few minutes later, he saw the target walking up the street from the direction of the cemetery.

The target stopped and tied his shoe. Then he walked right to his car and got in. When he was in his car, he made a phone call. Probably calling his boss to let him know the hit was all set. After he hung up, he started his car and left the parking lot. He never even looked around. Whoever this guy was, he had no clue what was going on around him. Max gave him one minute and then left the store and got into his car. He fired up his laptop and opened the tracking program. Then he called Lima. This was all going to be over by the end of the night, no need to tail him closely. Just let the computer do the walking. Getting a ticket for speeding right now would be a bad, bad idea.

■■■

Jorge Gonzalez had dinner with a much younger girl he was trying to get into bed. It was the second time he had taken her out and all signs were pointing to him going home alone. Again. This is exactly what happened on their first date. Oh well, he would play it out. This girl was at least six years younger than him and had the sweetest ass he had seen in a long time. All he could think about was burying his face in her perky breasts and making her scream to stop fucking her so hard.

The date ended at her car. She gave him a long, lingering kiss, right on his lips. It was a kiss that promised good things to those that waited. Gonzalez was the perfect gentleman. He didn't beg, didn't try to force her and he surely didn't try to make her feel guilty about the $250 meal they had just shared. His pants were uncomfortably tight as he watched her drive away. Yes, she was definitely worth taking the time for. By his estimation, he would have his way with her naked and maybe bound as if it were her idea, within the next two dates.

Gonzalez climbed into his own car and started driving home. He would spend some time in his office reading his e-mail and he would relax with a glass of his favorite wine and probably some hard core porn to get over the disappointment of being alone tonight.

■■

On my way to Gonzalez's house, I drove by the plaza that had the moving truck in it. It was still there and it hadn't moved. It didn't make sense for the moving truck to be there. It was out of place. I figured the van would play a part in my pursers plan to get me. I knew a cleaner on the east coast that owned several moving vans, just like this one. In the back of his vans, he had everything he needed to "clean" a job.

I had used the cleaner before on a few different jobs. He did all his work on the east coast with a very limited area of travel. He was the best at what he did though. His normal rate was $25,000 to do a "cleaning". The cleaner never participated in the hit. A cleaner's job is to come in after a killing has taken place and "clean" the scene. This could include making a body disappear to cleaning up blood and bodily fluids to repairing bullet holes in walls and repainting and everything else to hide the fact that a murder had occurred. I had used this guy on a few jobs when I was paid to make someone disappear completely. I was still making $25,000 on the deal after paying the cleaner his fee. It made the work go by faster and it was safer for me.

I bet if I could get into the back of this van that's what I would find. Since a good cleaner never took part in the hit, that meant there were two people looking for me, if not more. It was starting to come together now. These dudes were so sloppy I bet dollars to donuts they were staying in one of the empty houses in Gonzalez's neighborhood keeping watch on Gonzalez.

Since I had seen the rental cars on the street behind Gonzalez's house, I now had a pretty good idea of what house they were in and how long this had been going on. What I didn't know was who had sent them after me. I kept thinking about it and the only thing I could come up with was O'Malley. I must have pissed him off so much that he called his uncle or whoever and hired a crack pot team to take me out. They picked me up at Gonzalez's house and have been following me ever since. Once I eliminated Gonzalez, I would take out O'Malley as well, the minute I was done taking care of this rag tag hit crew. Too bad for them. I wondered how many people were after me? I saw five cars and a van. Was it six people, or were there more?

■■

SHIT! Max was starting to sweat and definitely panicking. He followed the target on the laptop tracker to Dallas's historic district and couldn't find him. He found his car and parked in the same lot paying the $20 premium to hold his space. There were too many bars and clubs. Max wished he had Angelo there. He didn't know if he should start searching the bars or stay with the car. He didn't want to call and ask for advice. Lima and Angelo already talked down to him and he didn't want to give them another reason to make fun of him he knew he was not near as dumb as they say he looked. He would sit and watch the car. The target had to come back to the car, must have just needed some quick pussy or maybe a drink to get him ready. Whoever this guy was, he was a poser and clearly not as good at his job as he made it seem. Max would wait it out; maybe he would get a drink too.

■■

I wasn't sure if I should take out the shooter first or my target. I decided to sneak into the neighborhood and scout both houses. There were pro's and con's to both approaches and deciding the value in each was of the utmost importance.

If I took out the shooter first, I would not be rushed or worried when it came to taking out Gonzalez. However, if something went wrong, the shooter got a shot off with his gun, or if one of the neighbors were walking their dog at the wrong time, someone might hear or see something and call the police or add another element to the situation causing collateral damage I wasn't prepared to be a part of. If that happened, I would have to get out of the neighborhood fast and miss my chance with Gonzalez. Plus, I didn't know how many people were in that house waiting for me. I had seen five rental cars and a moving van. I had to assume there was at least six people, but it could have been anywhere from six to twenty-one. Hiring twenty-one people to kill one person, even a professional as good as I was, just didn't seem logical. Hiring six people didn't seem logical either, but it was more rational.

I was hoping Gonzalez had already had his wine and was passed out, at least that would make him a non-moving target. If I took out Gonzalez first, then I would have the time to stash his body and then I could eliminate the shooter in the vacant house. If it all went to hell then, at least Gonzalez would be eliminated and secured in the trunk of his car and I would just have to jump in it and drive away.

I needed to scout sight lines to see if it was possible for me to gain entrance to Gonzalez's house without being seen from the house where I assumed the shooter was. I also had to verify Gonzalez was passed out. I didn't want to break into his house only to find out he didn't drink the wine. If I could get to the front door, I could just ring the bell. If Gonzalez opened the door, I could just put him down right then and there. Decisions, decisions, decisions...

■■

Lima called Max for an update.

"I'm sitting on his car right now. I watched him walk into a club here downtown. I don't know what he's doing. Maybe killing time?"

"You're probably right Maxie. I bet he's going to come in the middle of the night. We got a watch on his house so if anything is going to happen, we'll know about it. Besides he hasn't had a woman in a while according to Bear, bet he needs to get off." The two men laughed at the thought of the desperation as if they could get any woman they wanted knowing they both resorted to lap dances and paid for sex regularly.

Hearing the name "Maxie" made Max's blood curdle. When this was over he would have every opportunity to take out Lima making it look like their target did it before he died, and who would be "Maxie" then, he thought.

Instead, he said "I'll call you when he gets back to his car. It's awfully quiet in this parking lot. I could take him here and dump him in the trunk. You guys could take out the other guy and we all could be out of here by morning." Making himself feel smart and valuable for all of three seconds.

"Yeah, um, no, Maxie Pad, let's stick to the plan. If anything changes, I will let you know. Call me the minute you see him, and quit thinking for fuck's sake. Just do your damn job and do it right this time, I'm not covering for you this time that is all I am saying." The line went dead.

Lima hung up the phone and told Angelo what his brother said. Angelo chuckled and said he should have let him stay home in Buffalo, but Bear had set this shit up, they had a plan and they were going to follow it so Bear could take his rightful place in the organization and then promote Lima and Angelo to the top of the list.

They would be patient and their patience would pay off, so long as ol' Maxie could do his damn job. "The patient killer". No, the "patient *assassin*". Yeah, that was better. Lima liked the new nickname he gave himself. Maybe he would have it tattooed in Italian Script backward on his bicep as soon as they all got home, and only he and his reflection would know what he meant.

■■

Even with the neighborhoods street lights, there were still deep pockets of darkness for me to melt into. I was taught how to blend in with my surroundings and had a lifetime to perfect it. I scouted the sight lines and figured with a little luck and some great timing; I could get to Gonzalez's front door unobserved. I would only be exposed for a few seconds. I needed a small distraction.

■■

Max was getting real nervous now. It had been almost an hour since he last saw the target. Sure he told a little lie to Lima about actually *seeing* the target but what difference did it make?

The guy was down here somewhere, probably trying to score some ass. That's what Max thought he should be doing right now; the ladies kept getting more and more drunk and definitely needed a ride.

He was thinking that maybe he should call Lima and ask for direction. While he was mulling the decision over, Lima called him.

"Maxie, give me an update. What the hell is going on?"

"Nothing Lima. I haven't seen him since he walked away. He's probably picking up some fine southern ass right now. What should I do? You want me to stay or head on back?"

"Well, if he is going to take Gonzalez, we'll know it because we're sitting just down the street here practically on top of the house and we have the tracking device. Come on back."

"Ok. See in you in about 15 minutes." As Max was hanging up his phone, he thought he heard the doorbell ring in the background of Lima's phone.

▪▪

While Lima was on the phone, Angelo was watching Gonzalez's house with binoculars. Everything was quiet until the doorbell rang.

"What the hell? Hey Gio, you expecting someone?"

Giovanni Lima hung up the phone with Max.

"No Ang, I ain't expecting anyone. Go see who it is. If it is a realtor or something, get them in the house and we'll take them out. Maxie is on the way back."

Angelo went to the front door. He opened the door with his left hand and kept his right hand, the one holding a pistol, out of sight.

"Domino's pizza sir. That will $23.86."

"I didn't order no pizza. You got the wrong house kid."

"Are you sure sir? This is the address I have. Let me call the shop-"

"Get lost kid. No one ordered anything from here." Angelo then closed the door.

"Fucking dumb ass pizza guy. Can't even find the right address."

▪▪

I was across the street hiding next to the neighbors shed. The darkness was complete here and I was unseen from the street. I waited twenty-four minutes and saw the familiar lighted sign of the pizza delivery driver. He drove by Gonzalez's house and made the turn. I closed my eyes and pictured the driver pulling up to the house. I estimated his speed and the distance he needed to drive and I counted the seconds off in my head and when I thought the guy was at the front door, I made my move.

If I had planned better, I would have taken out the street light in front of Gonzalez's house. This was a mistake on my part and I was hoping it wouldn't come back to haunt me. I made it to the front door but I had no idea if I had been seen or not. Things were going to happen quickly now. I wasted no time and leaned on the doorbell.

My senses were on high alert and I was waiting for either the door to open or for someone to come around from the side of the house. After a full minute, I used my electric lock pick gun and popped open the door. The interior alarm started to beep. I went to the panel on the wall and disarmed it. I stood silent and still. I slowed my breathing down and listened for any sound at all.

I had to walk through the kitchen to get to where the alarm panel was but I didn't see an open bottle of wine. I learned over the years when a home owner hears a noise in the house, they stay quiet for about forty-five seconds. Some a little longer, some a little shorter, but forty-five seconds seems to be the average. Then they feel compelled to investigate.

I stood still for four minutes. The Army had taught me the value of absolute stillness. In that time, I got the sense that the house was empty. It very well could have been. I wasn't even sure if Gonzalez was home. I wasn't familiar enough with Gonzalez's alarm system to just set the exterior doors or perimeter. It was time for action. I quickly moved from room to room in the down stairs and cleared the first floor. I didn't find anything. However, a quick peek in the garage confirmed that Gonzalez's vehicle was parked in there.

I slowly crept up the stairs. There was a light on in one of the rooms. If I remembered correctly, and I was sure I did, that was the home office. I quietly walked to the open door and peered in. Slumped on the floor, behind the desk, was Gonzalez.

I quietly backed out of the room and cleared the second floor of his house. I didn't want there to be any surprises. I cautiously approached Gonzalez. I knelt down next to him and looked for signs of life.

After 15 seconds, I could make out the rhythm of his shallow breathing. There was an empty wine glass on the desk next to him. I was happy Gonzalez was still alive. Normally when people die, they empty their bowels. It's not pretty but it's a part of death. Not having to clean that mess up would definitely save me some time.

I stripped off all of Gonzalez's clothing. I carried him to the bathtub in his master suite and laid him in the tub. If Gonzalez was going to leave behind any bodily fluids, I wanted to be able to easily rinse them down the drain. I pinched his nose closed and covered his mouth. In less than a minute, he had left this world and went to whatever is next. My job was half way done. Time to make him disappear.

■ ■

Back in the vacant house that currently had two killers in it, Berrazino was calling for an update. He called Lima because Lima was in charge of the operation. He was really only calling because Mazzio was calling him and demanding an update. Berrazino was already regretting helping out Mazzio. What could he do though? He owed him a favor and he was getting paid fantastic money.

"Gio, where are we at on this thing? Is it gonna happen tonight or not?"

"I don't know Bear. I thought it was going to but our guy is still downtown. He still has time. Expect a call in the middle of the night. If he shows, we're going to finish this."

"Ok. Let me know. There are other people involved and I have to provide updates to them."

"Not a problem Bear."

Berrazino hung up with Lima and then called Mazzio. He gave him the latest update. He told Mazzio not to worry that his team assured him it would be over by dawn.

■ ■

I searched around Gonzalez's house until I found his luggage. I carried two matching suitcases back to his master bedroom. I opened his closet and took a bunch of clothes and filled the suit cases neatly. I also grabbed a few pairs of shoes and all of his bath room stuff to fill up his toiletry kit. When someone came looking for Gonzalez, I wanted it to appear that he had left town.

After packing his suitcases, I started a more thorough search of Gonzalez's house. I was looking for a hidden safe. Guys like Gonzalez always had a safe. After Gonzalez disappeared, if the police were searching his house and found a safe full of money, it wouldn't make sense.

It took me about twenty minutes, but I found it. There was a lose corner of carpet in one of the spare bedrooms closet. I pulled it up and found a latch. I opened the latch and found the safe. I tried to lift the safe out but it wouldn't budge. It was a key lock, not a combination. Now all I had to do was find the key, shit.

I found Gonzalez's key ring and started there. I tried every key but neither one was the correct one. So I started searching the house again. I found two key rings in a drawer in the kitchen. I found a single key in the desk drawer in his office. While I was in his office, I took his empty wine glass and brought it to the kitchen. I washed it with soap and water and then dried it and put it away. I took the wine bottle from the fridge and put it in the back seat of Gonzalez's car. I would need to take that with me and dispose of it later.

I tried all the keys I had but none of them worked. I could use my lock pick gun, but on a pad lock like the one on his safe, there was a chance I would damage it. I didn't want Gonzalez's disappearance to be questioned at all so I kept searching for the key. Pockets, I would check the man's pockets.

■■■

Max was taking his turn watching Gonzalez's house. He almost missed it, but he thought he saw their target enter Gonzalez's bedroom.

"Aww, hey Ange? Can you check this out? I think I seen something."

"What did you think you saw?"

"I think I saw our guy in the bedroom. He walked by the window. See where the blinds are flipped up? I am pretty sure it was him."

"The tracking device says he is still downtown. It can't be him. Hey Gio, check this out a minute. I bet it is just this Gonzalez guy. Don't worry about it."

Lima came back into the empty bedroom where they had the best view of Gonzalez's house.

Ho took the binoculars and watched the master bedroom window. A figure walked past the window quickly carrying something.

"I don't know. It's possible he left the car downtown and got back here somehow. Shit, this thing could be going down right now and we're missing it! There is no way this guy is on to us, no way."

Lima was the leader and the Ferraro brothers looked to him to make the decision. He asked how Max thought their target gave him the slip. Max said maybe the target just slipped out the back of a club and took a cab. Lima thought about it. It seemed plausible enough. He was a great killer but he lacked leadership experience, and he only cared about himself. He knew they would only have one chance at taking out Stevens and he didn't want to blow it. He knew this was his big chance. If they were wrong, they would just kill Gonzalez and wait for Stevens and kill him when he showed up.

"Fuck it. I'm gonna go get the van and pull it in the driveway. I want one of you guys on the street in the front of the house and one of you guys in the back of the house. If our target comes out, waste him, and use silencers idiots, we don't want to disturb the universe. Don't go in the house until I get back. Ok?"

The Ferraro brothers grabbed their guns and left. Lima called Berrazino and told him it was going down right now. He said he would call him back when they were finished. Lima then got into one of the cars and drove to where the van was parked.

■■■

After hanging up with Lima, Berrazino called Mazzio.

"Dom, it's Bear. It's going down right now. I just spoke to my team."

"Right now? Is it over? Is he dead?"

"Jesus Dom, take a drink and chill out, not yet. They just said Stevens was in the house and they were going to take him out. My guy is going to call me when it's over."

"The second he calls, you call me. You understand Bear? The very second I need to know!"

"Ok, Dom, ok. I got it. I'll let you know. Calm down."

Mazzio hung up without saying good-bye. He called Ragulli into his office and told him it was time with only his eyes and a head shake. Ragulli cracked a big smile as he left Mazzio's office and headed towards the east wing of the estate. It wasn't every day he got to murder a mafia don.

CHAPTER #13

Searching around in the musty room that I noticed smelled like cedar, cheap cologne and stale cigars mixed with wine, dust, and now piss was making matters worse. The particles in the air were so big I was worried they were bugs and not just the result of totally crappy air quality and old carpet in this God forsaken place. Damn! Not in the pockets, this was pissing me off.

Finally, I found the key in the last place I looked as usual, taped like someone who never thinks anyone is after their stuff would, right under the desk drawer in the office. I opened the safe and emptied it out. There was only about $9,000 in the safe and some illegal narcotics I would flush later. I took it all out and put it with the wine bottle in Gonzalez's car.

I popped his trunk and cut apart a bunch of garbage bags from Gonzalez's kitchen. Using a roll of duct tape, I spread the bags out and sealed up all the seams. I took a sheet from his linen closet and went back to the master bathroom. After rinsing off Gonzalez's body in the aqua blue porcelain bath tub, I had to take a minute to think the last time I had seen a blue porcelain bathtub? Probably never...Not only that, but who uses those metal covers that go over tissue boxes anymore? I was doing the world a favor getting this guy off the planet.

I gingerly pulled him out and wrapped him in the sheet. I was getting ready to pick him up and carry him out down the stairs to the trunk of his car when I heard the front door crack open, making the curtains move in the downstairs hall near the entry way. I saw them sway just slightly from the top of the stairs, it was all I needed to know that digging two graves was a blessing in disguise, and then wondered if the next person getting ready to breathe their last breathe in this house would wait the full four minutes. The count began and my senses were on high alert, like a cat's ears or radar, I dissected each click, slide, or muffled tone with precision.

■■■

Ragulli walked quietly through the house glad he had worn his shoes with soft soles tonight; he didn't want to miss a moment of this event. He was told to kill the old man in any way he wanted. Shoot him, stab him, choke him, it didn't matter, the choice was his. Mazzio didn't even care.

No one was to know the real way or reason DiFlippo was killed, but Ragulli knew it would eventually come out. Just like when Gotti and Gravano killed Paul Castillano in NYC. All the details leaked out years later to save reputations and make new ones. It was securing his name and place in mafia folk lore that he was interested in, the pride was welling up inside him as he thought about the way in which he killed the old don that would be talked about forever. It would help establish Ragulli's reputation amongst the families and make him and his closest relationships untouchable.

The more he thought about it, the idea of crushing the life out of the old, frail don with his bare hands and watching the fear and anticipation of death overtake his eyes excited Ragulli. Sal should definitely know who took his last breath from him, not that he was going to tell anyone, but it would be ironic to say the least. Maybe he could be known as Anthony "Bone-Crusher" Ragulli. Oh no, maybe skull crusher. That also had a certain charm to it that made Ragulli stop and smile.

He wasn't worried about encountering any of the old man's personal body guards because Mazzio sent them all home earlier this evening. He told them the old man wasn't feeling well and that the two of them would be staying in all night. Everyone had taken him at his word. After all, Mazzio was the #1 guy right under the old man. He was the under boss, the next in line for the crown. After killing the old don, Ragulli would be Mazzio's under boss.

When he got to the old man's room, he stopped outside the door and listened. He didn't hear a sound coming from the bedroom. The old man was asleep. Just in case, Ragulli drew his favorite knife; it was his Golgotha fixed blade tactical knife from Bench Made. His knife was a few years old and he had spilled a lot of blood with it. It was eight inches of solid stainless steel death. He liked it because the blade was only four and a half inches long and it was very easy to hide in his big hands. As the unlocked door slid open just a hair above the beautifully thick carpeted room he stopped to listen some more. Quietly, he opened the door, inch by inch, and silently crept into the bedroom listening for his heavy steady breathing knowing that this was too bad that it was the last breaths he would breathe.

■■

Lima left the car parked next to the moving van and drove the van back to the house.

Once he was in the neighborhood, he turned the headlights off and slowly drove down the street to Gonzalez's house. He wanted to back the van into the driveway but he remembered the damn beeping sound that happened every time it was put in reverse. He decided to pull it to the curb in front of the house. After Stevens was dead, they could make all the damn noise they needed to.

He met with Max in front of the house. He told him what he wanted him to do. Then he went around to the back of the house and met with Angelo. He told Angelo to take Max in the house and handle the 'wet work'. He would keep a watch on both the front and backdoors from the side of the house. He told Angelo they were going up against a pro and to take no chances and just shoot and kill everyone in the house.

Max and Angelo went to the front door. Angelo was able to silently pick the lock and open the door. They stepped into the house and closed the door quietly.

■■■

I was upstairs when I heard the front door open and close. What the fuck? It could only be one person, my pursuer. He must have figured out I gave him the slip downtown and came here. I didn't hear another sound from anywhere in the house. I shouldn't have heard anyone else come in the house. If the guy was a professional, like me, he would be doing the same thing I was; standing still and listening. He also wouldn't have made any noise coming in.

After two minutes went by, I thought I heard the floor creek downstairs. Nobody ever waits as long as I do. I slipped my shoes off and walked as quiet as I could to the hallway that led to the stairs. I had the tactical advantage of not only having the higher ground and knowing the layout of the house, but my pursuer could only approach me from one direction; the common one, the stairs. I had another advantage and that was the fact that he would have to walk through what is called a choke point. The choke point here was the narrow place between the hallway doors leading to the stairs. When he came into the choke point, he would be back lit from the light behind him and not have any idea where I was. This was going to be easy.

■■■

Salvatore DiFlippo had lived a good life. He was fortunate enough to have fallen in love with the woman of his dreams.

It was heartbreaking when she passed on and he never really got over her death. He was also blessed with a beautiful daughter. She was a grown adult now and ran a profitable accounting firm in Florida. He was very successful in his business. He was lucky enough to have never spent one day in jail. He was liked and respected. He was also feared. He lived through two mob wars and made more money than he could spend in several lifetimes.

People often under estimated the old man. They thought because of his advancing age he had grown soft, feeble and weak. There was a rumor circulating that he was contemplating retirement, which was completely absurd. Mafia Don's didn't retire. They were either murdered or died in prison. This old man may have been a lot of things, but he wasn't stupid. He also wasn't ready to die.

When Ragulli walked up to his bed and pulled the covers away to kill the old man, he wasn't there. Ragulli dropped his knife and drew his pistol. He searched the room only to find it empty. Where could the old man have gone? He checked the bathroom but that too was empty. He left the room in a hurry to find Mazzio. This would not end well.

■■■

After waiting a full two minutes, they had literally counted off 120 seconds in their heads; the Ferraro brothers searched the downstairs but did not find their target. They knew he was in the house but they hadn't heard a sound yet. They quietly came up the stairs. Max was in the lead and Angelo was close behind him.

When the brothers got to the top of the stairs their plan was to split up. One would search the rooms on the left, and one on the right. In one step less than a second had passed and Angelo heard two quick pops, saw a bright flash, and then felt the heavy thud as his brother's lifeless body was being thrown backwards on top of him. They both fell down the stairs and Angelo's last thought before losing total consciousness was to wonder where all the blood was coming from, Max or me?

I pulled the trigger, twice, quickly, and the man's head and face at the top of the stairs disappeared. He tumbled backwards and fell down the stairs. I walked to the top of the stairs and looked down. I did this cautiously because I was now the one standing directly in the choke point.

I was surprised to see a second person lying under the man with brand new holes in his face bleeding all over the other one. The second man appeared to be unconscious, but I wasn't taking any chances. I kept my gun trained on him as I walked down the stairs. Shit, there was blood and slivers of fleshy brain matter all over the place. I checked the unconscious man and he was still alive. He looked familiar to a degree, but I didn't recognize him. Maybe I had seen him following me and it didn't compute until now? Either way, his time was up. I was about to end his life when I heard the front door open again. What the hell? I quickly slipped back into an open nook under the stairs and waited…four minutes would seem like an eternity.

■■■

"What the fuck Anthony? What do you mean he's not there? Where the fuck is he?"

"I don't know Dom. His room was empty." Ragulli said eyes darting around, sweat starting to bead up on his forehead.

"He's got to be here somewhere. Shit! I only have two other guys here tonight. For Christ's sake it's damn Pete Parrione, and Sonny De Luca, get them and search the damn house and grounds! We have to find him Anthony. We have to find him *right* fucking now!" Dom screamed in a deep growling voice that sounded like he was chewing gravel and getting ready to sink his teeth into the profusely fearful man standing in front of him. Ragulli scattered off screaming for Pete and Sonny.

"Where could he have gone? He has to be here some place." Dom whispered and slipped his gun out of his holster vest and opened a nearby drawer with a false bottom and ripped off the hidden panel and filled up his pockets with bullets, each chamber was at the ready…this would be over, soon.

As his pockets became heavy laden with bullets, Ragulli and Sonny showed up looking like they had seen a ghost or were waiting to see one. Their eyes screamed for direction from their mighty ruler, "WHAT the HELL are you doing back!? Did you find him? NO? THEN GO FUCKING FIND HIM! HE AIN'T IN THIS ROOM WITH US! CHRIST ALL MIGHTY Anthony! What the fuck am I paying you for?"

"I'm sorry Dom, I'll get right on it." Sonny said as they hustled off to find Sal.

■■■

Lima heard the shots from outside. It was two quick bursts that blended into one. The sound was muffled outside and he was confident that none of the neighbors would have woken up. He walked to the front door of the house and went in. He was gonna chew these jokers out right before blowing their heads off and leaving their body's for the buzzards in the desert for not using their silencers as he'd instructed. He wanted their cut of the profit anyway and felt he deserved it after all the babysitting he had done.

■■■

What the hell is this, Grand Central Station, I thought to myself clicking off each minute waiting to hear the next move. As I heard the person who came in walk through the kitchen and heard him bark out their names, Angelo and Maxie, I thought I was going to see two little ankle biting dogs show up to lick my face or something. What idiotic names. No wonder they were so sloppy. I tried to walk around the dead man and his unconscious partner but I accidentally kicked someone's gun across the floor and it banged into a coffee table. I stood their silent for a second but it was time to move. I took a deep breath and moved.

I stepped through the room as fast as I could, keeping my gun in front of me and my finger tight on the trigger. Just like I had been trained to do and just like I had done 1000 other times before. My breathing was under control and I was eerily calm, not even a bead of sweat had left my body, I was completely in control, I was in the village and nothing would survive.

The silence was pierced by a bullet ripping just inches past my ear. Then I wasn't calm. I was anything but calm. I didn't have to think, I just reacted. I dropped to my knees and fired five rounds to where the bullet came from throwing my body down and forward. My knees slammed the floor; I and came up in a combat crouch with my gun extended in front of me safely on the other side of the room.

A few seconds later, I heard the front door open and close. Reinforcements had arrived, or my shooter was making a retreat. This wasn't the time to be patient or quiet so after dropping one magazine from my gun and hearing it slam to the hard wood floor with a loud heavy clacking noise, I instantly added a fresh, full clip.

As if all in one motion, like I was swimming through the thick air, I moved as quick and as carefully as I could towards the front door wondering how many people had their sights literally set on my chest. I kept looking for red lights, as surely they were out there.

I checked carefully around the corner and didn't see anything. I eased the front door open with the side of my foot using the force of the spring loaded hinges and as expected, two more bullets ripped into the door and frame.

Son of a bitch! I didn't like getting shot at and now I was really pissed off. The door was still open and I could hear the shooters footsteps fading in the distance. Good thing I knew where he was headed at least, but SHIT! There was the same moving van I had seen earlier parked in the plaza. I wanted to follow him outside and chase him down so I could kill him. I didn't though, I stopped. I didn't know if there was another shooter waiting for me to leave the house.

I figured the person that shot at me was gone, and he made a hell of a lot of noise before he left. I am sure someone in this neighborhood would call the police to report the noise. I am also sure the police would respond fairly quickly to this neighborhood. I figured I had about seven minutes before I had to get out. Not enough time.

I ran out of the house into the van. The keys were still in it. I backed the van up the driveway all the way to the garage door; the damn beeping noise was surely going to attract onlookers. I jumped out and quickly picked the lock on the back of the van. I opened the roll up door with a bang and ran back into the house as it finished its ascent. I hopped over the men, ran back upstairs and grabbed Gonzalez throwing him over my shoulder and carried him down the stairs, through the garage and tossed him in the back of the van.

I opened Gonzalez's car door, grabbed the money, drugs, and wine bottle from the back seat and threw all of it into the van with Gonzalez. I popped the trunk and quickly ripped out all the trash bags and duct tape I put there earlier. As I jumped up to grab the door cord and yanked the roller door down, I thought of how much information I didn't have. I needed answers and I didn't have the time to screw with the guy I let live at the bottom of the stairs. I needed to wake and question him now, but I thought I heard sirens in the distance and decided I didn't have the luxury time. I threw the dead man off his stomach. I grabbed him and carried him to the van. He moaned a little bit and I thought he was going to wake up. I tossed him in the van front seat, slammed the door and climbed in in the driver side after him.

At least I was right about the van. It was completely functional and loaded ready to be used to "clean" a scene. I found a roll of duct tape and pulled a strip around the unconscious man's eyes and mouth. I also held his hands together and taped them. This would have to do for now. I had to get rolling. I did a quick walkthrough of Gonzalez's house. While upstairs, I put my shoes back on and grabbed both suitcases. In the living room, I picked up the clip from my gun that I dropped when I reloaded. When the police investigated, they would find the dead body and Gonzalez would be gone. During the investigation, they would question his friends and neighbors and learn the great news story about the lawsuit with O'Malley and hopefully just assume Gonzalez was the killer and left scared. It wasn't perfect, but it would have to do. I closed the house up and locked the doors. I made sure to set the alarm as well. I took Gonzalez's garage door opener from his car with me. As I was driving away, I closed his garage door, it was the least I could do; the last thing I wanted was his car to be stolen.

I needed a place to go and I needed it quickly. I couldn't go back to the motel near the interstate because there was still at least one shooter out there. I could get on the freeway and drive until I figured it out. I would drive until I found a quiet, remote place so I could 'interrogate' the unconscious man. I also needed to call Buffalo and talk to Sal. I had to warn him that someone had tried to take me out and this job had gone to shit. I started to think in a circle asking myself questions like who would want me dead that could find me. What clues did I leave behind, and how can I get this other guy or guys taken care of and out of the picture? How come I didn't take the time to dig out another grave?

CHAPTER #14

I needed a safe place to get out of sight for a while so I decided my best bet was to call Sal. I needed to make him aware of what happened at Gonzalez's house. I was also hoping he could provide me with a safe place in Dallas where I could "question" the unconscious man who was still lying in the truck. I dialed up Sal in Buffalo.

"What?"

"Dom? It's me. I need to speak to Sal. It's important"

"Listen kid, he ain't here. He's meeting with the New York families. He should be back tomorrow. Maybe there's something I can help you out with?" he said a little too quickly.

I didn't want to talk about what happened with Mazzio. I didn't like him or trust him, but I was in a bind and I needed help fast.

"Look I was at my last job when someone took a shot at me. It was close but I took care of it. There-"

"What? Someone took a shot? You ok kid? They didn't hit you?" he cut me off acting like he cared. What was bothering me was how fast he was answering me, as if his response was planned, and Dom didn't study at Julliard.

"No they missed. I was lucky but I…"

"Listen, kid, you gotta come in. We have some good people in Texas. We can get you some place safe so the shooters won't have another shot at cha. The boys here and I, we can protect you but you gotta tell me where you are."

The hairs on my neck were standing at attention again feeling like needles and ice were driving through my veins. I didn't have the time to think about it, I just had to decide.

"No, it's ok, I'm safe right now. I just need to talk to Sal. Who is with him? Who can I call to get through to him?"

"Sorry kid, strict instructions not to interrupt him. Some big important meeting. You sure you don't want me to set you up at one of our safe houses? I mean, really, it's no problem."

"Thanks, but no thanks. I am safe right now. If you talk to Sal, tell him I need to talk to him."

"Sure kid, no problem. I'll do that. Why don't you give me the number you're using and I will have him call you."

Something about my conversation with Mazzio wasn't right. Maybe I was being paranoid but paranoid has kept me alive in this business for a lot of years. No, it was clear I wouldn't be giving Mazzio any more information about where I was or what I had planned. "After I hang up with you, I have to ditch this phone. Just have him send me a message on the bulletin board. I will be checking it every hour or so. If anything changes, I'll call you back."

■■

Mazzio slammed down the phone. "MOTHERFUCK...!" He screamed and rambled. Ragulli came in from the next room.

"What's going on Dom?"

"What's going on? What's going on? We're fucked is what's going on! These losers, they missed! They missed Stevens! How the fuck could they miss him? Please tell me you got a line on the old man. Please Anthony."

"I'm sorry Dom, but he's gone. Vanished like a ghost or sumpthin. I tried calling everyone, no one knows anything."

"If it gets back to Stevens that we were behind taking him out, he's going to come after us. What have we done?"

Ragulli had worked with Mazzio for a lot of years. He had even been with Mazzio one evening when someone took a shot at him, but this was the first time he had ever seen him even look afraid. Ragulli couldn't believe how frightened Mazzio was. "Don't worry Dom. If he comes, I will handle him."

Slowly, and with a crazy look in his eye, Dom turned toward Ragulli, "You can't handle shit! I sent you to handle an old man and you messed that up! You don't understand what Steven's is. He is death. Pure and simple. Once he has a target, he will not stop until that person is dead! He's killed more people this year than you and all your boys have in your entire life. The fucking leading cause of death in this country is heart disease. Stevens is #2 and when he is done with us and our crew he will be closing in on #1. This is very bad Anthony. Very bad. I need to call Berrazino right now. He has to know." With that Dom stormed off leaving Ragulli to listen closely to the silence left in the room wondering if he was being watched right now.

Mazzio called Berrazino and quickly lined out the situation in a bullet pointed manner. Berrazino was in a bad position, a lot worse than Mazzio ever was.

Berrazino would have to explain why he had some of his best hitters doing a job "off the books" and without approval and why one or all of them got "taken out" by Stevens. He hoped he could smooth things over with his bosses, but he wouldn't be getting promoted anytime soon.

This was a career if not a life ending mistake. Past that and even more disastrous if Stevens found out the hitters were sent from Berrazino, a family war could erupt that would definitely destroy his personal family starting with his wife and children. Stevens wouldn't stop there. He would destroy the entire organization and everyone in it that Berrazino worked for.

Berrazino knew that Stevens would come for him and most likely kill whomever was around at the time, and he wouldn't care about the kills being sanctioned by Sal or not. This was a bad night for everyone involved. Berrazino said he would contact his shooters and find out what happened and call Mazzio back. Neither man was going to be going to get any sleep anytime soon, until Stevens either showed up, or was killed, it was crunch time.

■■■

After flipping my phone closed and ending my call with Mazzio, I pulled into a half gas station half junk food joint with a blazing yellow sign screaming free Wi-Fi and started up my laptop. I had been preoccupied the last day or so and didn't get on to check to see if I had any messages on my private bulletin board. Once I accessed the board, sure enough, I had a message. It was short and cryptic, but there was only one person it could have been from. Salvatore DiFlippo. It said:

"Son, my worst fears have come to light. There is a disease. It hasn't gotten to me yet, but until I can figure it out, I am going underground. I will be alone because I don't want to infect anyone. Be safe. You may also have the same disease so be on the lookout for it. I will be on the move. Stay in touch and I will do the same when I can"

Son of a bitch. I couldn't believe it. I knew someone was going to try to kill Sal. Who could it be? My first thought was Mazzio. Maybe. But my concern was that my complete disdain for him was clouding my judgment. Should I call Mazzio for help? Sal must have made up the story about going to New York to meet with the families to give him some time to disappear.

I typed a message back to Sal explaining what had happened to me in Dallas so far. I told him I had a "lead" I needed to "explore" and that as soon as I had information, I would send it along to him.

As I logged off and ran my sweep program, I started to replay my conversations with Mazzio over in my head. Something about the way he had talked to me had bothered me each time we spoke and I couldn't put my finger on it. The laptop started to power down, and I put it back in the soft sided carrying case. As I went inside, I ordered a hot coffee.

Walking back out to the truck wondering why coffee sizing had to be all confusing and the pricing so expensive it hit me like a ton of bricks. All of a sudden, it was like all the tumblers in a lock falling into place. When I was talking to Mazzio, I told him someone took a shot at me and then he said he had to get me someplace safe so the shooters wouldn't get to me. Over and over I said this to myself. I could almost hear it like on an old style message machine in real time. "shooters…"

"I never said there was more than one." I said aloud under my breath. Then the questions started running around in my brain, how did he know there was more than one shooter? Was I looking too closely at his words? If this is true, should I stay in Dallas or go into hiding? Was the cryptic message from Sal real? Did Sal trust even me? Should he? Would I? As I locked the truck door once inside, I stared at the bottom of the Free Wi Fi poster. It said in smallish print in comparison to the bold main message, "Wi ask Wi, high speed here!"

THAT was a good question. Why ask why about Dom? I didn't trust him, that's why! I put the moving truck in reverse and headed out to do some digging. I didn't know for sure who was behind the hit on Sal, but I knew it was connected to the hit on me. I didn't know who I could trust, but I knew one person I could get the answers from; the unconscious man bound in the seat next to me. All I needed now was a place.

It was very late; the time was quickly approaching 4:00am and sleep was not even close to the forefront of my mind. I figured Bramwell would still be at his club counting his cash. I called Geoff who proved at 2am his time that he can find everything even when I was sure I heard a young female voice in the background, but he was able to get me the unlisted, private number for the Salty Kitty. I thought maybe he was fast not because he wanted to keep me happy but I have a feeling his own happiness was at stake if he didn't hurry.

"Salty Kitty, this is Micky. How can I help you?"

"Micky, this is your Buffalo friend, remember me?"

"Well, hello there Buffalo. Sorry we got off on the wrong foot yesterday. I remember you fondly. How can I be of assistance?" He said in a slightly shitty 'I'm not going to mess with you' kind of way.

"I need to speak to Bramwell right away."

"Sorry Buffalo, he ain't here."

"Where is he?"

"The Hairy Drain."

"What?"

"He's at The Hairy Drain. It's another bar he owns and runs. He wants to make sure he caters to all possible demographics man; this is the club for the alternative crowd. You know, the Goths and shit."

"Where the hell is that? Is there a number? How do I reach him?"

"Let me give you his cell. He can always be reached on his cell. Be thankful he ain't at his other bar. The gay one he owns. He ain't gay or nothing but he says its good money owning a gay bar."

"All right Micky, I'll bite. What's the gay bars name?"

"The Man Hole."

He gave me the cell number and laughed under his breath while saying "Man Hole" and I hung up. I dialed Bramwell on his cell phone but all I got was voice mail. I pulled into a grocery store parking lot and turned my lap top back on. I used Google and Map Quest to find The Hairy Drain. I started heading in that direction. I called Bramwell back on redial about 20 times in a row but I got his voicemail every time. I wanted him to think it was an emergency and answer. All I knew was that I needed to keep moving until I could figure this all out.

■ ■

Lima was finally able to call and update a very angry Berrazino. He explained the operation and what had occurred. He assured Berrazino that he was not identified by Stevens. He also said that the Ferraro brothers had been eliminated. There was no way for Stevens to track any of this back to Berrazino. He told him to relax and not to worry. He asked Berrazino if he wanted him to stay out in Dallas and hope for another shot at Stevens or come home on the flight that left in the early afternoon. Berrazino said to stay in Dallas. Keep working the target and try to eliminate him. Lima's number one priority now was to find and kill Stevens.

Berrazino called Mazzio and passed on the update. Both men felt a little bit better but there were still too many lose ends that needed to be tied down. Obviously the old man had found out someone was going to kill him and disappeared. Mazzio's best chance at survival now was to set someone up. He needed a way to make it look like someone wanted to eliminate the old man and Stevens. It had to be someone fairly high up. He also needed to make it appear that this person was trying to set up Mazzio. He needed to think, with that he headed to the bar across the room.

■■

I was able to find The Hairy Drain. The outside of the building looked like it had once been a traditional catholic church. It had double wooden doors as the entrance, one single bell tower and everything was covered in drab rounded off gray concrete stones that were crumbling toward the top of the walls and gargoyles sat outside the corners as if they were guarding the place.

I imagined some sort of saint or cross may have been in their place years ago. After walking through the double doors, I was in the vestibule of the old church. I stood there, having remembered that I made a promise to never set foot in a church again many years ago. Maybe God did have a sense of humor after all, although this was far from entertaining. In my time of need, I once again turned to the church, only this time the music was so loud I thought my ears would bleed.

I paid another cover charge (at least this time it was only $10) and made my way to the bar: it was shaped like a phallic symbol and was pretty gross when added to the name Hairy Drain. There was no way I would drink from this bar. Behind and above it were suspended fishbowls of colored gel looking material with shrunken heads, skeletons of small animals, and various human organs. The one that caught my eye was a yellow gel with the skull of a cat and a collar right where the neck would have been.

I was really hoping I wouldn't have to go through what I did the night before. After being ignored by the two bar tenders for five minutes, I "accidentally" sent the napkin holder flying off the bar and into the bottles that were lined up behind the bar. One of the sullen looking bartenders with a white painted face and huge black rings of liner around his multi pierced eyes finally approached me.

I told him I was a close personal friend and business associate of Bramwell and told him I needed to speak to him immediately. He shrugged his wide suspender wearing shoulders and pointed me to a door that said "PRIVATE" on it and flipped his long bangs back over his shaved head and stammered off into oblivion to the deep and hard bass that overtook the whole building.

I walked through the door and into a long hallway again, and eventually I found an office, knocked on the door and Bramwell told me it was open, come in. He looked up at me, and with little surprise said:

"Seriously?"

"Just like Arnold, I'm back. I am also in some very serious trouble and need help. I have no one I can turn too and I am not even sure if I can trust you."

"Trust me? Shit, you can trust me. I am just relieved you aren't back here to kill me."

"What? Why would I kill you Bramwell?"

"Uh you know, I mean, I saw your face and all that shit. Come on man, that's a little hit man humor."

"Thanks, I actually don't' have a lot of time to appreciate the humor. I'm really in a bind. I can't say much about it but I need a place. I need a place that is distant and quiet, where I can make a lot of noise and where no one will bother me. I need a place I can have a killer time at. How's that for hit man humor" I said with my steely look of fear that I knew would incite him to give up a place.

"Yeah, let's stop with the humor, um, no problem. You know where the industrial park is? The place called South Town? There are the regular buildings and then when you get back in there a ways, there are the few fenced in buildings? I own one of the fenced in buildings. I can give you everything you need right now to get in there. I own two big warehouses out there. There is a front and a rear warehouse. They backup to each other. The front warehouse is currently occupied. The rear warehouse is empty. Feel free to use it for as long as you need."

"Bramwell, I can't thank you enough, but I will. When this is all over, you're going to get a package in the mail from me. It will be a gift for all of the trouble I have caused you."

"No trouble at all. Keep your hit man mail, uh just, the next time you see 'the man', put in a good word for me." He said referring to Sal. I was just hoping that I would get to see Sal again. Everything was getting far too complicated.

After getting the directions to Bramwell's warehouse, he walked me outside and we went to his car. He gave me the keys that would open the lock on the front gate. He also gave me the alarm code for the building. I gave Bramwell the narcotics I had found in Gonzalez's safe and the $9,000. It had been a long day and I was exhausted, but I still had work to do. If I wasn't already, what I was about to do next might damn me forever.

CHAPTER #15

We were in some Middle Eastern hole in the wall country doing not even the President knew what, and we had just secured a terrorist training facility. The top guy in the facility, some captain, had information our government needed. The General on duty sent in a professional "interrogator". I was outside the building that they were using to "interrogate" the Middle Eastern Captain. I don't know what they were doing but I could hear his screams even through the thick concrete walls, and too this day if I hear a sound resembling it I am transported back to that time.

The second time I saw someone tortured was a few years ago in New York. I was hired by one of the New York families to abduct and kill a man. They said after I abducted him, I was to bring him to an address they had given me before I killed him. They said there would be a man there to question him and another man to dispose of him after I was finished with him. I grabbed the guy and went to the address. As expected, two men were there waiting for me. I knew the cleaner from previous experiences.

I had a chance to talk to the "interrogator" while he was taking a break from his work. Dave Travis was the interrogator's 'name'. He looked like an everyday guy. There was nothing about him that stuck out as not average. If you were at a party and were introduced to him, you would forget him completely five minutes after meeting him. I learned a lot about torture from watching him. I wasn't sure I would ever be able to put aside the human that was still left in me to actually do any torture but I will never forget about fifteen minutes before he finished with my guy, he told me "The key to torture Steven's is to make the person believe they are going to survive."

"You see…" He said "…The thing is, if they know they're going to die, they kinda just shut down on you. In their mind, it's like you can't touch them. They go off to a place in their mind and then you're screwed. The key is making them believe they are going to live after they give you what you want. That's why I never kill a person I am interrogating. That is what you are for, am I right? I'm not a liar Stevens, I am NOT going to kill them, but they are in fact going to die".

He Continued "When people are in the chair, they can read that shit in your eyes. Think about this, when I am talking to them, I can honestly say I am not going to kill them. They know I am telling them the truth. It adds to my credibility and they believe what I am telling them. It always helps me get the information I need faster."

"Another thing. If you have time to research a person and find out their biggest fear, don't use it right away. A lot of guys make this mistake." He said matter of factly cleaning off a knife. "These armatures, they think they know everything, shit, if they find out someone is afraid of drowning, the first thing they do is water-board the poor son of a bitch. I mean, what if it doesn't work? What then? Where you gonna go from there? You used your ace and it didn't work. Always keep that in the back of your mind. Their deepest fear always works best after you have worn a guy down a little bit."

"This guy here? His worst fear is getting strangled. Notice I didn't go in there and strangle him right off. If it comes to that, and I don't think it will, he's close to cracking now, but if it does, it will work better after I have broken a few bones or removed a few more fingers. I got all kinds a shit I use to wear 'em down. Sometimes I use a hammer, sometimes I use tooth picks. I saw in a movie once a guy used a cigar cutter to take a finger." He laughed in disgust, "I tried that shit and what a disappointment, yeah its total bullshit. It makes a hell of a mess and it's not sharp enough to clip through the bone. I also ruined a great Parisian cutter I got when the wife and I went on vacation a few years before that. If you want to take a finger, just get down to brass tacks, be a man; use a pair of bolt cutters. Maximum amount of torque, you know? It also cuts real slowly. It's more dramatic and it works every time."

He continued "A lot of guys will also start with burning a person's hands or feet. I don't like that shit either. I could never get used to the smell. I mean the rest of the time you are with them, you have to smell it, usually they vomit too, and that's gross enough in itself. I learned to keep a bucket nearby, it can hold all their parts and they can vomit in it. Burning, while effective, just smells horrible. Hey, use what you're comfortable with is all I'm saying. I mean maybe you don't notice the smell." He said as if he was grocery shopping and pulled a rope out of his nearby bag made sure he could get it tight enough and put it in his back pocket for later. He then went back into the room and continued asking questions.

It took Dave Travis just over an hour in total to get the information he needed. It was very ugly and at times even I had to turn away. When he was finished, he washed his hands and told me it was my turn. I went into the room and untied the guy from the chair he was slouched over in. I helped him to his remaining foot and was helping him walk to the door, as if to leave. He thought I was his friend, I even smiled, he seemed woozy from the loss of blood and I was shocked he didn't realize this was coming.

What would he tell people about where his foot went? How was he going to continue going after I let him out the door? So I let him get one step ahead of me and just before all these realizations came to his mind, I slid in quickly behind him as if to bolster his weak, blood deficient body but instead I easily slipped the garrote wire around his neck and strangled the life out of him. He must have pissed someone off very badly to have ordered me to kill him in the way he feared most after being tortured.

When I was finished, I left and my cleaner friend who had been listening to music and reading a book in another room came in and cleaned the scene. That was one of the easiest jobs I ever had to do physically, but it also took me the longest time to get over what I had witnessed and done.

I didn't know what tools were in the back of the truck, so I stopped at another gas station on my way to Bramwell's warehouse. Purchased some bottled water, a few screwdrivers, tooth picks, a utility knife, pliers, a box of matches and a few lighters. It would have to do.

When I got to the warehouse, it was large enough that I could pull the truck in and close the door. I mentally prepared myself for what I was about to do. In my mind, I knew I was crossing a line, a line I had set many years before and never wanted to cross.

What could I do though? I needed information and I needed it quickly. Maybe I would get lucky and the guy would just spill more than his guts and I could get the information from my prisoner quickly. The only other option I had was to go on the run. I could go into hiding and use Geoff and all of my resources to try to figure this mess out. It would be more dangerous, and take longer to find the information I needed, assuming I could find it at all. Besides, running was not in my blood and I refused to accept it as a valid option.

After turning on the lights inside and closing the large overhead door, I opened the passenger side door of the truck and grabbed my prisoner by his legs and dragged him out.

With his hands taped, he was unable to protect himself when he landed on the concrete floor. I then climbed up into the back of the truck and looked around. Whoever these guys were, they were good. They had everything they needed to kill me and then eliminate my body. I was as impressed as I was pissed.

I decided to be nice and maniacal, if I was going to do this, and it was clear I was, I should start now. I took a deep breath, picked up a pile of white cloth that was a pair of painters' overalls and changed, as I zipped it up, I too changed in my mind. I felt the switch, it didn't feel as bad as I thought it would, but parts of my brain and heart that I had long since closed off, were up and running, this was going to be fine, I lied to myself.

I grabbed a gallon of bleach, the hacksaw, some zip ties and an ax and walked to the back of the warehouse into what was an office. I grabbed the office chair and rolled it into the warehouse. I picked my prisoner up and put him in the chair. I did a quick pat down and found he was carrying a Taser stun gun.

In the Army I had learned how to use electricity to incapacitate a person. The Taser was a nice weapon because a person could use it shoot someone from across a room, or they could use it like a hand held stun gun. I knew if I held the electricity to a person's stomach for fifteen or so seconds, it would render them unable to move for up to 30 minutes. It completely messes up a person's central nervous system and they can't control their muscles. With a very loud clicking and the smell of burned hair the 15 seconds felt like 60.When it was over I cut the tape off his hands and feet and re-secured them to the chair using the zip ties and more tape then I removed his shoes and socks.

I drank some of the chilled bottled water while I waited for him to come around. I couldn't remember the last time I had been this tired. Just as I began to wonder if I had the mental and physical capabilities to do what I was about to do, I saw his right eye open slowly.

"I am going to remove the tape from your mouth. We are in a very empty, very secluded building in the middle of nowhere, somewhere in America. It has been several days since we first met, you've been drugged during this time, and I bet you remember who I am and where we met. You are welcome to yell and scream as loud and as long as you want." I let him think about that for a few seconds.

"When you are done with that, I am going to ask you some questions. Make no mistake; you will answer the questions I ask. It doesn't matter to me, easy or hard, but you're *going* to answer them."

He mumbled from under his taped mouth and tears streamed down his face from one eye in both fear and defiance and maybe even anger. "I absolutely will do horrible, painful things to you. Well ok, only if I need to, so you will give me the answers I need, understand? No matter what I do, or how much pain you are in, I promise, I will not let you die. It's important you understand that. I'm a charitable guy. I have done this before and I know what I am doing. I look at what I do like it's a form of art," I said while now holding the ax, "In the end, everyone talks. After they talk, they go home."

I slowly removed the tape from his mouth. After a few minutes of screaming and another few minutes of threats, he seemed to settle down and go quiet. I figured I would start out nice, maybe I would get lucky and he would see the light and then we could move on to my actual job, killing him.

"Would you like some water?"

"Go fuck your-self."

"Ok. I was afraid it was going to be like this. We're getting off on the wrong foot. What is your name?"

"What are you deaf? Go. FUCK. Your-self!"

I gave him a sad little smile, and noticed I no longer felt like me and I wasn't too upset at all about it. I thought about it for a second, acted like I was hanging a piece of art on the wall, placed the end of a large flat head screw driver on top of his big toe letting the cold metal sit against his skin knowing the feeling probably burned with anticipation of the ridiculous pain he would feel in just a few moments. I felt like a game show host who was waiting more than 10 seconds to tell the last two contestants who would win and who would lose. I always hated that on TV these days. I could feel him watching me, trying to decide when to tense up and try to move his foot, but he couldn't even when he tried.

Using the back of the ax as a hammer I felt his bone break like in a chicken breast and blood spewed from his foot as his toe flopped around. He screamed a scream that would make your blood run cold if you were human, but after three or four more tries to get the toe completely off, he vomited and off it eventually came.

Sure, I could have just used the ax to remove his toe, but this way seemed like I would get more bang for my buck. There was a lot more screaming and threats and again I quietly sipped water and just stared at him as I waited him out.

"Listen, listen, I know that has got to hurt, but it doesn't have to be this way. If you tell me what I need to know, we can both walk out of here. Well, ok, so I'll walk and you'll limp, but you don't have to suffer or lose any more body parts man. Just tell me your name."

"You're a piece of shit mother-fucker! You're going to burn in hell! I ain't telling you shit!"

I walked over to the truck, and took the top off the gallon of bleach. "I think you got this to clean up my bloody mess, after you killed me, right? Too bad I am not sure when to use this. Am I supposed to use it before or after your dead? I mean look at all this blood! I think I will use it now. If you think your foot hurts now, just wait until I pour this bleach on it!" I said as I poured it on the stump where his toe used to be causing a lot more screaming. At one point, I thought he was going to black out, but he hung in there.

"This is how it's going to go. I won't lie; this is how it always goes. I ask someone some questions, they tell me to fuck off. I start carving them up and hurting them and before you know it, they answer a few questions. I carve them up more, and I really start hurting them. They answer a few more questions and beg me to stop. I bring them to a whole other level of pain; maybe I take a hammer to the vertebrae in their back and paralyze them from the waist down. I really start causing them some pain, pain you can't even imagine right now, and they answer a few more questions. Now, we're a few hours into this and they are really hurting. This is when they start begging me to kill them. Seriously, I mean absolutely begging me to die because they are in so much pain. And guess what? I don't kill them. I let them live. Why? Because I promised! I mean I am a man of my word. Once I get all of the information I need, I leave them. I call 911 and they are rushed to a hospital. Some can walk, most can't…ever again. Most are horribly disfigured and will remember me very well. A lot of them are burned really badly. They're all missing pieces and parts. I don't see the harm in telling me your name. What is it?"

"Angelo Ferraro." He swallowed hard, "Ange..lo Ferra..ro.." he repeated and trailed off with what sounded like a tissue was in his mouth. Unfortunately for him, the name was unfamiliar to me.

"Well Angelo, nice to meet you, I would shake your hand, but you already know a lot about me, and that isn't fair, but I want to know, don't you wish you had of given me your name earlier? I mean that wasn't so hard, was it? If you would have told me that a minute ago, you still would have all ten toes. Back at that house, who was the guy I shot and killed?"

"That was my brother, Max. You fucking killed my fucking brother right on top of me!!"

"I would say I am sorry, but Angelo, shit happens. Stop looking at me all pissed off. You guys have obviously done this sort of work before and know the risk. I have to thank you for getting me all this cool new stuff I am sure to hurt you with. I'll tell you what, your brother got off easy compared to you, don't you think. There was a third guy, who was he?"

"Look man," he said with the thickness of his voice coming hard and with a growl spit splattering out from his mouth, "That's all I'm saying. I don't care what you do to me."

I took a few tooth picks and jammed them into the stump of his foot where his toe used to be. "Oh now you asked for this, or I guess really I told you this was going to happen, be quiet and let me work…" I said to him over his screams.

I jammed in a few of the match sticks and set them on fire. Then I took the screw driver and ax and used them on his other big toe. This time my aim was better and I was able to sheer it off in only two tries. I dumped some of the bleach on it for good measure. I wasn't done. I grabbed the hacksaw and sawed two more of his toes off. This time, Ferraro actually did pass out. SHIT! I went too far? He can't die before I find out who the other guy is and what is going on! I used some of the bottled water and a few slaps to the face to bring him back around.

"Angelo, you don't look so good. I don't think you are suited for this type of abuse. This guy whose name you are trying to protect, do you actually think would he go through this abuse for you? Fuck no. Probably not. If he was smart, he would have started talking before I took his first toe. Who is this guy that you want to protect so bad?"

"His name is Giovanni Lima and he is the baddest mother fucker out there. He has killed more than 50 people and he'll kill you too."

I laughed at him, "Baddest? More than me? Bull-shit! Look where you are now…you don't even know what state you are in, what day it is or how to walk with 6 toes and haven't eaten in probably several days, oh and your brother is dead and no one will ever find him, well I can, but no one else ever will." I didn't let on but this was a name I recognized. I didn't remember which family he worked for, but I knew it was based in New York. I had never met the guy before, but he had a good reputation. He was an efficient killer.

"Which family does he work for? Who is it?"

Angelo just looked at me without answering. I used the back of the ax and slammed it down on top of his right foot. We both heard bones crunching and breaking. After the screaming died down, I asked my question again. This time, Angelo answered me.

"He works for the Camarillo's. Out of Rochester." His voice came like the whisper of a child asking for water in the middle of the night, trying not to wake a parent but needing to wake a parent.. "Please…. please don't hit me again. I'll tell you everything I know." Tears, vomit, and I was sure from the foul odor coming from him, he had now shit more than once. He was shutting down but I wasn't done. He still knew things I didn't.

"Now we're getting somewhere. Was this a sanctioned hit or was this off the books? Who did the actual hiring?"

"Man, we are just crew. Maxie, tell him, tell him we are just crew." He said delirious thinking Max was close by and talking to him. "We don't know exactly. Lima said we were helping out a guy from Buffalo. He never said who put us on the job. Lima is a part of Paul Berrazino's crew. He does almost all of his work through Berrazino." He was starting to panic I had to calm him down, so I got him some water, didn't even ask him, just poured it in his mouth.

As he slopped around trying to get all the water he could, I thought about what I knew. I really only knew a little bit about Berrazino. He wasn't a main guy in the family. He was maybe mid-level and I didn't think he had enough pull to order a hit on me. Even though I was technically an independent contractor, all the top people in the NY families knew of my close relationship with Sal. Permission would be needed from the top on down to make a move against me. Suddenly it was all starting to come together now.

I was not a sanctioned hit.

Someone close wanted me dead. Someone in Sal's organization asked Berrazino for a favor? It had to be someone pretty high. Mazzio was my first thought, but I needed to be sure before I went after him. "Can I please have some more water?" he weakly asked.

"In a minute. How did you get on to me?"

"We don't know all the details. All I know is Lima said we had an important job to do out west." I gave him some more water, he was on a roll, it streamed down his chest because his tongue was swelling up and drying out from blood loss, "I don't even know who you are. We came out here and we were told to follow that Gonzalez guy. Lima said we would find you through Gonzalez. We found you when you followed him to his businesses whatever day that was. We got your plate number. Lima has this computer guy." No way was Geoff involved, I started checking people off the list, "He, he, he, it's cold in here man, can I have a blanket? Maxie, you cold too? Can Max have a blanket too? I mean we searched for you but we couldn't find your hotel. We sat on Gonzalez's house and when you broke in the first time, Lima dropped an electronic transmitter on your car."

"Why didn't you just kill me then? Why wait?" I ask pouring water in his mouth again.

"I don't know man. Lima was running this thing. Holy SHIT it is cold, are we in Colorado? That's it isn't it? I keep getting light headed and it is so fucking cold. Lima said we had orders to wait until you eliminated Gonzalez and then we were to take you. That's all I know. Please call 911 now. I am fucking dying, I know I am …please…" he trailed off starting to sob.

"I wouldn't doubt it Angelo. You lost and looks like from this mess are losing a hell of a lot of blood. Do you know who Michael O'Malley is? Or Salvatore DiFlippo?"

"Fuck man, help me please! I told you everything I know! I don't know O'Malley or Difilo? Filipio, what did you say? I don't even know who you are, I just know your our target, that is all! Tell him Max!"

"You don't know who I am?" I laughed out loud and slapped my knee before standing up tall and looking at him in a way that he wouldn't forget (Not that it mattered because, he would be dead soon enough). "I'll tell you. My name is Rick Stevens. That name ring any bells with you?"

Ferraro didn't say anything at first. He just stopped mumbling and crying, looked at me for a solid ten seconds and started to weep a deep hard sob that meant he did in fact know who I was.

The last shred of hope he was clinging to quickly slipped away. I saw it leave his eyes before he started screaming at me. "Yeah, I know who you are. You're the devil! You're fucking death man! The grim reaper! I heard about that family you killed in Syracuse and all those people you wiped out in Tulsa. You're a sick fuck. You're going to kill me now aren't you? If I would have known you were the target, I would have left the country. I swear to God! Ask MAX!"

"I already killed Max, and you can swear to God all you want. He doesn't care, I personally know that."

I could only come up with one more question. I asked Angelo where Lima was staying and he told me about the hotel and the vacant house. I had a good lead on Lima but I also wanted to talk with O'Malley. Angelo Ferraro had out lived his usefulness to me. I pulled my gun out and pointed it at his head. His last words were "You miserable, lying prick!" and then he was gone.

My gun shot was loud and echoed around in the enclosed warehouse. I wondered if I should have cut out his tongue, a few more fingers and then let him bleed out instead of the mess his brain made all over the concrete floor. Bramwell would need a power washer for sure in here.

I decided since I gave him the easy way out, I too would take the easy way out and used the ax and cut off the rest of Ferraro's fingers and toes. Then I moved his body and the chair into the back of the truck. I changed out of the bloody painter's overalls and back into my own clothes.

Then I called Bramwell on his cell phone.

"Hello?"

"Bramwell. You know who this is?"

"I sure do. Don't you ever fucking sleep man?" he laughed, I didn't.

"I am done with your warehouse, but it's a mess. There is spilled product everywhere. You know a good, reliable cleaner in town?"

"You don't know anything about me, do you? I got my start back in Buffalo cleaning. I did some good jobs and I was at the right place at the right time to meet the man. We talked over dinner and hit it off. He thought I could be better use to the organization than cleaning."

"Damn Bramwell, that's some of the best news I have heard in a while. I have two packages, lots of damage and a moving truck that need to be cleaned. How much will it cost me to make it all disappear?"

"How about we trade services? I have a situation that needs to be resolved. *You* have a situation that needs to be resolved. I help you resolve yours and you help me resolve mine. How does that sound?"

"Sounds fair, but I have to be honest with you. I have a few other things I need to get to first. They can't wait. Once I have them done, I can come back to help you out."

"Perfect. Just knowing that this problem is going to disappear will be a load off my mind. Leave everything as is and I will take care of it. Just make sure to set the alarm and lock the front gate when you leave."

"Done."

"You ever come here when you're not on business? If you do, we should meet up. I'll buy you a drink."

"I might do that. Thanks again." I hung up with him and realized I didn't have a car with me as my rental was still in town.

I kept the stun gun and all of his fingers and toes. I wrapped them in some paper towels I found in the office. I left the warehouse and walked to a laundry mat that was about a mile and a half away. I used a pay phone there to call a cab and had the cab drop me off in the other plaza where my rental car was. As I sat down in the car, I knew I needed sleep. I got on the interstate and drove for a few miles. I saw the sign for a cheap motel chain. I rented a room using another alias. It was the last one I had on me. I would need to go back to my safe house or my safety deposit box to get more. I didn't worry about that. I locked the door, pushed a chair under the handle and passed out fingers still in my pocket.

PART TWO

CHAPTER #16

I was at home making a ham and cheese sandwich wishing I had rye bread when I only had whole grain wheat. Considering that it was the kind with nuts and not just plain wheat, I decided I could make it ok. The normalcy of the day was making me wish I could go fishing or golf, but tonight would be a fun night at the drive-in movie theater and I had waited and waited until it was at the drive-in. I wasn't cheap, I just really didn't want to see it and if I was going to see it, the comfort of my own car would make the difference. It was almost like renting a movie and just staying in, but date night was always fun for both of us. I decided to spice it up a bit and slice up some banana peppers to add to my thick sandwich that had two slices of cheddar and one baby Swiss for some extra flavor and make up even more for the lack of rye bread. Out of nowhere there was a knock at the front door.

Standing side by side were two New York State Troopers. My American Flag that I always hang right outside my door was flapping slowly and lying back and forth on the taller man's head. He in particular looked a little nervous and was holding his hat in his hand as if he didn't want to tell me the flag was bothering him.

"Good evening officers, how can I help you? Would you like to come in?"

"Um, Sir, are you Mr. Rick Stevens?"

"Yes sir, I am. Come in, come in, that flag is attacking you there. What can I do for you gentlemen?"

The shorter one said, "I'm sorry to say this, but there has been an accident."

I didn't think much of what he was telling me. There had been other times when the State Police had come to my house to inform me about car accidents. It wasn't uncommon for a family member in my congregation to send the police to get me. One of the things I did as a pastor was comfort people in troubled times.

I reached for my wallet in my back pocket and my keys in the front pocket. Turned around and grabbed them off the small shelf that separated the front room from our dining room. The walls were a light mustard color that I hated but my wife just loved. The dark wood touches were shellacked with a high gloss that offset the white crown molding and made the Berber carpet blend in perfectly.

We had just redone the house a few years before and all we needed was a new couch, she said. For our anniversary this year I was going to surprise her with couch shopping. I just hoped she was as excited as I was about it. I had been saving for a year and had nearly a thousand dollars saved up. It was the least I could do for such a giving woman. Right this second she was out there giving her time and loving on a person in need and handing this sweet sprit on our precious daughter too.

Selfishly I was hoping this visit wasn't going to take me away from our date night plans, the sitter was coming in an hour and I was very concerned someone in my congregation had died or was in need of my evening.

"Oh, officers, I'm sorry to hear that. Give me a minute to change into some dress clothes. Has anyone died in the accident?"

"Yes sir, they have."

I just stopped, wanted to smack myself in the face for being so selfish, someone had died here and I was worried about a movie we could see tomorrow night. I was pretty sure it was showing tomorrow too. Someone was not ever going to be seeing another movie again; here I was worried about popcorn and dancing hot dogs. "That's just terrible. Oh my goodness, who was the person that died?"

"Sir?" He paused and I will never forget his confused look or what he said next. "Mrs. Julie Stevens and a young girl we presume was your daughter, Faith? I am really sorry to have to tell you all of this."

Nothing. Absolutely nothing.

My life had ended with Julie and Faith's. One moment, one car, one life, and then two, and now three. Standing there, alone in the kitchen you have it all, banana peppers, whole wheat bread, and the promise of tomorrow. Everything I ever wanted or needed and the next moment it is gone. Taken in the blink of an eye. Everything after that moved in a blur. The trooper brought me to the hospital, but there really was no need, I was not allowed to identify the remains. They instead ask me direct questions about what they were wearing, birth marks, or any other distinguishing marks, hair color, etc. I answered each question hoping for a look, a pause, a breath of grace; not my family.

From what the state police and the doctors told me, they said my wife was driving under the posted speed limit of forty-five miles an hour when another vehicle, a black pick-up truck, crossed over the double yellow line to pass them. Another vehicle, some sort of SUV, was traveling towards them and instead of hitting the vehicle head on, the driver cut back into my wife's lane, and slammed into the front end of my wife's car with the rear of his truck.

My wife lost control of her car and went off the road and hit a telephone poll. With my wife and daughter still in the vehicle and unconscious, the car caught fire. The person that caused the accident didn't stick around, no one saw him or her because they were focused on my family, my sweet precious darling wife whom I had or hadn't I couldn't remember told I loved just a few moments before they took her, stole her from date night, from couch shopping, from lemonade stands, and graduations. This person, this unnatural being took every laugh, scraped knee, lost dog, and prom dress. They didn't care to check to even see if anyone was hurt or needed help. This person who breathes air forever just drove off with untied shoes, grandbabies, baptisms, arguments over curfew, and retiring in a small town with a horse and a small orchard. By the time the SUV was able to pull over and stop it was too late. The fire had consumed my wife's car, it was too hot to get in, a gentleman standing by the corner walking his dog saw it happen, let his dog go, and ran to help, the fire was so hot and all consuming, nothing could be done to help them.

Sometime, while I was at the hospital, long after they told me to go home, Sal showed up. He just sat next to me. I didn't even say hi. I didn't even turn to him. I just sat there, thinking of nothing and everything all at once. We sat there for an hour, neither of us moved. Sal had amazing patience and I believe was actually staring at the same tile of carpet that I was. Green with yellow flecks and a blue swirl of color running through it had me mesmerized, or bored, I wasn't sure. I just knew that I was thinking, and Sal was helping me think, there were no thoughts before the carpet. He was a comfort to me and a great help during my time of need. Without him there, I doubt I would have made it through the night of which I spent staring, listening, coming awake out of my own coma, crying silently, curling up in a ball in my chair trying to die to be with Julie and Faith. Instead of driving me home, he drove me to his house, I didn't even care, he got me inside, and I swear he must have carried me, I don't think I walked.

There was a bit of irony in the fact that I was there with him the day his wife died and he was there the day with me when my wife died. We sat up all night talking and not talking, pretending like tomorrow would be better. We both shared stories about our families; we drank coffee and ice water with lemon. Nothing that we drank or snacked on in the next hours tasted like anything. I figured that Mana must have tasted like this, tasteless, plain and nourishing. I must have dozed off at some point, but when I opened my eyes, Sal still sat there, stirring his coffee, reading the paper, or praying. Sal had a lot more stories since he and his wife had been together for so long. The only part I remember and may never forget, I asked, "Sal this pain, the same now as when it happened, does it ever lessen." Sal never answered, he just talked about what it felt like to smell her shampoo that he kept a few ounces of in a drawer near his bed for when he wanted to feel less alone. The answer was never admitted, but I knew the truth and tears sloshed down my cheeks in waves as if they had made a trench to my chest where my heart was exposed and bleeding out, not for him, not for me.

"Rick, you have to prepare yourself for the fact that the person that caused this to happen will never be found or arrested. He or she may never have to answer for what happened, ever."

"I know Sal." I said in defeat of my own occupation and the knowing that I had in what was left of my heart, "They will answer, they will have to answer for it before God someday, I am sure it will get me though." I wanted to roll my eyes, at Sal, at God, at the truth, at my moment, at being a child in a man's body who was screaming out for saving but felt alone, and empty, dry, charred.

"Yes he will. It would be nice if someone could arrange for that part of his or her life to happen sooner rather than later."

You know Rick, Sal went on "I was never a very vengeful person. I always believed if you did good things, good things would happen to you. Call it karma or God's way, just whatever. You know and I do that people reap what they sow. I don't know if I believe that anymore. I would really like to be alone with whoever caused this to happen. Even for five minutes. Rick, you killed people before when you were in the Army, yes?"

"Yes, what are you asking Sal; I have."

"Killing in the service of one's country and killing out of revenge or anger or spite is completely different." Sal said reading the paper or at least looking at it like it was a cue card as if he was reading his script to me to help me, like he knew what to say and what not to say.

"I don't know if I agree Sal. I understand your point, but when you boil it right down, killing is killing. The end result is the same. When I was in the Army, there were times we were given direct orders to kill people. That's really no different than a mafia don giving orders to one of his soldiers to kill someone, or a police officer shooting and killing someone in the line of duty or killing the son of a bitch that murdered my family. The end result is exactly the same. Death."

"That's an interesting point of view. Especially for a man of the collar."

"I don't think I am cut out to be a pastor anymore. I just don't know if I can do it anymore. It all just feels like a lie. I preach forgiveness, and yet here I am, fantasizing about killing the person that murdered my family. I seem to be at odds with myself. I am going to take some time off and pray. I am going to talk to an old friend who is coming into town for the funeral. He was my mentor when I was in seminary school."

"Do you really think you could kill a man in cold blood?"

"I do Sal, I do. Especially the bastard that killed my wife and daughter. Let me ask you something now."

"Go ahead."

"The day your wife passed on, do you remember the question you asked me?"

"Yes, Rick, I do remember."

"The answer to your question Sal is yes. I think He would take away our loved ones just to punish us. It's the only thing that makes sense. Now can I ask you a question?"

"Yes"

"I know why God is punishing me. Why did God punish you?"

And he told me.

CHAPTER #17

I slept, hard, until almost 8 o'clock at night. The sun was just disappearing away under the horizon and dusk this night could easily be confused for dawn. I had dreamt of my precious wife and daughter. I tried hard but didn't remember the specifics of my dream, but I awoke with the feeling that she was fading away like the sun was doing, as if in colored pencil, she floated around in the deep reddish gold hues of my dreams.

She was disappointed in me for the choices I made following her death that much I knew. What she couldn't understand, what no one could really understand was, that the person I had been before her death, the person who cared, who filled his life in white crown moldings, manicured lawns and prayer had also died.

Not for the first time, I felt ashamed in a part of my heart that I wondered if I should just kill myself, then we could be together, but maybe that was what she was disappointed in. The God we served at her death would never allow me to see her. She would be standing there back to me, never hearing my voice, praising the Almighty with the golden locked beauty of our sweet darling. I would hear her voice singing and watch her bounce lightly to the songs of Angels, they would never hear me, or see me, and I would be tortured with their memory.

Their God would see death as taking the easy cowardly way out of the life He created me to be a part of. At this point, if God was ready to have a conversation with me, He would have to call me. I saw him turning right stopping to look at me....I almost jumped out of my skin, straight up in bed. I had fallen back asleep...The Savior had abandoned me, and it was only 10 o'clock. Until he spoke to me again, I would keep sending him souls.

I took a shower, changed my clothes and wiped down every surface in the room, checked out of the hotel and checked my car for more tracking devices; luckily I didn't find any. I made sure no one was following me and drove back to my Dallas house. I needed supplies for my imminent survival. There were also two loose ends I needed to tie up. The other shooter, if he was still in town, and O'Malley to collect the other half of my fee.

■■

After checking into a new hotel, Lima called Berrazino to update him on the situation. The update was, there was no update. The status hadn't changed. Berrazino screamed and seethed at Lima ordering him to stay in Dallas and try to track down Stevens again. Lima had no idea how he was going to do that. Through Berrazino's wild swings of anger on the phone, Lima got all of O'Malley's contact information. Lima figured before Stevens left Texas, he would want to question O'Malley. Being the last lead Lima had, if he failed to find Stevens, he would return to New York a failure. This was the last thing Lima wanted to do, New York, like Lima would be just a memory if Stevens wasn't eliminated.

Lima rented a hotel room and attempted sleep for a few difficult hours. Early the next morning, he returned to Gonzales's neighborhood. He didn't believe what he was seeing, and was surprised when he got there. The neighborhood was as he left it. There wasn't any sign of crime scene tape on Gonzales's house. The vacant house they had been staying in was still vacant. The only thing different was the missing moving van.

Lima acted like a new real estate agent, attempting to resell the vacant house and took everything the Ferraro brothers and he had left inside and loaded it quickly into his car that he had parked very close to the back garage door. After that, he wiped what he had hoped was everything they had touched down, grabbed his suit jacket, returned the lock box to the front door and the for sale sign to the front yard. After he was satisfied everything was as he found it, he left after taking a few pictures of the property as if he was a real estate agent caring about the sale of the home. It was time to go find O'Malley and see if Stevens showed up, and he pulled out on to the street in his rental car.

■■■

DiFlippo was always an intelligent man. Even when he was younger, and still a captain within the Magidino family in Buffalo, he knew the importance of a great "rabbit- hole". He always paid attention to the older, higher ranking members in the family. When the police or the government was getting close to indictment, they would go on the run and disappear. Some were better at it than others.

Some men had apartments in different cities and others would just get in a car and drive off. One of the reasons why DiFlippo eventually became the head of the Accardo family was because he was always prepared.

No matter what occurred, he was always ready to deal with it. His recent attempted assassination was no exception.

Shortly after DiFlippo and his wife were married, they purchased a condominium in Toronto, Ontario in a false name and never spoke about it. No one in the Magidino or Accardo family, not even his right hand man, Mazzio, knew about the condo. Toronto, ninety minutes from Buffalo, is very easy to get to just across the shared US Canadian border.

Sitting alone in his beautiful space, he settled in to a traditional dinner of pot roast and fresh vegetables. This place was very La-Tee-Dah he could almost hear his wife telling him as he sipped a bottle of cold sparkling water. They always disagreed on luxury; her idea was to be with him in the wilderness, the mall, or just sitting at home reading the paper. He wanted to spoil her, this beautiful creature who had loved him, every single cell of him, in spite of who he was and what he did. Sal could never tell his wife "No", and never wanted to. He wanted her to have everything she desired.

Leading up to the day DiFlippo disappeared; he had been under a lot of stress. There were numerous rumors on the street that he was going soft, losing his nerve or maybe even contemplating retirement. People in his own organization were questioning his decisions. Then, that wanna-be, Fat Ritchie was refusing to pay him back the money he owed.

DiFlippo had been planning on this time, he moved carrots around on the plate and remembered the day he knew for sure it was only a matter of time before someone tried to eliminate him. He wanted to talk to Rick about it but with the Dallas job on the docket, there had been no time. He knew if he told Stevens, Stevens would refuse the Dallas job and stay with him until they had the threat eliminated. The only problem with that plan was that DiFlippo wasn't sure who was responsible for wanting him dead.

Mazzio was at the top of the list. They had been together for a lot of years. DiFlippo was the idea man and Mazzio made sure his ideas were implemented. It was a good partnership and had worked well for both men for a long time. If Sal did decide to retire or was killed, Mazzio would replace him as head of the family.

The thought made him physically nauseous. He just didn't want to believe it could be Mazzio, and chose to avoid overeating because of the anguish in his heart about his life, this life, the one he had created, could be ending unless handled properly.

The only other person he suspected was one of his captains, Jack Carlotti. Carlotti along with a small, twelve man crew worked out of Niagara Falls New York. Niagara Falls is a quick 30 minute car ride on the I-190 from Buffalo. He was responsible for all of the action in Niagara Falls. Book-making, loan-sharking, construction, prostitution, and protection money were all his. Carlotti was one of the people that sometimes questioned DiFlippo's decisions. Carlotti wanted to expand the business by getting some of the action on the Indian Casino located in downtown Niagara Falls. Everybody vested would make a lot of money, but there was only one problem. The Tribal leaders of the Seneca Nation, the people that actually owned the casino, didn't want to share any of the money they were making with either Carlotti or his organization.

Carlotti wanted to strong-arm them into allowing him access to their business but DiFlippo, after weighing his options, had said no. He singlehandedly decided that all of the trouble that would be caused by fighting with the Tribal Leaders would not be worth the end result. In DiFlippo's experience, it never paid off being in a business relationship with someone who didn't want to be in business with you. It was always one headache after the next, and never a smart way to do business.

DiFlippo opened his secured mail and was glad to know about the attempt on Steven's life was tied into the attempt on his own, whoever was behind this knew it was a two for one deal if breathing air and not the Hudson was to be a part of their future plans. The only way Carlotti could have planned Rick's part was with a lot of help. After reading Stevens posts, it did appear another family had been involved. What DiFlippo was unsure of was who the other family was and who sanctioned the hit on Stevens? The waters were very muddy right now. Like when you lift a rock from the bottom of a pond, a lot of dirt is stirred up. DiFlippo had an idea he wanted Stevens to implement. The only question was, would his idea clear the water or only muddy it further?

■■

Mazzio knew if DiFlippo or Stevens lived, they would never stop until they found out who tried to kill them. If Mazzio didn't come up with a likely candidate and some convincing evidence very soon, by default, he would be the one that was blamed.

The thought shot icy shingles down his back and over his arms, just then he got an idea; Carlotti.

Mazzio knew that Carlotti up in Niagara Falls was unhappy about DiFlippo's decision to stay out of the very lucrative casino business. Now all he had to do was figure out how to tie Carlotti in with the botched assassination attempt, possibly eliminating both Sal and Carlotti, doubling his family size and getting the casino's to boot. He had a few ideas but he would need Berrazino's help. Berrazino would have to keep quiet about the whole thing,. He was fairly certain that Berrazino would remain quiet and help Mazzio out again if the taste of promotion could stay fresh in his mouth. If Berrazino couldn't stay quiet, Mazzio's second option was to frame Berrazino for the hits. His plan formed quickly and he thought he had an excellent idea on how to pull it off.

■■

Lima parked down the street from O'Malley's house. O'Malley had finally shown up at home around 8:30 that night. He was with his wife and since going into the house, he hadn't seen him; only the light in an upstairs room illuminated the home with passing shadows from time to time. Lima was hoping to see some sign of Stevens. So far, there had been nothing.

Lima sat there watching lights flip on and off until about midnight. Then as the still silence of the street encroached around the neighborhood, Lima sat, staring at the house until 2:00 am. As if no thoughts had crossed his mind except the vision of O'Malley's extremely young wife wrapping her underdressed body around the dry cleaner mogul's, pulling dollars out of his wallet with every flip of her hair which made him feel like Arnold Schwarzenegger in True Lies as he watched Jamie Lee Curtis tantalite him from the shadows, he awoke from his staring contest and hit the steering wheel hard.

This is a waste of time Lima thought. Stevens wasn't going to reach out to O'Malley. It was over, and he knew he missed his chance. He knew Stevens was gone. Stevens would lay low and regroup. Then he would try to find out who took a shot at him meaning he would have to be very careful until Stevens was finally dead.

Lima left his lights off as he started the car and drove back to his hotel, only turning them on as he reached a main street as to keep attention to himself low.

He had a very nice room at a Comfort Suites waiting for him, the lack of sleep and over all comfort was making him jittery, he started to think of a new ad campaign for the big coffee chain stores, something about drinking coffee instead of water to help your body ....but he was too tired to even rhyme the last line. Should have been an ad exec, then I would have a beautiful piece to sleep with at will every night and a house no one wanted to break into with a life no one wanted to rip apart. He parked in the parking lot and used the side entrance to go into the hotel.

He took the elevator to the fifth floor and walked to his room. When Lima opened the door, the first thing he noticed was an envelope on the floor with his name on it. He bent over and picked it up thinking the hotel must think he was checking out, but as he was opening the envelope, he sensed movement behind him.

■■■

After I had everything I needed, I left the Dallas house and headed towards the interstate calling O'Malley and told him the job was complete. I informed him he had sixty-minutes to transfer the remaining money into my account. O'Malley suggested we meet some place and he would give me the money he owed me in cash. I told O'Malley if we were to ever meet, I would kill him on the spot, I was in no mood.

As silence enveloped the line and I started to brake the car to turn around, O'Malley must have heard my brakes and turn signal in the background broke the silence and said the money would be transferred within the hour.

I knew who my shooter was and I knew what hotel he had been staying at. I called Allen and gave him the name of the hotel and the alias Lima used the first night he was in Dallas. I called out to Cali and asked Geoff if he could hack into the hotels computer to get the credit card info Lima used to rent the room.

I was willing to bet that Lima didn't have multiple aliases like I did and if he was still in town, he would be registered under the same name in a different hotel. All of this relied on the information I was able to get out of dearly departed Angelo.

If the information was correct, and I was pretty sure it was, Geoff should be able to get me what I needed. It took about 35 minutes but when he called me back, he had a hotel and a room number for me.

I found Lima's room and knocked on the door, stepping quickly to the left of the door so I couldn't be seen from the peep hole and to stay out of the way of any bullets directed at me. I waited and listened, knocked again. If I heard any sound at all from his room, I already decided to go in shooting and kill everyone in there. Lucky for him, I heard nothing. Picking electronic hotel room door locks is a lot easier than it appears, especially when you have a device that does all the work for you. Several years ago, Geoff made a device that would open any electronic key card lock. It looks like a black credit card with a wire attached to it. The wire runs into a little computer device no bigger than an Mp3 player all the kids had these days. All I had to do was put the card in the lock, press the on button on the mini-computer and wait just under eight seconds and the lock opened. According to Geoff the computer would be able to check millions of combinations of passwords in seconds.

Once in the room, I closed and locked the door, cleared the room and found it empty. I didn't know how long I would have to wait until Lima got back. I opened the desk drawer and took out an envelope. I used the hotel's stationary and folded a sheet of paper and sealed it in the envelope. I wrote Lima's name in script as if from a woman on the envelope and placed it on the floor, about three feet inside the room. I left the lamp on the side of the bed and turned it to the lowest light setting.

The hotel room was set up like a million other rooms I had been in. You walk into the room in a narrow hallway. On the left hand side, there is a small closet and on the right hand side there is the door to the bathroom. After that, the room opens up and there is a bed, a dresser, an armoire with an old tube style TV inside, a desk and a chair. My plan was to leave the envelope on the floor to draw Lima's attention. With their only being one light on in the room, the bathroom would be covered in shadows. When Lima bent over to retrieve the letter, I could come up behind him and disable him. I planned on eventually killing him, but I needed to question him first. I didn't feel prepared to torture him like I did his cohort and I was definitely not in the right location to do that. I had another card up my sleeve though…fear.

I waited in the bathroom all night. It was a very long time to wait and I was very bored, but stood my post. I would have made my drill instructor proud. In my opinion, patience is the most underrated gift there is. A little after 2:00 am my patience was rewarded.

I first heard Lima slide his key card into the lock, it didn't work the first time he tried it, I smiled at his bad luck. As the door finally opened and Lima stepped into the room. He closed the door behind him and then took a step into the room and just as I had planned, bent over to pick up the letter. He took another step into the room then started to yawn as he was opening the letter. I quietly slid in behind Lima and put him in a vascular restraint hold. The vascular restrain hold is one of my favorites, come up from behind a person and put your shoulder into their arm pit. You take your right and left hands and clasp them together, one in front of the person and one from behind the person. You drive your shoulder up into their arm pit and at the same time you use your clenched hands to pull down on the side of their neck. The pressure from your shoulder in their arm pit cuts of the blood flow to their brain from the carotid artery and your hands pulling down on the side of their neck cuts off the blood from the other carotid artery. The result; the person passes out almost immediately.

Once Lima was out, I helped him slump to the floor and then moved him to a nearby red and white striped chair using duct tape to tie him down. I covered his mouth with the tape as well. Once secured, I slapped him three times, hard, in his face.

This brought him back to the world of consciousness. I just sat on the edge of the bed in the shadows where he couldn't tell who it was. It took him about a minute or so to figure out where he was and what was happening. He didn't immediately see my figure sitting on the bed due to his incredible fear and thinking I was behind him or next to him. Once I stood, I saw it all form and crystallize in his eyes: first confusion, then understanding and finally the last drop of unadulterated complete and frozen fear. That is exactly what I wanted to see. I didn't want to torture him but I concluded that I would if I had to; surely the warehouse was cleaned by now. With his mouth taped, I figured I could still cause a lot of damage to him if the need arose. I was hoping I wouldn't have too, I needed him.

"Giovanni Lima, a pleasure to meet you. It's unfortunate that we meet under these circumstances, but what can you do? I have heard a lot about you. Your reputation exceeds you. Or, is it precedes you? I'm not sure the correct verbiage, it's late, but either way, I have to say, I am a teensy bit disappointed. You had two chances to kill me last night and you missed them both." As I said this, his eyes got wide and he shook his head left and right hard as if that would matter.

"Come on Lima," I said casually like we were sharing a few cold ones at a back yard barbeque, "we both know it was you. Now let me tell you something you didn't know. When you sent the Brothers Ferro into Gonzalez's house, I only killed one of them. I believe his name was, oh yes, Max? I took Angelo prisoner and interrogated him. He had a long night last night, but not as long as yours will be..." I paused a long time and got some ice out of the bucket in the room drew some water into the cup and sat back on the edge of the bed. After the excruciatingly long pause, I started again, "In the end, like everyone does, like you will here tonight, he talked. He answered all of my questions. That's how I knew it was you that tried to shoot me last night." Lima was really shaking his head left and right now, with a glassy look in his eyes like he was trying hard not to cry. Trying to tell me a lie through his eyes, trying to get me to side with him, to understand him, to let him be on my side.

I grabbed Lima's right hand and used my knife, one of the items I brought from my safe house, nothing special, just a four inch Spydereco Barong, to cut off the finger nail of his trigger finger. I smiled the entire time I did the cutting.

Lima was rocking back and forth in his chair and trying to yell, but the duct tape was silencing his screams. Once I had the nail loose, I used a pair of vice grips to remove the nail from the finger. A little blood from the cuticle spread out over the exposed nail bed. I was sure he didn't notice from the way he was thrashing and shaking his head.

"Look, I just want you to know how serious I am Lima. As a matter of fact, Angelo wanted me to give you something. I have it right here in my pocket." With that, I took out a zip top bag containing Angelo's fingers and toes. I dumped the bag out on Lima's lap. He was trying to jump out of the chair to avoid the body pieces. His body wretched like he was vomiting and swallowing it from the horror.

"You see , I took Angelo to a very secluded place. We had a wonderful little chat. I found out things about him that he has never shared with anyone else. After about the third toe, Angelo really wasn't trying to be tough anymore. It was a miracle, he was answering all of my questions by then. Unfortunately, by then I was really quite enjoying myself and just continued to carve on him while we talked."

At this point, I stopped talking for a few seconds. I stared off into space as if I was reliving the experience. I let my eyes get glassy. Then I smiled a huge smile and looked back at Lima.

"By the end of our conversation, he was a fucking mess. He was missing pieces and bleeding all over the place. He even pissed himself, it was awful. Which gave me an idea. I wish I could tell you how Angelo died. To be completely honest with you, I am not really sure myself. You see, I don't know if he choked on his own dick or bled to death. After he pissed himself, I reached down between his legs and used this knife, the same one I just took your finger nail with, and cut his pecker off. Then I jammed it into his mouth. He was still alive when I put it into his mouth. With such a little pecker, I really can't believe he didn't last much longer after that."

I figured a little lie here would help convince Lima to talk to me.

"Now before I get started carving you up, before I get carried away, I want to give you an opportunity to answer a few questions for me. If you answer them and more importantly, if I think you are honest, I might let you live. In the very least, I will be kind and kill you quickly and painlessly.

I am not really that bad a guy, but if I think you are lying to me, even just one time, the things I did to Angelo will seem like a day at the park compared to what I will do to you. Now I am going to remove the tape from your mouth. You can answer my questions or yell for help. Actions and consequences. The decision all yours." I stood back using my hands like an old style scale to animate the weight of the moment standing there, smiling, knife in hand, like I was the good guy.

I removed the tape from Lima's mouth. He coughed a little bit, spitting out the remaining vomit left in his cheeks, cursed a string of ridiculous gibberish, and said in a slow growl, "Ask".

"YOU are a winner! I mean I am not going to give you a new car or anything, but you're a lot smarter than Angelo. So to me that is a winner....who sent you to kill me?"

"Paul Berrazino."

"Why?"

"Fuck you man, I don't know, I just got a call in the middle of the afternoon and was told he had a job. He said it was very important and I needed to pick two of my best people to help out with. I chose the Ferro brothers, worthless pieces of shit."

"Dead ones too, Did he tell you specifically who the target was? Did-he-say–my-name?"

"Yes."

I laughed then stopped quick. "Oh now, what else…don't stop, you will regret it…Tell me a story Lima, it's late, maybe a bedtime story before your eternal rest…"

"Look, he said we had an unlimited budget, he said I could get whatever I needed. He said I had to wait until you took out Gonzalez and then we were free to take you. We had to make you disappear; completely. I was the only one who knew your name or who you were. Angelo and Max had no idea. Man, are those really his fingers?"

"I am not the liar here, and you better not be either. Of course they're his fingers. Who else would they be from? Count yours, are they all still there? Well then, yep they are Angelo's. Back to the point here, why, why does Paul Berrazino of all people want me dead? Who is he working with?"

"Shit man, I don't know. I swear I don't. He's my captain, I do what he says. He told me I would make a shit load of money and be famous in the organization for eliminating you. He did say something about reporting to someone else on the hit or something. I am not sure what he meant. That's all I know. It was nothing personal. You know how it is."

"Yep, that I do Lima, that I do. So how do I get to Berrazino? Where does he operate out of?" I said flipping out my knife again

"Fuck. My finger, oh God take this shit off my legs man, I want to fucking vomit…Bear owns a strip club outside of Rochester. The Tickled Tuna. It's a middle of the road place. He always has a few guys with him. He's pretty well connected with Vince Augostino, head of the Camarillo family right now. I think he and Berrazino went to school together or something. They go way back. You can't make a move on him without Vince's okay."

"Bull-shit, I don't need anyone's okay to make a move Lima. You think someone told me to do this? I am not a small-time order taker like you; I am in business for myself. If he is so tight with Augostino, why is he only a captain?"

"I think it's because Vince's brother, Mario, is his number 2. Either way, I don't know nothing about a hit on DiFlippo though"

I tried not to act surprised by this nugget of goodness coming from his mouth, I almost for two seconds wanted to make him more comfortable, but it was a fleeting feeling, "What do you mean a hit on DiFlippo?" I said as unsurprised as a kid who already opened his present's way before Christmas.

"Man, there was a rumor floating around that someone was going to try to take out the old man. I didn't hear anything specific, it was just a rumor."

"You are an asshole, that doesn't make any sense." My haunches were raised, "Who would want to eliminate Sal? The Camarillo's and DiFlippo have been doing business together for years without any problems. It makes me wonder if Vince knew about the hit or not. You know, I am thinking this is a lie…you remember how I feel about lies. You a foot or a finger man…." I said picking up one of Angelo's severed digits and wiping it under his nose for effect

"I don't know. I really don't. Hey, you don't have to kill me you know. I can get you into Berrazino's club. I can schedule you a meeting or a sit down with him. I would be willing to help you. I would be eternally grateful."

I laughed out loud. As much as I didn't like to admit it, I was starting to like Lima. For a brief moment, I thought what it would be like to have a partner. Especially someone as skilled as Lima was. He wasn't as good as me, but he was still pretty capable. Clearly he followed directions well. I didn't even have to spill a lot of blood; a pink rainbow bandage would fix that little missing finger nail right up.

"You ever let someone live you were supposed to take out?"

"No Stevens, I never did."

"Well?"

"But you're not supposed to take me out! I can pay you. Whatever your fee is, I will double it to let me live. I'll also pay you to take out Berrazino. How's that sound?"

"I just told you I don't answer to anyone, ever." I stood, Lima was getting desperate, he was going to stop talking soon and I was really, really tired. He was starting to remind me of a drowning man gasping for his last breath. It was time to end this.

"Sorry Lima. I have to do what I do now. I will make it painless. I am a man of my word…"

"Wait! Don't I get last rites or something?" he begged. I moved closer to him.

"Don't I get a chance to confess my sins and go to the afterlife or where-ever with a clean conscious? I, I, I heard you were a priest before you started killing people for money." That slowed me down for a second, but I kept moving to keep him guessing and keep my body moving…I was actually tired.

"Where did you hear that?"

"It was a rumor I heard a long time ago. I never put much stock into it. Is it true?"

"You've heard a lot of rumors Lima. First one about DiFlippo and now one about me. To answer your question, yes it is. I was once a man of the cloth."

"Holy shit! Sorry, I mean, how do you go from saving people and helping them achieve eternal life to killing them for money?" It was a good question. It was a question a lot of people wanted to ask me but never had the nerve to. It was also a question I had asked myself on more than one occasion.

"Well, you ever see those guys in prison? You know the ones, the serial killers, the mass murderers. They kill a bunch of people and get sent to prison for life. Somewhere during their sentence they get religion and find God? They repent their sins and change their ways. Who really knows if that is real or just for show?

The closest I can explain it is it's the same thing but only opposite. I had religion, I knew God but somewhere along the way I realized it was all bullshit." I swung my knife around for affect, "I realized religion was a sham and this wonderful, all seeing, all knowing and compassionate being that lived in the sky was nothing more than a man-made guardian to help us all feel better about us and our failures.

If something good happened to us, we should thank God for the blessing. If something bad happened to us, we should pray to God for help. He was only testing us and our faith. God would never give us more than we could handle and we would be a stronger, better person in the end for having suffered through the hardship, right?"

"Yeah, I heard that."

"Well Lima, its bullshit. It's the biggest cop-out I have ever heard. When everything goes right, God is there to take the credit and glory. When it all goes to shit, the short comings are our own. Gambling is bad and we shouldn't do it, right? Take a look at all the different churches, big shining Catholic ones especially, and what do you see every Saturday night? Their bingo hall, filled. I guess gambling is bad, but bingo is God's game of chance." I ranted.

"The body is a temple, right? Well, then why do they sell pizza and candy at the all those Bingo Halls? Why are they always filled with cigarette smoke?

It must be ok to abuse the temple when you're dropping dollars for God. God has unlimited amounts of love for all of creation. Then, according to his own book, the Bible, he's going to send 2/3 of us to Hell? I guess God's unlimited love is tough love of the hardest kind. God loves children and then he allows pedophiles and other sick fucks, sometimes their own parents, or even His own priests, to rape, abuse and murder them.

What the hell is that? Is that love? If it is, I ain't interested. You want your last rites Lima? You really want them? You want to ask forgiveness to an absentee owner who could give two shits about you? Go ahead, be my guest. Beg for forgiveness. Better yet, pray that He strikes me down and allows you to live! Go ahead I will wait." I sat back down, head in my hands, elbows on my knees and waited....

Lima just looked at me. I can imagine what I looked like. I pictured myself as looking like one of those crazy Southern Texas Evangelists, all wide eyed and frizzy hair. All I needed was a cheap white suit and someone to occasionally yell "AMEN" and the look would be complete. I took a deep breath to compose myself.

"Sorry, sometimes I get carried away. It looks like God isn't taking any calls this evening. No surprise, right? I guess Psalms 50:15 is bullshit."

"I am not familiar with it. What does it say?"

"It says, 'In times of trouble call on me, I shall deliver you, and you shall glorify me.' I did my part. I put you in harm's way. You're definitely in trouble. You did your part. You held up your end of the bargain. You called on him right? Where is he? He's not going to deliver you and you won't have chance to glorify Him. That's ok though. You're about to meet him. You can then file a grievance with him in person in a few minutes." With that, I stepped behind Lima and snapped his neck. Was God up there, somewhere in the heavens listening to our exchange? I didn't think so. I was pretty sure God stopped listening to me a long time ago.

■■■

After killing Lima, I stripped him down and laid him in the tub of his shower. I know this was the second person in as many days that I killed and then stripped naked.

I didn't feel good about it this time either. Like last time, I had a good reason. First, I put a Band-Aid on the finger where I had taken his nail off, turned the shower on and left his body at an unnatural angle. This would help out in two different ways. If I had left any trace evidence on Lima it would be washed away in the shower and secondly, when his body was finally discovered, he would have appeared to have died from a slip and fall accident in the shower. The Band-Aid was to help make the Lima's missing nail seem more natural.

After cleaning up Angelo's fingers and toes, I searched his hotel room but didn't find anything useful other than the pistol he was carrying. I looked through his wallet but he didn't have any cash in it. I didn't want Lima's death to even have a hint of suspicion about it so I took sixty dollars out of my own wallet, all in twenty dollar bills and put it in his. When the police searched the room, they would find his wallet, watch, credit cards and cash and hopefully this would quicken their decision in saying Lima died of natural causes. I made sure there was no duct tape residue on the chair or him and took his car keys and went to the parking lot.

I found his car and searched through it finding several guns, and a lap top computer. I took everything from his car and put it in mine. Then I returned to Lima's room for one last walk through. There was some blood on Lima's shirt and pants from where I had removed the nail. I didn't see any on the floor or the chair. I took out a pair of pants and a shirt from Lima's suit case and left them on the floor. Once I was sure the room was as clean as I could make it, I took his bloody shirt and pants and left.

When I got in my car, I turned on my lap top and checked my account. As promised, there was a deposit of $25,000 waiting for me. O'Malley was a smart man after all. Just when I thought my work in Dallas was done and it was time to head home, I had a message waiting for me in my secured website. After hearing the message, I knew I would be in Dallas for at least another day.

CHAPTER #18

Salvatore DiFlippo spent his entire life growing up in the mafia. His father, Armando DiFlippo, worked for Stefano Magaddino. For 50 years, Magaddino was the dominating presence in the Western New York underworld. He is the longest tenured boss in the history of the mafia.

Magaddino was also deeply involved in national La Cosa Nostra affairs. Magaddino was a charter member of Charles "Lucky" Luciano's Mafia Commission and attended important underworld summits such as the 1946 Havana Conference in Cuba and the 1957 Appalachian Conference in Appalachian, New York.

Magaddino was an old-style boss who preferred to stay in the background and not draw any attention to himself or his criminal activities if possible. He was the owner of the Magaddino Memorial Chapel, a funeral home in Niagara Falls, New York. This is where Magaddino kept his office and this is where Armando started out and worked.

Armando was a great worker and very loyal to Magaddino. The two could often be seen eating lunch at The Como Restaurant on Pine Avenue in Niagara Falls. When faced with serving five years in prison or offering up Magaddino for a lighter sentence, Armando gladly did the five years.

Sal started working for the Magaddino family when he was 12 years old. He would deliver packages as a courier, usually filled with money, to the different police officers and politicians that were on Magaddino's payroll. Sal was a shy, quiet kid and didn't say much. Some people even in the organization thought Sal might be a little slow. They couldn't be more wrong. Sal pad attention to every little detail, he watched, learned and filed away the lessons that had been taught to him. He worked his way up through the ranks of the family and years after both his father's and Magaddino's death, he would eventually become head of the family.

In the late 1960's, Sal understood that the next big money-maker would be illegal drugs. Heroin, marijuana, cocaine and other drugs would be what alcohol was during prohibition. While prohibition was in effect in the United States, Magaddino ran a profitable bootlegging business smuggling Canadian alcohol from Canada across the Niagara River and Lake Ontario into New York State.

Using the same supply lines that Magaddino used during prohibition, DiFlippo was able to stay ahead of the curve and be out in front in the drug business when it started to boom. DiFlippo was a lot like the old mafia don that taught him. He liked to maximize his profits while limiting his exposure. That is why in the early 1980's, DiFlippo, in effect, sold his drug business to several street gangs that operated in New York.

At the time, this was unheard of. When you have a cash cow, especially one that was running so smoothly, you didn't sell it. You milked it for all it was worth. But once again, DiFlippo proved to be in front of the curve.

DiFlippo knew that law enforcement would come after drug dealers and suppliers harder than they had gone after the rum runners during prohibition. He wanted to be out of the drug business before the full power of the federal government was focused on what would later be a war on drugs. DiFlippo had two stipulations when selling off his drug business: The first was the street gangs had to use his supply line for five years. What that meant was even though DiFlippo was out of the drug business; he would still be collecting money on it for five years. All of the illegal drugs flowing into Western New York were designed to come through DiFlippo's supply line. The second condition was anyone that wanted to sell drugs in DiFlippo's territory had to have his approval first. Getting DiFlippo's approval was easy; you just had to pay for it. Once you had his approval, you were assigned a section of the city. What if you wanted a bigger section? Easy; all you had to do was pay DiFlippo more money. Two years into the deal, the head of the street gang that was currently in charge paid DiFlippo off, in advance, for the next three years. DiFlippo was also paid a lump sum to cover all his future approvals.

When the government was seizing property and freezing cash assets, DiFlippo went on his way without a worry. All of the cash the feds could find was all backed up by the various legitimate business holdings DiFlippo had. While other mob guys were scrambling to hide their assets in other people's names, DiFlippo continued to keep everything in his own name. The IRS audited DiFlippo four times in six years and each and every time, DiFlippo walked away clean. The final time they audited him, DiFlippo's lawyers found an error the IRS had made and the government had to refund tens of thousands of dollars back to DiFlippo.

When people were being gunned down in the streets, and rival gangs were going to war with each other over drugs and territories, DiFlippo never batted an eye. Everyone knew which section of the city was a "No Sell Zone". One dealer from a large organization attempted to violate the "No Sell" rule. The next day, every other leader of all the other street gangs received a package in the mail. Everyone got a piece of the dealer that violated the rule. Some of the people received their piece hand-delivered by police officers. It was subtle reminder of who was in charge. It was about as subtle as a 20 pound sledge hammer.

When low ranking soldiers and mid-level lieutenants in other people's organizations were getting hit with RICO charges, flipping on their bosses and being sent away for long stretches of time or entering the witness protection program, DiFlippo never lost a wink of sleep. Nobody could point a finger DiFlippo's way. DiFlippo only gave his orders to one man, and that was Mazzio. DiFlippo was also not very greedy. He was not afraid to spend his own money on bribing police officers, federal agents and judges. The police officers that worked for DiFlippo received better benefits then the state could supply.

DiFlippo's organization wasn't the biggest in New York, and it didn't generate the most money, but when the old Don requested a meeting with another family, it was always granted, immediately. Magaddino may have been the longest tenured boss in mafia history, but DiFlippo was holding steady in second place.

"Hello?"

"Hello, Mr. Augostino please."

"May I ask whose calling?"

"This is Salvatore DiFlippo."

"Hold on please."

A few minutes later, the head of the Camarillo Family, Vincent Augostino, picked up the phone.

"Salvatore! Hello my friend. I hope you are well?"

"I wish I could say that I was but I do not want to lie to you. I hope you are doing well. I have been having some trouble and I need to talk to you about it."

"I have heard some things on the street regarding this trouble friend. I was wondering if there was any truth to what I was hearing. How can I help?"

"I need to meet with you. I have set for you a doctor's appointment on Friday, two days from now, at 2:00 pm. Will that work for you?"

Several years ago, an older man came to DiFlippo and asked for a loan. He said his son just completed medical school and wanted to set up a practice with several other doctors. The older man had borrowed money from DiFlippo before and always made his payments on time. However, the amount of the loan the man was asking would be far too much for the man to afford when it came time for collecting the debt. The man was a blue collar guy and was loyal to DiFlippo. DiFlippo wanted to help the man and his son out.

Instead of refusing the man, DiFlippo saw opportunity. Instead of giving the man a loan he knew would never be repaid, DiFlippo offered to fully fund a private practice for the older man's son. The only stipulations DiFlippo wanted in return was free medical care for anyone he sent there and use of any of the examination rooms whenever he wanted. The man couldn't believe his luck and gratefully accepted DiFlippo's offer. DiFlippo knew one of the few places the federal government was not allowed to wiretap was a doctor's examination room. He would now have a place he could meet with people and not fear being recorded. Also, if one of his soldiers suffered a gunshot wound, they would be able to receive care in a doctor's office without it being reported. It was a costly investment for DiFlippo that paid off tenfold over the years.

"The same doctor as last time?"

"Yes."

"That will work my friend. I'll have Dante and Franco with me. I trust that this is all right?"

"Sure. Bring whomever you feel comfortable with. I will have a guy of my own there. Thank you for helping me out."

"It is my pleasure. See you on Friday."

The meeting was in place. DiFlippo anxiously waited for a report from Texas. He was counting on Stevens to come through for him. He was taking a huge risk and his plan had to work out perfectly. He was betting his future, and his life, on it.

CHAPTER #19

It was dark; I was waiting in another man's house to kill him. I had killed a lot of people and been on a lot of jobs, but nothing was as even close to being as complicated as this one was. I vowed when this job was over to go someplace warm and tropical and spend some time on a beach.

The house wasn't hard to break into. It had an alarm system, but it wasn't armed when the owners were home. Lucky for me the man's wife was home when I got to the house so I went in through the garage. I knew she was home so I was patient and silent. I could tell she was in the kitchen getting dinner ready. There was a roast and baked potatoes in the oven. I hadn't even realized how much I missed home cooking until that moment. It almost hurt my stomach and my heart at the same time. I knew the man would be home soon and I was informed that he always parked in the garage.

When it got close to the time for the man to come home, I laid down on the garage floor between the wife's car and the wall of the garage. Just like I had planned, the man came home and parked in the garage. After the man went into the house, I waited fifteen more minutes and then followed him in.

I crept silently into the house and heard the husband and his young wife eating dinner in the dining room. I walked through the kitchen and towards the dining room, stepped through the dining room door, smiled my new trademark smile that said "you are too late" and fired a round from the Mossberg into the woman's head as she chewed. I pumped the shot gun, ejecting the spent shell casing, and then trained the weapon on the man at the table.

O'Malley sat fork still in hand looking like he was in shock. Most people are when they are confronted with sudden, instant, unexpected death. Even more so when it's their own. I thought of saying something cute, but decided not to waste it on him. Before he could react, move a muscle, pray, cry, or say anything at all, I pulled the trigger and his chest disintegrated. Before he could fall to the floor, I pumped the shot gun, ejected another shell, and fired at O'Malley again. This time I hit him in the upper shoulder and face. I knew he was dead. No one could survive two close range shot gun blasts from a 12 gauge, and if they did it would be short and painful. I ejected the spent shell and let it fall to the floor with the others.

It was time to move fast now. The shot gun blasts were deafening and I was sure someone would call the police. I removed a zip top bag from my pocket containing several pieces of hair I had removed from Gonzalez's hair brush at home. I dropped them on the floor and left the house taking the shot gun with me.

If the Dallas Police Department was as good as I thought they were, they would find Gonzalez's hair at the murder scene. I know they would find the spent shell casings. Since the shells came from Gonzalez's shot gun, and he was the one to load it, I knew the shell casings would have his finger prints on them.

The detectives would run the prints and come up with Gonzalez's name if he was in the system. If he was not in the system, when they started investigating O'Malley's murder, they would discover the nasty law-suit between him and Gonzalez. They would go talk to Gonzalez and find a crime scene there. Once they made an ID on the body at Gonzalez's house and found out he was a professional shooter and had connections to organized crime, they would assume someone sent him there to kill Gonzalez.

It would look like the shooter failed in his attempt. Following the evidence, they would run across a purchase statement from a gun store on file for Gonzalez and his 12 gauge. They would have the slugs from his gun at the murder scene and Gonzalez wouldn't be around to answer any questions. What else would a person think? O'Malley missed Gonzalez and instead of hiring a killer like O'Malley did, Gonzalez did the job himself and then disappeared. It would all tie together nicely.

The icing on the cake would be when they started looking for Gonzalez. They would check his credit cards first to see if he made any travel arrangements. With Allen's help, they would find some. The police would see Gonzalez purchased a one way ticket from Dallas to San Diego. Also with a little help from Geoff, the airlines would have a computerized record of Gonzalez being on the flight manifest from Dallas to San Diego.

The credit card receipts would show one final purchase at a fast food restaurant within walking distance of the San Diego/Tijuana boarder. The final piece of the puzzle would be when they checked the boarder's computers to see if they had a record of Gonzalez crossing over into Mexico. Since 9/11, records were better kept at the boarders and Geoff would be able to place a record indicating Gonzalez had crossed over. The evidence in Michael O'Malley's murder would lead them to Jorge Gonzalez and Jorge Gonzalez would lead them to Tijuana Mexico. After that, the trail would end.

I left O'Malley's house and got on the highway stopping at Lemon Lake Park. While I was there, I broke down Gonzalez's shot gun. I needed this gun to disappear. Half of the pieces of the gun went into Lemon Lake and the other half of the pieces went into the Trinity River. That was a fantastic gun and I was very disappointed I had to get rid of it. As soon as I got back from my warm tropical vacation, I decided I would buy myself one; well one of my alias' would anyway.

I stopped at my safe house in Dallas and unloaded all of my supplies and weapons. I showered, changed, re-packed a carry-on bag and signed into my e-mail. There was a message from Mazzio saying someone had tried to kill Sal and Sal was in hiding. He told me he was telling everyone that asked about Sal that Sal was sick in bed. Mazzio asked me to come to Buffalo so we could have a face to face meeting. I deleted his e-mail without replying. I composed an e-mail to Sal telling him we were all set to go on our scheduled fishing trip and I would be at his house by the morning, lures in hand.

After locking my house, I drove to DFW again. I turned in my rental car and took the free shuttle back to the terminal. I had a few hours to kill before my flight left so I purchased a book from a gift shop and then had dinner at an overpriced burger joint in the terminal. When it was time, I checked into my first class seat and settled in for my flight to Toronto, I was asleep before my ginger ale ever made it to my seat.

CHAPTER #20

After my wife and daughter were killed, I was lost. I didn't know what to do, or even if I could do anything at all. I was also shocked to find out that a man not only that I respected but considered one of my closest friends was a leader in the criminal underworld and he expected and trusted that I would be ok with that. It was a lot for me to process, and I did what I usually did when I felt lost, I prayed. I prayed for clarity, wisdom, rest, death, silence, amnesia, death, and more death…it never came, none of it. I knew then that God was not real, not in my life, not caring about me about my family. Nothing mattered, only death.

I essentially closed down my church by not showing up, returning checks and leaving any money donated at the entrance of the church for anyone to come and take. I alienated everyone by telling all the well-wishers to stay away. I locked myself in and without embarrassment or pride, and I prayed. Over the course of the first two days, that's all I did. I fasted without a cause but my own, I didn't sleep, I just talked to God. I talked silently as I stared at a wall, sitting in a corner, beating my head against the wall periodically, waking up having fallen asleep from exhaustion. I yelled, I screamed, cried, wept, begged, and cursed. Anger is an honest human emotion and I was angry so I displayed that to God. He made me this way, full of anger, full of emotion, He the God of pillars of fire, drowning kings, and deep honest painful love and vengeance to be envied.

I wanted an answer as to why this tragedy occurred. I wanted an explanation of why my family was taken from me. Why was I spared? Why wasn't it me that was killed? I read some scriptures, but didn't find any comfort in their words. I searched for direction and found none. I was truly at a crossroads. I considered taking my own life. It would be a quick end to my pain and misery, I had pushed away all that cared and made them hate me. They wouldn't be hurt further by loss. Four days into my rant, as I started to stop feeling my body's hunger pains, I had lost consciousness and slumped to the floor. The only thing I remember is a pair of clean polished black men's dress shoes with black top stitching and a square shaped toe, tied at the top and reptile skin accents in the same midnight black tone.

I woke up a few days later with an IV in my arm, a nurse reading a romance novel at my bedside and Sal sitting at the foot of the bed. During my conversation with Sal the previous week, the day after my families' deaths, he implied I could come to work with him and his organization. Here he was making my decision for me, I wouldn't have a choice to leave or stay. what had I gotten myself into? Alone, I felt broken down, like a moving box that is coveted from the time you decide you need it, until you get it, to when you use it, to be marked, cared for and considered, up until its function is no longer needed, it is broken down, stomped, piled, and thrown out. My function; as a community leader, a healer, a confidant, a loyal friend, a lover, and a daddy, were no longer needed. I didn't even know if I cared or had any position concerning the situation that sat before me in the form of Sal's twisted life. So instead, I sat silent for days, I never moved more than a few times here or there in the bed, went to the bathroom, never bathed, never brushed my teeth, nothing. Just moved back and forth on the amazingly soft and comfortable California King sized bed and seriously considered what it would be like to work in an organization like Sal's. I wondered what he would have me do. I figured I wouldn't be answering phones or mopping floors, though I wasn't even qualified to do that at this particular point in my life.

I also considered taking a sabbatical and joining a monastery somewhere to be alone and pray. There are monasteries on the coast of Italy that remain untouched from the beginning of time that could be a haven for someone like me. I could work, pray, live. I wanted to reflect on my life and what I had done thus far. I knew I couldn't function anymore, not here, not in any real sort of way. The day to day minutia of having a job and paying bills seemed like an impossible task to face alone.

After enough time had passed that I started to feel my skin, I pulled out my IV, put on the clean folded clothes that sat at my bedside untouched, put the five hundred dollars that was in the front pocket in the offering plate of a local church and spent several days there, taking communion several times a day as my only nourishment.

Without receiving any answers from God, I decided to take a break. I went back into my house, where the kitchen was clean, the yard mowed, and the door to my daughter's room was closed. My bathroom was set up like a hotel with towels and toilet paper that was folded to a triangle at the end and I showered until I ran out of scalding hot water.

After sleeping like a rock for a few hours smelling comfort in my wife's shampoo on the pillows and knowing the sheets had not been changed since the last time we made love, I was awoken by a knock at my front door. When I answered it, my old friend and mentor, Bill Jenkins was standing there.

I invited Bill inside and we sat down in the living room. Our conversation started off innocently enough. Bill asked me how I was holding up and I told him I was struggling. Bill asked if we could read some verses from the bible but I told him what I had been doing for the past two days.

Bill said "Your resolve in your faith to God is being tested. That is normal in a circumstance like this. I would be concerned if you weren't struggling a little bit."

I just sat in stunned silence before my pointed and heavy response, "This is more than a little bit Bill. I just can't understand…why."

"That's the hardest part, isn't it?" He was smiling at me as if I wasn't in on the joke, as if I didn't get it, "God has a plan. He has a plan for each and every one of us. He reveals his plan to each of us on His time, not on our time. That's where faith comes in. Having the faith to believe that even though you suffered a horrible loss, it is all a part of His plan. Down the road, when more of his plan is revealed to you, you will be a stronger person for having endured this. You may never know or understand why your family was called back to Heaven, but you will endure it and be a better person because of it." and another pity filled smile crept across his lips as he sipped his bottle of water that was magically in my fridge, just like everything else in my house, it was like pixie's came and took care of it while I just sat and decomposed in my own sorrow.

"I honestly don't know if I believe that. I don't know what to do. I am so lost…"

"Rick, you don't need to know what to do next. You don't need to plan. You should take your days an hour at a time. Right now, we are talking. When we are finished, you will eat. After you eat, you will go to bed. After you sleep, you will wake up. You see? Take it hour by hour. Eventually, you will want to do more and incorporate more into your daily routine. Before too long, you will be back to work and your life will continue on. It will not be like it was, but it will continue. You will laugh and smile again. As foreign as the thought is to you now, it will happen."

"I don't know if I can go back to work. I don't know if I can trust God. I know my faith is being tested, but I don't understand why. I don't think I can handle it."

"God never gives us more than we can handle. I can't even imagine the pain you are suffering right now. I'm not here to give you false promises or hope. You will be in pain for a while, a very long while. But by putting your faith in God, and trusting him to carry you through this, you will recover and be a stronger, better person."

"Maybe you're right. I think I need to spend some more time praying."

"An excellent choice. I am heading back home in four days. Why don't you join me? You know I have the guest house on my property. The mountains of North Carolina are beautiful this time of year. When the sun rises over the mountains in the morning, it truly is majestic. You can stay for as long or as short of time as you like. I could counsel you while you were there. What do you say?"

"Thank you for the offer. I am not sure. I will pray about it and get back to you. Thank you for coming over." he stood, opened his blazer and pulled an airline ticket with my name on the front and placed it on the table next to me. I chose to ignore it, didn't even tell him thank you, I just walked him to the door. While it was a nice gesture, it was making me want to kill myself all over again.

After Bill left, I got down on my knees and prayed some more. I was so confused, I prayed for a sign. I prayed that God would lead me where he wanted me to go. I fell asleep, exhausted, while praying. I didn't feel any better the next morning when I woke up. I was still hoping for a sign, or for my beautiful wife to come and bring me a coffee or my daughter to have the cartoons on the television too loudly. A few hours later, I got a sign, but I really wanted cartoons instead.

I was just returning from a run. I only did two miles, but I felt better. It felt like a fog was lifting from my mind. When I got home, Dominick Mazzio was waiting for me.

"Hello kid. Don't you have a cell phone or something? We've been waiting for about 30 minutes already."

Even though I knew this large powerful man was Sal's business partner, I didn't like him standing there with his plaid shirt, white beanie style golfers cap, and khaki pants looking like he could go play golf and bury you on the 9th green before holing a birdie putt. There was a depth of violence I sensed in him that hid below the surface of his calm business casual look.

"I apologize, but I didn't remember having an appointment with you Mr. Mazzio." I said bent over to my knees, catching my breath, looking up at him like I didn't care that he was standing there attempting to look imposing.

"No we don't have an appointment. Mr. DiFlippo sent me to pick you up. He said he had something he wanted to show you. Very important. Come take a ride with me kiddo."

"I am all sweaty. Let me take a shower and change. Give me 30 minutes."

"Kid, I've been fucking standing here for 30 minutes all ready. I told you, it's important. Get in the car and let's go."

I kept walking toward my door, I simply turned to him with my hand on the front door knob, "Mr. Mazzio right? I didn't invite you here. I didn't ask to go see something with you or even with Sal. I'm going in to take a shower and change. If you are still here when I come out, I'll take a ride with you. If you're not, oh well. If this is so important, you'll wait another 30 minutes." I smiled a smile that said go fuck yourself, and went into the house without waiting for his reply.

I took an extra-long shower with extra hot water, made sure every surface of my body was clean, twice. After my shower, I looked out my bedroom window and saw Mazzio sitting in the car talking or barking on his cell phone, since I could see his mouth moving I figured he was barking for sure. He didn't look too happy. I took my time in getting dressed, changed my shirt a few times, made sure to hang each one up as I found it, and then headed down stairs to my strappy brown day sandals.

I got into the car with Mazzio and we left without a word. At least if he was going to kill me he would be doing me a favor and I was all clean to go meet up with my wife. Instead, he drove me to Chef's Restaurant on Seneca Street in Buffalo. Mazzio pulled up front and let me off.

"You're not coming Mr. Mazzio?"

"Naww kid, Only you today. Have fun!" and he sped off laughing. There was something about the way he said the last part. *Have fu-un!* I wanted to punch him in the face as hard as I could. Instead, I took a deep breath and went into the restaurant. At a corner booth in the back of the restaurant, Sal was sitting alone.

When I approached, he got up and we embraced. "I am glad you could make it Rick. Please, sit down." After we both were seated, I asked Sal what he wanted to show me. "After we eat." He said as a waiter with salads appeared out of nowhere as if on command, "Lunch first, business after."

On Sal's recommendation, I ordered the chicken parmesan. It was, of course, excellent. After we finished our meal, Sal poured us each a glass of red wine and we got down to business over tiramisu.

"Rick, has there been a break on the case? Are the police any closer to catching the person who caused the accident?"

"I spoke to the detective in charge the other day and he said so far, no, no leads."

"Rick, the police are overburdened and under staffed. They don't have enough man-power or time to investigate a crime properly. It is not their fault. Crime continues to happen every day. They have to stay on top of it. They will work the cases that they have the best chance of clearing."

"I know Sal, and it sucks, sucks so damn bad, I am so frustrated. I think the police are tired of hearing from me."

"Rick, you must prepare yourself for what I am about to tell you. You may find this upsetting."

"Ok Sal…" I said with some hesitation wondering if I could take the words back and turn around and just leave, but something kept me planted right there in that uncomfortable black seat…"just tell me."

"The man responsible for the deaths of your wife and child will never be arrested or charged with causing the accident and their deaths."

"What? How do you know?" I said eyes wide as plates and filling with tears quicker than I had expected.

"I know a lot of people in this area. I have many different business interests. I took all of the information I could from the police and gave it to my own people. I have had my people checking collision shops, auto part stores, and garages. I have called in favors and asked for help from many different people. Something like this couldn't be hidden. Not completely. The vehicle would need to be repaired; someone would talk to someone else. You with me so far?"

While I was pretty sure I wasn't breathing as I comprehended his words I said, "Yes. Please go on." Though I thought I would maybe regret my auto-response.

"I got a call three nights ago from a guy that owes me a favor. He said he had just received word on what I was looking for. He said he repaired a vehicle that matched the description I was looking for. He also said the damage was consistent with what I was looking for."

"Was it him? Did you find their killer?"

He continued as if I hadn't spoken, "Not wanting to see an innocent man get hurt, I took the information I received from my friend and investigated it. The man that was driving the truck that killed your wife and daughter was driving on a suspended license. He had already received his third DUI charge and was supposed to be locked up in jail. He had a decent lawyer and his lawyer was able to get him probation instead of going away. This man is an alcoholic, he was stone drunk when he caused the accident. He wasn't supposed to be drinking and he wasn't supposed to be driving."

"Oh my God. We have to go to the police. We can give them this information and he will be arrested." I said in complete resolution.

Sal raised his eyes to me from stirring his freshly poured coffee around in a circle inside his cup. "Rick, you're not hearing me. His vehicle has already been repaired." He set the spoon down, took a sip of the hot drink, made a clicking sound with the back of his cheek and teeth and then looked back at me in a serious tone, "There is no longer any proof that his vehicle was involved in an accident. He will no doubt have an alibi for the time in question. Going to the police will do nothing."

"Come on, can't they get a statement from the collision shop owner? Won't that help?"

"They can get a statement and then when the driver is questioned all he has to say is one of his friends was driving the vehicle and the vehicle was damaged in a parking lot somewhere. The proof is gone. There is nothing to tie him to the accident scene."

"So you're telling me that you know who the killer is and he's going to get away? Isn't there something we can do about it?"

"Now Rick, there is always something we can do about it. We can leave the police and the courts to themselves. They're not interested in justice anyway. They're interested in law, but not justice. Understand, there is a difference between the two. Don't ever forget that. Usually, the law and justice have nothing in common. We can make sure justice is served. The decision is all yours."

"Mine?"

"Yes, yours. I will do whatever you decide. We can follow what the bible says. We can turn the other cheek. We can let this man live. We can hope that he has learned his lesson. We can hope that he will not drink or drive anymore. We can hope that he will not kill another family while he is violating *their* precious law by driving intoxicated. Or, you can ask me to take care of it for you. You now know what it is that I do. All you have to do is ask, and I will send one of my people to make sure this man never has the opportunity to hurt or kill anyone else. I will never ask you for anything in return. This will be a favor between friends…there is one other way as well."

"I know."

"I am sure you do. I can give you this man's name and let you handle it. You can decide if this man deserves to live while your family is gone. You can be the judge, jury and executioner."

I slumped my shoulders in defeat of my religion, in defeat of my burden to be a man above men that God trusted with His people. "The only one that has the power or right to judge someone else is God. I don't need to be the judge and jury", I said and sat there silent, staring at my hands in my lap, thinking of my life in the Rangers, raising my eyes slowly to meet Sal's gaze, "I can just be the executioner."

"Understand something Rick. This isn't like the Army. There is no higher cause or better purpose here. You killing him is nothing more than revenge. You will have gone from being an enlisted soldier to being a paid mercenary. Once you do this thing, it cannot be undone. There is no going back. Can you live with the guilt?"

I could feel the stone cold silence of my brain that I had craved for days, the emotionless muscle relaxation under my facial skin, knowing I had pushed the button inside me that let me go through life without feeling or emotion that mattered, "It doesn't matter what I kill for, the end result is the same; death. Country, money, revenge, the end result is me with blood on my hands and someone dead." Like a light switch I was back to myself. I felt like I was wrestling with the good angel and the little demon on each shoulder, both yelling so loudly I couldn't tell who was saying what. "Maybe this guy is sorry for what he has done? Maybe he has learned his lesson and will not drink or drive anymore? What if he has decided to change his life for the better and I end it?

Sal Replied "He may be sorry, but I doubt it. If he was truly sorry, he would have turned himself into the police, no? If he was truly sorry he wouldn't have gone out last night and gotten drunk, would he? There is no such thing as being sorry without consequences. I am not going to force you into a decision. We can forget this entire conversation." He lifted his hand and the tiramisu plates were lifted from our table as if on invisible strings, coffee cups replaced with ice water and I could hear music in the background that I couldn't remember hearing before.

The coldness was back, the emptiness overtook me, the screaming in my head stopped. "No. Everything I have read about grief says the individual suffering the grief needs to have closure. I will not have closure as long as this man is allowed to go on with his life while my wife and daughter are gone. What-is-his-name?"

Sal slid a file across the table to me but didn't let go, his eyes locked hard with mine, "This, Rick Stevens, will leave blood on your soul. Will you be able to live with yourself if you do this?"

"I know I won't be able to live with myself if I don't."

With that he let go of the file and I was driven home, Mazzio silent. I read the file from cover to cover. I stayed up all night vacillating between good and evil, right and wrong, the angels of death and life playing on my soul. I sat praying and trying to make the right decision until sleep overtook me. The morning came as the Bible promised but without grace as the other half of that verse stated. I knew what I would do.

That evening, I went his house. It was a hot day and as the sun set, the temperature started to fall. A breeze was kicked up and blowing in from Lake Erie. It was a pleasant evening. I waited outside. He had all of the windows open in his house. I was watching him through one of the windows as he sat on his couch and drank a 12-pack of Bud Lite. As the hour got later, and the man got drunker, and with the crack of each can's opening, I got angrier, and angrier, and my head got more and more silent.

I was angry that this piece of shit was allowed to live while my innocent and pure family was killed. I was angry that he was continuing on with his life as if nothing had happened while I was tormented and in constant misery. Mostly, I was angry at God for allowing it all to happen. The anger came in waves and it washed over me. I was consumed by it.

Sometime during the evening the man got up from the couch and went into the bathroom. At this time, he was working through his second 12-pack. When he walked back into the living room, he was not alone. There was a cold blooded empty hearted killer waiting for him in the living room.

The anger continued to wash over me and there was a pounding in my head and ears. The second I opened the door to his house, I felt a tremendous sense of calm enter into me. It was like being in a small room with a radio playing really bad music extremely loud and then having someone cut the cord. I went from going a hundred miles an hour to zero in the distance of a breath.

I wish I could tell you I said something enlightening to him, or something witty. You see it in the movies all the time. The action hero will get off a zinger of a one liner right before he kills the bad guy. No, there would be no conversation. There would be no redemption for either of us this night. I didn't drag it out or make him suffer. I just swung the tire iron I had and crushed his skull. Blood squirted across the room and his eyes rolled back into his head. The sound was like a coconut exploding. Just for good measure, after he was lying on the floor, I crushed his skull in further with another swing of the tire iron. He didn't say anything enlightening to me either. His final words on this planet were, "What the fuck?" I could imagine my wife's last words were, "My baby" my daughters' were probably "Mommy". I wonder what mine will be.

There was no need to check for his pulse. I could clearly see he was dead, his chest was still. I wish I could say I felt sad or disgusted at what I had just done, but I didn't. I was still riding the adrenalin high and I actually felt at peace with myself. I left house. I thought about all the steps I took and realized that I didn't need to wipe anything down because I hadn't touched anything. On my way home, I stopped at a McDonalds and changed my clothes. I put everything I had worn during the murder into a bag. Then I took a drive to the upper Niagara River. As I stood on the bank, I first threw the tire iron into the water. It was immediately swallowed in the murky current. A few minutes later, I threw in the shirt I had worn earlier. A few minutes after that, the shoes and pants I had worn also went in. After that I drove home. For the first time since was my wife and daughter were killed, I slept the entire night through

Consciously, I had made a decision. I stood at the crossroads and chose which path to take. I prayed, begged, pleaded, and cried for advice and direction, but the Heavens remained silent, God remained silent as if He had what He desired, my wife, my child, and me going to Hell. I asked for help and none came.

I called my old mentor Bill and declined his offer to spend some time with him in North Carolina. I ended up going to work for Sal almost immediately. I read in the paper while waiting to drive Sal from a meeting one day a few weeks after my brush with my new reality, all about a decomposing body found by a water meter reader in a house that smelled so bad it caused the man to vomit as he left a notice on the door that the water was being turned off for non-payment. His skull was crushed and body identified by family.

I started out as Sal's driver and body guard. Slowly, as these things usually do, my responsibilities increased. One day Sal asked me to pick up a gun and kill a man. I didn't know anything about the man personally; I only knew what was provided in the folder in front of me. I eliminated the man and time marched on.

As I honed my skills and became a better killer, my reputation grew. As my reputation grew, so did my job offers. With Sal's help, I stopped working directly for him and went out on my own. Pretty soon, I was doing jobs all over the country for all of the major crime families. Finally, I became who I looked at in the mirror each day: my facial muscles were relaxed and calm, I loved a good one liner, and I tried to make my own story for people who would find the left over carnage. I saw a person with empty eyes and a damned soul that didn't care if he lived or died.

I often think back to those many days I spent in prayer. I wonder what would have become of my life if I decided to move to North Carolina. I wonder what would have happened if when I came back from my run that day, instead of Mazzio Standing there, Bill was standing there. Instead of getting in a car with Mazzio, what if I got on a plane with Bill? Instead of driving into Buffalo, what if we had flew to North Carolina? I asked God for a sign and I got one, but I would always wonder if that was from God or from the depths of Hell itself. The Lord sure does work in mysterious ways.

CHAPTER #21

While I was somewhere over the United States, Sal was on the phone with Dolan Gillespie of the Westsiders. Sal was going to deliver the unfortunate news to Gillespie about his cousin, Michael O'Malley's murder.

"This is Dolan, what do you want?"

"Mr. Gillespie, this is Salvatore DiFlippo. I am on a secure, untraceable phone. Are you?"

"Yes I am. Mr. DiFlippo! Thank you for calling me back. I tried calling you earlier today, but I was told you were in bed with the flu. Did you get my message? Are you feeling better?"

Sal coughed for effect, "I am getting there. Why were you calling me?"

"My cousin from Texas called me yesterday and told me his problem had vanished. I just wanted to call and say thank you for your help."

"Dolan that is why I am calling you. I didn't handle the job in Texas. I was in a position where I was unable to help you. I had to send the work out to someone else."

"Hey, it's cool Sal. I don't care, I am just happy it is done. I was going to send you a little something to show you my thanks...."

"I hate to have to tell you this Dolan, but the people handling this job for you screwed it up. They screwed it up badly. No one has called you to inform you of this yet?"

"Mr. DiFlippo, you must be mistaken. Nothing got screwed up. Michael called me yesterday and said the job was done. He paid the remaining balance on the bill. What got screwed up? Who should have called me? What the hell's going on?"

"I sent the job to another family. I gave it to a captain. He sent three of his people to take care of the situation. They missed. They messed it up. One of the people sent on the job was eliminated from action. Another one had an "accident" and fell in the shower in his hotel. He suffered a broken neck. The third person is missing."

"What the fuck? What are you saying? My cousin lied to me?"

"No, your cousin was lied to. The third person sent out there was the only one to survive. They missed their target. Gonzalez isn't dead."

"How can this be? My cousin..."

"Dolan, I just heard from a contact I have in Texas that someone broke into your cousin's home last evening and killed him and his wife. I am very sorry for your loss."

"WHAT? Who the fuck did you hire to do this? WHO Sal, WHO did this?"

"It is early in the investigation, but my source tells me it was Gonzalez after he found out about the attempt. The shooters missed Gonzalez. Instead of owning up to it, the surviving shooter called your cousin and said the job was complete. He took your cousin's money and disappeared. It appears Gonzalez took his revenge on your cousin and he is now missing. I wanted you to know first before you read or saw it on the news. I truly am sorry. I wish I had been the one to take care of this for you."

"Thank you Mr. DiFlippo. I appreciate the call. I'm gonna find this fucking prick Gonzalez and I'm gonna find the shooter. Who screwed this job up? Who went out there?"

"That is another delicate matter. Now, you know your boss and I go way back. Your group and my group have always been on the same side of things. You know we have never had any bad blood between us, right?"

"Yeah, I am familiar with our history. You're one of the few Guinea's we never had a problem with."

"That is why I need to ask you for help. I believe the person that botched the Texas job for you, is the same person that is planning on taking me out. Have you heard any rumors to this?"

"Mr. DiFlippo, I heard that maybe you weren't really sick, that maybe you were hiding in fear of your life. The word on the street is you are in the process of being replaced, but what no one knows is who by."

"That's what I thought. This captain that took this job, I think he didn't tell his boss. This captain is running operations behind the bosses back. I am going to meet with the boss. The boss will give me the captain. Once I have the information I need from the captain, I will give him to you."

"You sure the boss will give you the captain?"

"Positive. Keep a low profile, say nothing to no one. Next month when Buffalo celebrates St. Patrick's Day, I would be honored to use all of your people for the celebration. Send me all your vendors, the carnivals, the booths, the food. Everything. Since it will be all your people, you can keep all of the proceeds. I don't want anything from it. Do we have a deal Dolan?"

"Mr. DiFlippo, you are too generous. Yes, we have a deal."

■■

The flight to Toronto was smooth and uneventful. I spent almost the entire flight locked in a dreamless sleep or sipping on extra bubbly ginger ale. When I exited the plane, I felt refreshed and ready to go. With the rest of the passengers from my flight, I followed them to baggage claim, even though I had not checked a bag.

In baggage claim, there was an old man dressed in a chauffeurs outfit holding out a sign that said "P. Rowe". As soon as I laid eyes on my friend, I couldn't help but laugh. Here was one of the most powerful men in Upstate New York and he was disguised as a chauffeur.

"I'm Mr. Rowe.'

"Very good sir. Do you have any bags Mr. Rowe?"

"Just the one I'm carrying."

"Follow me sir."

I followed my friend outside and we got into a black Lincoln Town Car. I got in the backseat and he got in the front seat.

"You know Sal, I can drive. It would be like old times."

"No, it's fine. I kind of like being inconspicuous. We have a meeting tomorrow with Augostino. We're going to go to the doctor's office. Augostino says he is going to bring two men with him."

"Do you believe him?"

"No. He'll have at least four, if not more. If I am reading this correctly, and I am betting our lives that I am, Augostino has no clue about the team Berrazino sent to Texas. If I am wrong and Augostino is trying to kill me, we might not survive the day."

"I'll be there with you Sal. I won't let anything happen. What is the rest of your plan?"

Sal told me his plan as he drove me to the hotel where we would be staying. I assumed this was not the same place Sal had taken refuge at. Sal said since it might be our last night on earth, we should enjoy it. We stayed at the five-star Fairmont Royal York in Toronto.

He had booked the Prime Minister's Suite for himself and the Royal Suite for me. We had an excellent dinner in the EPIC Restaurant. After dinner, we each enjoyed a glass of Remy Martin, Louis XIII and a Cuban Monte Cristo No. 2. Right before getting into bed, I had an excellent hour long massage.

All in all, if it was to be my last day on earth, it was a pretty damn good one, there was only a few things missing, but they had been missing for years.

■■

Back in Buffalo, Mazzio was plotting. He told Ragulli to call Jack Carlotti in Niagara Falls and tell him he was coming out the next day to see him. Mazzio's plan was to take Carlotti to the Native American Casino downtown. The casino was always packed on Fridays. Mazzio knew Carlotti would be pissed off just going into the place. He would see all the people and see all the money changing hands and be jealous that the biggest money-making operation in the area was in his backyard and he wasn't being cut in on any of the action.

Mazzio knew that after he plied Carlotti with alcohol, the short-tempered man would say things that no man should say about his boss, especially if his boss could have him killed. Mazzio planned to get it all recorded. While they were at the casino, Mazzio planned on having Sonny De Luca and Pete Parrione break into Carlotti's apartment and plant a few important things to make it appear he was going to kill DiFlippo.

De Luca and Parrione were supposed to hide photographs of DiFlippo's estate with copies of the alarm codes to get into the property. After DiFlippo heard the tape Mazzio was planning on making tomorrow, he would be very suspicious of Carlotti. At Mazzio's suggestion, they would send someone in Carlotti's apartment to search the place for more evidence. They would find the photos and alarm codes. That would sign Carlotti's death warrant right there. Mazzio would beg DiFlippo to let him kill the traitor Carlotti personally. It was all coming together nicely.

CHAPTER #22

While Sal and I were driving from Toronto to Buffalo, we set his plan in motion. The first thing Sal did was place a call to Mazzio and to tell him he wanted to meet with him at eleven am. He told Mazzio to meet him for lunch in Salamanca New York. Salamanca is about an hour and a half from Buffalo. Sal had no intentions on meeting with Mazzio but he wanted to make sure Mazzio and Ragulli would be away from his estate.

Next, Sal called his personal driver and body guard. He told them he wanted to meet with them at his house at 11:00am sharp. He instructed them not to be late and to be dressed for work. While Sal was on the phone with his driver, I called Geoff. I gave Geoff Sal's driver and bodyguard's information. I told Allen I needed a complete family tree on all remaining, living relatives for both individuals. I told him to e-mail it to me by 10:00 am.

Things were starting to come together now and I was sure once we got rolling, the day would move very quickly. I knew more people would lose their lives today. It might even be Sal and I. I was fine with it. Either way, I was fine with it. I just hoped my wife that really dances with Angels would turn her head to me one last time before my eternal drop into hell. It would sustain me. It had to.

■■■

"He said he wanted to have lunch with you in Salamanca, Dom?"

"What the fuck Anthony, is there an echo in here? That's what I just said! We need to be prepared. He's probably got the place staked out. I am willing to bet Steven's is there."

"We need to leave soon. Does he know how bad the weather is right now? Is he in Salamanca right now?"

"An-t-ony," he said with alliteration, "please! I don't know where the fuck he is, remember? Snow storm or not, I need to be there by ten fifty-five. He specifically said not to be late. I need to change, let's get on the road. I think he just wants to meet in a public place to feel me out. This is good. I can plant the seeds about Carlotti during lunch. This might work to our advantage."

After Mazzio was dressed, he got into a Lincoln Town Car. In the front seat Parrione and De Luca sat. Ragulli sat in the back seat with Mazzio. Everyone was dressed in an expensive suit and everyone was carrying at least one pistol.

■■■

Once we got to Sal's estate, I went in and made sure it was safe. After Sal came in, I got on line and checked my e-mail. Once again, Geoff had delivered exactly what I had asked for. Shortly before eleven am, Sal's driver, Mario Rossi arrived. I told Rossi I needed to meet with him before he met with Sal.

"Mario, please come in. I wanted to talk to you about a few things that have been going on. I am going to apologize now because the things I am about to say to you are going to be disrespectful and offensive. I need to say them anyway and you need to listen."

"Sure, go head. I got thick reptilian skin Stevens, I can handle it."

"Someone in Sal's organization is trying to kill him. I am not accusing you of being involved. If I even thought you were involved you would already be dead. I want-"

"Whoa, hey now, slow down. Don't you make fucking threats to me-"

I put my hand up to stop him, "Mario, if you ever interrupt me again, I will immediately stab you in the neck and watch you bleed to death. Just listen now. I want to make sure we are clear on something. Today, Sal is going into a dangerous situation. You will be responsible for his safety. If anything happens to him, anything at all, I will hold you personally responsible. I'm talking if someone takes a shot at him, or he has a heart attack or if you get in a car accident and he gets hurt, a paper cut, whatever happens…I am going to hold you responsible. And I will extract my revenge on you. Starting with your grandmother in Michigan."

I had Geoff run what I call a family tree on Mario and Carlo. I wanted to know what relatives both men had left alive and where they were located. I wanted to use the threat of violence against them as leverage for keeping Sal safe. I was not certain that Mario or Carlo were not involved in the hit on Sal and I. If they were involved and were having thoughts of making another run at either one of us today, I wanted to give them pause and have them think about it.

"After I brutally murder your grandmother, I will fly out to Las Vegas and kill your brother, his long legged blonde trophy wife and both of your nephews. I will make it real fucking messy too, they will talk about your family long after their bodies are discovered. After Vegas, I will head to Florida and take out your older sister. She isn't married, but I will kill her. I'll promise you though that because you are you and I am me, and we have this relationship here, to make it as painful as I can. Once your family is eliminated, I will come back here. I will kill all of your friends. I will kill your neighbors. I'll even fucking kill your tailor. When everyone you know and care about is dead, then I will come for you. I will slowly, over three or four days torture you. I will drag it out. I'll hire doctors and nurses to keep you alive as I do things to you. Eventually, I'll get bored and allow you to die, but it won't be very a very long time."

Silence.

I started with a whisper and leaned in real close to his face and spoke slowly, "I know you're pissed off and I know I have deeply offended you. Remember this, I don't care. The only thing I care about is seeing Sal survive the day."

"You're a sick mother-fucker. I heard some of the stories about you. I just thought it was all bullshit. I guess it wasn't. Fuck you man. Don't worry; nothing's going to happen to Mr. DiFlippo. We're on the same side here Stevens. How's about you remember that'

I lightened my body language and said as if we were pals the whole time, "If we are then, we won't have any problems. Thank you buddy. Sal is in the library. He wants to speak to you, now."

I didn't worry about offending Mario. His job was to drive and protect Sal. He didn't need to like me or respect me to do that. Most of the stories circulating about me are bullshit. I would never kill or harm a child again. Most of what I said I stole from shitty B horror movies, but when your reputation precedes you like mine does, you use it to your advantage. A few minutes after Mario went to meet with Sal, Carlo came in. I knew Carlo better than I knew Mario, but I went through the whole thing with him. The more I spoke, the angrier he got, yet he remained quiet and respectful. At the end of my speech which I changed up to make it even more grotesque, he got up, he told me he respected me for talking to him and informed me he loved Sal like he was his father and he assured me nothing would happen to him today, or any day. I wanted to check in with Sal one last time before I got on the road. I met him in the library with Mario and Carlo.

"So what do you think Sal? You ready for today?"

"Yes. The best lies have versions of the truth woven into them. I will be able to convince Augostino of what I want to convince him of. There will be just enough facts he can verify that he will have to believe the entire story. I just got off the phone with him and he confirmed the time and told me he would have two of his people with him."

"You still don't believe him?"

"No. I have known Augostino for a long time. He will have two bodyguards with him, but he will also have another two or three trying to blend into the area. I'm just wondering if we should bring another few people or not."

"We don't need them Sal. Mario and Carlo will be enough. They're both solid guys and I trust them" I looked each of them in the eye and smiled. "Besides, I will be there as well. Augostino and his men don't know what I look like. Mario and Carlo will cover you inside the building and I will take care of everything else. I am going to get over there now to prepare."

"Thank you. I will see you this afternoon."

"Hey Sal? How pissed is Mazzio right now? Does he know you're going to stand him up for your lunch meeting?" I couldn't help smiling when I said this knowing from past experiences how much Mazzio hated to wait.

"I just called him. I told him I was running late because of the bad weather. I told him to wait for me. He asked me how long he should wait. I told him until I got there and hung up. He's gonna be real pissed, but that's the way it is sometimes."

I left Sal's estate and made sure I wasn't being followed. When I was comfortable I was alone, I went to my safe house. I changed clothes there and packed a bag with what I thought I would need to survive the day. If everything went well, by midnight tonight, I would know the name of the person in Sal's organization that tried to kill us.

CHAPTER #23

Sal was right. Augostino came with more than the two men he said he would have. The first car that pulled into the parking lot had four people in it. All of them were big slabs of beef, pure muscle and heavy hitters. The second car that came in had three people in it. Two more bodyguards and Augostino.

Even though I had done several jobs for Augostino and his organization over the years, I had never met the man. He looked like an old Italian business man. He was smoking a ridiculously long and fat cigar. He appeared to be very confident. He was a man in control of his surroundings. Everyone moved around him as if in harmony like an underwater ballet practiced millions of times.

He went into the doctor's office with three of the bodyguards. The other three stayed outside. For the first 20 minutes, they were very good. They were spread out and observant. They all had little ear buds and microphones and were all keeping in contact with each other. Using a scanner, I was able to find what frequency they were using and listen in on them. Like I said, at first, they were very good. Then boredom set in. Instead of checking in and giving status reports, they started to comment on the women coming to and from the doctor's office. One of the bodyguards took coffee orders from the other two and got in his car and left. When he got back, the three of them sat together in one car and drank coffee and ate pastries.

If push came to shove, I would not have a hard time killing all three of them. Today, amongst other things, I was carrying two .45 caliber Glock pistols. The G21 is a great piece of armory. A little on the large side, but with two guns and high capacity magazines, I would be able to put 32 rounds of .45 caliber down range as fast as I could pull the triggers. I was confident in the power of the guns, and my ability to make quick work of a bad situation.

▪▪

Inside the doctor's office, Sal waited patiently in one of the examination rooms. Carlo stood silently outside his door as Mario tried not to look too board in the waiting room. When Augostino and his entourage walked in, every eye in the waiting room was on them.

The receptionist chastised Augostino for bringing his cigar into the doctor's office. He took the cigar out of his mouth, handed it to one of his men and sent him outside to wait by the car with it. Mario walked Augostino and his two other body guards to the examination room. There were a lot of stiff nods and hard looks between the four men hired as muscle. After Augostino and DiFlippo went into the examination room together, everyone seemed to relax, but no one moved.

"Mr. Augostino, my friend, thank you for meeting with me."

"No problem. Terrible weather, huh?"

"Yes it is, but not as bad as some of the winters we have had form a decade ago. Before we get started, would you like something to drink? Coffee, espresso?"

"No. Thank you. What business do we have to discuss today?"

"We've known each other a long time so I will not beat around the bush. I have identified a man in your organization that is working with someone in my organization to have me killed."

"What? Someone in my organization? No. No. There's no way."

"Please, let me finish. Like I said, I have identified the person responsible in your organization, but I have been unable to identify the person in mine. I would like to have a conversation with the person on your side to find this information out."

"You *can't* be serious? Who, who the fuck is it in my organization that is supposed to be involved in this murder plot against you, Sal?"

"Paul Berrazino."

"Bear? Fucking Ridiculous! I've known him forever! Since we were little bambinos! He would never do something like this behind my back."

"Please be careful of what you say. If he didn't do it behind your back, then maybe you are involved too?"

"You insult me DiFlippo. If we hadn't known each other as long as we have…"

"Stop. I didn't invite you here so we could argue or throw accusations at each other. I have proof. Did you know Berrazino sent a team down to Dallas Texas on a contract for the Westsiders?" Sal had painted Augostino in a corner with this question. If Augostino said he didn't know about the Texas job, then he would be admitting that he didn't have as tight a grip on things as he liked to make others believe. A mafia boss should be all seeing and all knowing. His captains shouldn't be running operations without his knowledge. It exposes him to liability and if a job is going on that he doesn't know about there is a good chance the money generated from that job is not being kicked back up to him. On the other hand, if he said he did know about the Texas job, he would be lying and if pressed for details, he could easily be exposed. So he did what every good politician and mafia don did, he hedged his answer.

"Texas job for the Westsiders? I remember something about Texas, but I don't remember the exact details."

"Oh, well then, let me refresh your memory. Berrazino was paid $50,000 to eliminate a man in Texas. The person that ordered the hit is a blood relative to someone very high up in the Westsiders organization. We're talking top tier here. Berrazino sent three shooters; The Ferraro Brothers and a guy named Lima. You know them?"

"Yes, I do. Lima's pretty good. He's one of the top hitters in my organization."

"Maybe was, but he won't be anymore. I got word out of Texas that this team Berrazino sent down there screwed up. They missed their target. One of the Ferraro brothers died in the targets house. Lima died in a hotel room not far away. The authorities are ruling it an accidental death. He 'slipped and fell' in the shower of his hotel room."

"Is that what really happened to him?"

"My sources tell me his neck was indeed broken and the scene was made to look like an accident."

"That's good luck for me then. The less the police look into his background the better it is for me."

"Let's just hope your luck holds out."

"What about the other Ferraro brother Max or Angelo, which one and the target? What happened to them?"

"The target and the other Ferraro brother have gone missing. I know where Ferraro is. However, my sources tell me the target disappeared to Tijuana. Before he disappeared, he took out the person who originally ordered the hit. He shot and killed him and his wife. My source in the Dallas PD is telling me they have DNA evidence at the murder scene. You knew about *all* this?"

"Shit. I haven't heard a word of it! I'll deal with Berrazino on this."

"Our Irish friends at the Westsiders are, needless to say, very unhappy. They paid your organization to take care of a problem and instead of doing it; you got one of their family members killed. I imagine they will be looking for retribution."

"Fuck them stupid micks. If they want to start a war, I'll wipe them off the map. I am not worried about them. I'll send them a case of Bushmills and refund their money. They'll be fine. Which Ferraro brother is dead?"

"Max, at the target's house."

"I figured. He was the dumb one. So tell me, where is Angelo?"

"He is 'indisposed' right now."

"Indisposed? What the hell does that mean? Where is he?"

"Angelo had certain information that I needed. Information pertaining to the attempted hit on me. He was the one that told me he was working for Berrazino."

"What the hell did you do to him?"

"I can assure you, I did not touch him. Unfortunately, Angelo tried to take out one of my people. Like the other job, he really failed at this one to."

"One of your people? In Texas? Sally, you 're not running *that* big of an operation. Did you have him killed?" Augostino was furious standing almost on his tip toes and was on the brink of yelling.

"Vincent, please calm down. Remember, *I* didn't send one of my people to kill one of yours. Please don't comment on the size of my operation. It isn't polite and you have no *idea* how large my organization is. If you knew about the Dallas job I can only assume you sent Angelo to kill one of my people. That would be a pretty big no-no Vince."

"All right! Fuck you Sal, I didn't know about the Dallas job! I had no idea about any of it!"

"I believe you Vince. Everyone in our business has ambition. Ambition and greed are what ultimately destroy people in our business, am I right?"

"You're right. I can't thank you enough for bringing this to my attention. I am going to deal with Berrazino personally!"

"Actually Vince, no, that's not going to work."

"What do you mean?"

"Berrazino knows who the traitor is in my organization. I would like to have an associate meet with Berrazino to make sure I get the real person's name."

"No. Out of the question. I will clean up my own mess. I will make sure to get the name from him and I will let you know who it is."

"As I said before and I will repeat it in case you missed it, that's not going to work Vince. You see, Angelo also told us that once I was eliminated and the new Don was established, he would work with Berrazino to have you removed so Berrazino could take over your organization." While this was a lie, it was a good lie. Every mafia leader throughout history has been a little paranoid. Everyone believes that there is someone in their own organization just waiting for the opportunity to take them out so they can move up and be the new boss.

"Maybe, maybe, it is possible that Bear was involved in a side job or two without my knowledge, and there is an outside chance he is working with someone in your organization to have you removed, but he would never, you hear me? NEVER make a move against me! Maybe your people aren't loyal to you, but mine are to me. Especially Berrazino. I mean hell, Sal, with all the rumors on the street about how weak you are can you really blame someone for trying to step up and eliminate you? It's the law of the street. The strong *will* eat the weak."

"Your arrogance blinds you. Don't believe the rumors you are hearing. I don't trust you to get to the truth with Berrazino. We have come to the point in our conversation where it is time for you to make a decision."

"Make a decision? Fuck a bunch of decisions? This is my family, my deal Sal, you can't tell me what we are going to do, I will tell you what I am going to do!"

Sal continued as if his peer had not spoken a word, "Simple. This is what I am asking of you. Leave here today and go back to your home. Stay away from Berrazino and let me send one of my people over to talk to him. By the end of the weekend, Berrazino will be gone and you will need to promote someone else to take his position. He will never be found. You can tell everyone he disappeared or went into the witness protection program, or he returned to the old country, whatever. It doesn't matter, because he will never be seen or heard from again. Through Berrazino, I will find out who the rat is in my organization and deal with them. By Monday, we'll both be back to business as usual."

"What if I don't? What if I say fuck you Sal, you're on your own. You already killed one of my people and I want payment for that. What then?"

Sal stood, and walked to the door and outstretched his hand to Vincent, "War."

"Bullshit! HA! You can't bluff me! I'm bigger! I have more resources, more money! I would wipe you out of existence! You wouldn't make it a week, especially since your organization is split. I should start inviting you to our weekly poker games. You have no poker face at all."

"I am not bluffing. Neither one of us wants to go to war. People will die, business will suffer. We will both lose a lot of money and we will both receive a lot of undue attention from the authorities. Not the smart decision ever."

"No, it would be a terrible decision for you. I said a week? You wouldn't last two days in a war with me. Maybe I make a call and you don't leave this office and all this non-sense ends today?"

Sal pulled out his cell phone and carefully placed his finger on the "SEND" button.

"You have your phone and I have mine. Before either one of us does something we cannot take back, let me explain one other thing to you. After I am done with my explanation, then you can make your decision. Is that fair?"

"Why not? What's another few minutes between *friends* anyway?

"If we go to war, the first thing I will do is contact the other families in New York. I will let them know we are at war because you sanctioned a hit against me. I will let them know that once I have won the war and it is over, I will not move in on any of your territory or businesses. I am very happy and comfortable with what I have in my control right now."

"So what?" Vince said with his hands up and slamming the table, "I can call them and offer them the same thing! You have nothing!"

"Yes, but as you have pointed out, your organization is bigger than mine. It is also closer to where they are located than where I am. I will also call my friends in the Westsiders. I am sure I will have no problem getting them to join me. They are already pissed off at you for getting a family member of theirs killed they would probably join me for free. But, they won't have too. I will tell them that once you are removed from power the other New York families will take over your area. I will offer them two million dollars, in cash, as payment for helping me eliminate you. You don't have an extra two million lying around do you Vince?"

"Fuck you Sal. I am willing to bet you don't either."

"A bet you would lose. I could easily offer them twice that much and have it not affect me. You know Vince; my computer guy can crack into any system in the world. For example, I know how much money you currently have stored in Cayman National Bank on Cayman Brac Island. The number starts with a 9, ends in a 7. I also know about the Swiss accounts you have in Toronto and your accounts you have spread throughout the various banks here in the United States. Now, I admit, I don't know where you keep *all* your money, but I know where most of it is and if I don't make a phone call by a certain time today, all of your cash will be gone and the feds might be sniffing around. You think you can fund a war without any cash Vince?"

"Bullshit. I don't believe you."

Sal put his hand on the door, refreshed his home screen on the cell phone in his hand, "Yes, yes you do. With just under $72,000.00 in the bank three blocks from your home address, you can decide, am I still bluffing Vince?"

Vince didn't answer. He was so angry his face was red and slowly turning into the color of a fresh eggplant. DiFlippo continued un-waivered.

"Finally Vince, if I am forced to press 'SEND' on my phone, the four people you have waiting outside will be killed. In addition to the two body guards I have in the office with me, I also brought one more. He has actually been here since last night and is ready to strike. You know who is out there…" Sal lowered his voice to a whisper, "don't you Vince?"

Vince's voice shook a little when he lied, "I ain't afraid of him Sal. I got ten guys that are better than him."

"You shouldn't be playing poker Vince. If I set Stevens loose today, it is you who will not walk out of here alive. If this visit takes longer than is usual or customary, it may be too late anyway. By the time you get to the front door of this building, your four body guards will already be dead. Maybe the two people I have in the office here, maybe they take your guys out, and maybe they don't. If they don't, Stevens will. We are out of time. I wish we didn't have to meet like this but circumstances outside of my control have made it necessary."

Sal had been in the game a long time. He was one of the smartest business people in the world. Through his conversation with Vince Augostino, Sal painted Vince into a corner. If Augostino went to war with Sal, he had to know he would not win. However, Augostino was very prideful and if he gave into Sal, he would always despise him and be afraid that Sal would tell the other New York families that he was weak. Augostino was truly a drowning man. It was time for Sal to throw him a life preserver.

"Now Vince, with the new Thruway project and the joint Art museums between Rochester and Buffalo, we both could make a lot of money. That is, if we weren't at war with each other. We would need to work together though to do so. So here I am Vince, asking you, an old friend for a favor: Please, let me have a talk with Berrazino. He's a thorn in both of our sides. Let me take care of this problem for both of us. If you do, I will be indebted you. I will owe you, one."

"There will be a hell of a lot of money to be made on that thruway project. It would be a shame if we were fighting and had to miss out on all of that." Vince said with a chuckle under a fearful breath.

"Yes it sure would. I have a few other projects that are going to get underway in Buffalo and Niagara Falls in the spring. As a tradeoff, you can have the entire thruway project. Once the work moves outside of the Niagara and Erie County line, it is all yours. Your organization is bigger than mine and that portion of the highway is longer. If I asked for a fifty-fifty split on the whole deal, it just wouldn't be fair. I am offering a sixty-forty split, you take the sixty, on the entire project. What-do-you-think? " He said all in one word like a true mafia boss might.

"How can I refuse such a generous offer? I am sorry I let my personal feelings get in the way of business. I have a responsibility to my organization and its continued success. Sacrifices must be made. Hell, look at us! Two old men sitting in a doctor's office holding onto cell phones! If this were 30 years ago, we would be holding pistols instead of phones."

"Well and I wouldn't be having an internal nervous breakdown thinking I need another rectal exam, damn I don't know what is worse, war with you or colonoscopy."

The two men chuckled and shook hands patting each other on the back like it had all been some big farce. They spent a few minutes talking about the old days. Their relationship was strained, but survive it would. Especially in the spring when New York State started to resurface the thruway from Buffalo to Rochester.

Power, true, real power, is getting someone to do what you want them to do, but at the same time, making them believe it was their idea and in their best interest all along. Sal knew this and understood this. He was able to get Augostino to do exactly what he wanted, but Augostino believed that it was his idea and he was the one doing the favor as well as reaping the benefits. The decision he offered Augostino was fixed. Sal knew Augostino would agree to his terms because by doing so, Sal was allowing Augostino to make money AND save face.

After Augostino got in his car and drove away with all his guards, I went into the doctor's office to talk to Sal. I wanted to make sure he was safe and Augostino agreed to his terms. He was still in the room where he met with Augostino.

"Sal, you okay? How was your meeting?"

"Yes, I'm fine. Thank you. The meeting went very well. We have the green light to continue."

"Very good. May I make a suggestion? Don't go back home tonight. Have Mario and Carlo stay with you. Find a hotel somewhere and take it easy."

"I will do that. I have to call Mazzio and cancel my meeting with him. I will instruct him to return to the compound this evening and wait to hear from me next."

"Very good. Once I speak with Berrazino, we'll know if Mazzio is involved. You should prepare yourself in case he is the one."

"I know Rick. I hope it isn't him, but if it is, I will make an example out of him. I have been in this business a very long time and I will do what is required to ensure I remain in this business even longer. After you are done with Berrazino, he must disappear, never, ever to be found."

I had an idea of how I wanted to take out Berrazino. I ran my idea by Sal to get his input on it. "You know Rick, you're the one that should be running the business. That is an excellent plan. I'll take Mario and Carlo and head over to the casino in Niagara Falls. I will call the Casino Manager, Chayton Takoda, invite him to dinner."

"You know the casino manager?"

"Yes, we are close. I met with him several times when they were constructing the casino. We got to know each other pretty well. Once I decided not to interfere with their operation, we became friends. Anytime I go there, he gives me the high-roller treatment. I stay in the best suite, eat whatever I want, all comped. When I am on the casino floor or in one of the restaurants, he is always with me. Not only will I have Mario and Carlo, but I will also have his personal body guards as well. I'll spend the weekend there. I will be safe. Don't worry. Besides I really want to try that new Wheel of Fortune slot machine."

I laughed a little at the thought of him scanning his card on a neck lanyard smoking a cigar and sitting around rubbing the machine for luck like the other poor saps that milled about the smoky casino halls, "That sounds good Sal. I'll be in contact with you."

CHAPTER #24

I always prefer to scout a target and an area prior to doing a job. Unfortunately I was on a tight time schedule and didn't have the luxury of doing things the normal way I do them. Instead of having a few days to learn the pattern of my target, I would have one night. It made my job harder, but not impossible.

In Rochester I checked into a cheap, run down motel several blocks away from Berrazino's club wishing I had one of those bed pocket sheet contraptions that keep the bed bugs and dirt away from your skin. I usually never stay in motels for a billion microscopic reasons but I liked the proximity of this one to the strip club. Across the street from the club was a convenience store. I parked in the parking lot. I wanted to watch the club for an hour or so to see what kind of clientele they catered to. I didn't want to walk into the club wearing a suit if everyone else was in jeans. My goal was to blend in, not stick out. After about 25 minutes of waiting and watching, I knew what to wear.

After checking into my motel, I used the phone book and called a cab company. While I was waiting for the cab to pick me up, I changed into a pair of jeans and a flannel shirt. I ditched my Ralph Lauren winter jacket and put on a Carhartt winter jacket. After putting on a pair of worn brown boots and a Buffalo Sabres ball cap, my look was completed. I would blend in perfectly in the strip club. I had the cab take me to a shopping center several miles away.

From the shopping center, I called a different cab company and had them take me to the Tickled Tuna. I don't know where these guys get the names for their strip clubs. Nothing I tickled should ever smell like or have any attributes of a Tuna. I paid the cab driver a decent tip but not one that would draw attention, and went inside.

When I walked in, there was a small vestibule in back of it was a long black curtain. On the left side of me was a small booth and cash register. I paid the $11 cover charge, bitched it was a bit high waited for my change in all dollar bills, and the curtain was swept back out of the way for me by an anorexic looking girl who couldn't have been more than a little over 21. There was an attractive woman wearing black fishnet stockings, a skirt that barely covered her ass, and a very tight, low cut black darted tank top that included tight corset style boning that did little to hide her large breasts. She simply said "Stage or table?"

"Table" I nodded and smiled at her like she was an object I could abuse at any moment. Once I was seated, she left with my drink order.

While she was getting my drink order filled, I looked around the room. The room was a large rectangle. On each end of the room there was a stage with at least one glitter and oil covered mostly naked woman dancing on it. In the center of the room was a square bar. Dotted throughout the room in no particular order were small, two and four person round tables. In the back corner, there was a DJ booth and a sectioned off area that was higher and partially hidden from the rest of the club: the lap dance area for VIP's. Cherry, again, strip clubs and the cherry mist. Made me want to hurl but again

Between the DJ booth and the stage, there was a door that said "VIP" on it. Standing in front of the door was a bouncer. I got my overpriced bottle of water ($4.00) and received all of my change in single dollar bills. I tipped the waitress and sat back and observed.

Occasionally, I would see a dancer and a man go through the VIP door. The guy was usually gone for approximately 30 minutes and then he would return to the main area. Other dancers were moving through the main room asking people of they wanted lap dances. I asked one tall topless deeply tanned dancer about the VIP room as she clomped past my table in extremely high platform Lucite heels with muti-colored blinking lights in the sole. She said there was a $100 minimum to go to the VIP room and six private rooms in the back. I asked her what the $100 got me and she winked and said if I wanted to know I would have to pay.

I didn't see any other doors in the club, other than the restrooms. I figured my targets office must be in the back, through the VIP room. So, strictly in the interest of scouting the area, I licked my lips, wiped my mouth with the back of my arm, paid the dancer $100 and went into the VIP room.

While we were walking to one of the private rooms, I saw another door that was different than the rest and was surprised to see that there was only one bouncer positioned in the hallway leading to the private rooms. He was sitting on a stool and looked bored reading a hunting magazine.

In the VIP room I was in, there was a small, leather loveseat that looked even in the dark dimly lit pink hued room like it had not been cleaned in a year, just filthy. I was told to sit there.

While we were waiting for the song to end, the dancer told me I had four lap dances coming from her. She said I could touch anything I wanted on her except her private area which she had no problem touching herself and showing me exactly what I couldn't have. However, she did say anything, everything was negotiable.

I sat through the four lap dances providing active responses to her so she would not think I was bored, though preoccupied, I was not bored. She was very beautiful woman in barely enough clothes to be legal, and I had already seen the rest of her show earlier.

Her hair bounced up and down her back and over her shoulder in milk chocolate and blonde streaked abundance with hot pink glittery extensions through the sides.

Her nose was not too big or pointed and her lips were full and painted with a glossy red that popped against her skin and the black lights. She moved her body like a snake around my lap, legs, and chest scraping my shirt with her long hot pink tipped nails decorated with sparkling jewels and flowers. She would look into my eyes with a deep hollow abandon that made me think she was knitting or washing her hair in her mind.

I didn't see a person in her gold flecked hazel eyes, or a soul, but a beautiful woman with curves exactly where a man's man would want them and a moan that when whispered directly in my ear with her lips so close I could almost feel them on the edge of the fine white peach fuzz length hairs around my neck nearly sent me over the edge to forgetting what I was here for.

She was very skilled at what she did. I would be lying if I said I did not enjoy my time in the VIP room. Unfortunately, I had to shake myself out of the fantasy spell the fourth song was trying to sprinkle on me; I was not here to enjoy myself. I was there to kill. I opted not to spend any more time or money in the VIP room when my four songs were done; I tipped the dancer very well, made a mental note of her name Delilah, and as she was getting dressed for her next visitor I headed straight for the door that didn't match the rest of the VIP rooms. As I was opening the door, I heard the bouncer call out to me. I was only able to catch a quick glimpse of a staircase heading up and one heading down.

"Sorry, I thought this was the way out. Is there a restroom back there?" I said with a big drunk looking wink.

"Naww man. No restroom. Only a few offices and the beer cooler downstairs in the basement. The restroom is across from the bar."

"Thanks."

I headed back out to the main area. Pretended like I was sidetracked from the bathroom by another half dressed woman covered in bubble gum scented body oil and went to the bar to order another bottle of water. As I sat at the bar, I watched as beer and liquor were sent up to the bar on a dumb-waiter style pulley system. Empty beer bottles were dropped into a PVC tube and sent down to the basement to be recycled.

This job was going to be a little harder than I had anticipated. There was one bouncer standing guard outside the VIP room door and one bouncer monitoring the action from inside the VIP room. The offices were up stairs and that was most likely where my target was. Normally, I would just kill the bouncer that was standing guard inside the VIP room's door and head up stairs and take out my target. I couldn't do that because I needed this target to disappear.

I clearly wasn't going to be able to take him in his club. I would have to get him coming or going. I left the strip club and walked back to my motel. I retrieved my vehicle and drove back to the convenience store. I parked in the shadows at the far end of the lot. I could see the entrance to the strip club and the parking lot. At around one thirty in the morning, the last of the customers stumbled out and left. After that, there was a parade of young women dressed in sweat suits being escorted by the bouncers to their various vehicles. Around two thirty in the morning, my target left the club. He was escorted to his vehicle, a big Pearl White Chevy Suburban, he got in alone and drove off.

I followed the Suburban for a few miles to see if there would be an opportunity for me to approach my target. The snow storm that was predicted all week was in full swing by now. The roads were icy and the snow was falling hard. My target pulled into a Denny's parking lot. I kept driving. I drove up the street and turned around and headed towards the Denny's. I pulled into the parking lot and I could see my target, sitting alone in a booth through the windows reading an early edition paper and drinking a coffee.

I cruised through the parking lot and looked for security cameras. I didn't find or expect any. I parked my vehicle right next to my target's Suburban and waited. From where I was sitting, I could see him eating his breakfast.

He ordered something with sausage because he sent it back twice. What an asshole, I thought to myself. I hoped the rest of what he ordered was something good; my stomach growled just smelling the iconic foods being cooked inside. I was thinking how ironic it would be if he was eating my personal favorite, moons-over-my-hammy, because this would be his last meal. When I saw him at the register paying for his food, I got out of my vehicle and hid behind the rear quarter panel of his precious Burb.

Because of the storm and the late hour, the parking lot was nearly empty and the streets were deserted. I heard him approaching. When he was between the two vehicles, but before he could open the Suburban's door, I was on him and I could see the defeat and fear in his eyes.

■■

Back at the Seneca Nation Casino in Niagara Falls, Mazzio, Ragulli and Jack Carlotti were having a miserable time. The casino was very busy. Everywhere you looked, people were either feeding money into slot machines or dropping money by the fistful on table games. The casino was doing a very brisk business this particular night and raking in a lot of money. All of which would not be shared with Carlotti.

"See Dom? This place is a cash fucking cow! I should be making 1% on all of this, and I'm not!" Carlotti was complaining loudly and nearing drunk again to Mazzio and Ragulli.

"I agree with you Jack, but Mr. DiFlippo decided to stay out of the casino business."

"Maybe he has enough money, but I don't. Being cut in on an operation like this would change my entire life. DiFlippo doesn't give a shit about me out here in the Falls. He doesn't care about all the money I can be making right now. The only time he ever calls anymore is if I am late on a payment or when it's a little light. I try to tell him it wouldn't be so light if we were in the casino business but he refuses to listen to reason."

"Well, as long as he's head of the family, it is *his* decision."

"Yeah well, the old fuck doesn't have much longer to live, from what I hear. It's only a matter of time."

"Hey Jack, you shouldn't talk like that about Mr. DiFlippo. It's not right you know."

"I know, but it's the truth. Rumors are on the street that his time is limited. I say good. I hope the next guy is more reasonable. I hope the next guy is interested in making money in this decade and not in the 1950's."

So far, Mazzio's plan was working perfectly. Mazzio knew if he could get Carlotti just a bit more drunk and bring him to the casino, he would start not just complaining about all the money he wasn't making but want to do something about it. Mazzio had received a text message from Sonny De Luca saying they were able to hide maps of floor plans and alarm codes of DiFlippo's house in Carlotti's apartment. Mazzio didn't think it would be hard to get Carlotti to continue to talk bad about DiFlippo. Every word he was saying was being recorded. Mazzio had no doubt that after DiFlippo heard the recording; he would be convinced that Carlotti was the traitor. Mazzio would soon be in the clear.

■■■

It was so cold out the amount of outerwear being worn by not only this big man but myself was making it hard to keep a hold of him. Once I grabbed him, I put the barrel of the gun I was carrying tight as I could against his ribcage. I wanted him to know that even though he was bigger than me, and very possibly stronger, all I had to do was pull a trigger and there would be moons-over-this-parking-lot. I told him all I wanted was information. If he was honest with me, I would drift silently back into the night and he would never see me again.

Luckily for me, he did what everyone does in this situation; he talked. "Look, Rick, I didn't know what was really going on, I mean, Mazzio, he is the one that did this, he wanted to have Sal taken down, I didn't know when I got in about you. I mean I was just told it was a target, I had no idea, have mercy on me Rick."

"Bear, Bear, Bear, oh you poor thing, that is not the truth and you would have to ask Lima and Angelo what I think about liars. Tell me the truth now. Confession is good for the soul."

"Look…" Berrazino went on and on about Mazzio and gave me his plan to have both Sal and I eliminated so he could take over as new Don. It was a pretty good plan, and I only saw two flaws in it. The first flaw I saw for Mazzio was an ace in the hole for Sal and I, Anthony Ragulli. Ragulli was the leak. He was the one that told someone else about the hit on Sal. That's what started the rumors that ultimately saved Sal's life.

If Ragulli would have kept his mouth shut, Sal would have no idea someone was trying to kill him and he would have been home, in bed, when Ragulli went to murder him. My mother always told me when I was a child that just because you think your secret is important, the person you are telling most likely will not feel the same way. Mazzio's and Ragulli's moms must have left that out of their child rearing plans.

The second flaw in his plan was his failed hit attempt on me. They gambled, bet their lives, and lost, that Berrazino's men would be able to take me out in Texas. I hate to admit it, but they came very close. It was now time to make payment.

I told Berrazino thank you, released my hold; put the gun back in my pocket. I instructed him to slowly pull out his cell phone and the keys to his vehicle. Once He did I told him to drop them on the ground. Once again he complied with my demands; this was going well. I told him thank you again, and to get into his vehicle and count to one hundred with his eyes shut before he got out of the vehicle and retrieved his cell phone and keys. He said he would count to two-hundred.

I opened his vehicle's door for him, patted him on the back, told him a lie about how he was a valuable member of the family and as he was stepping up into the vehicle, completely unaware, all hackles down, I grabbed him hard by the back of his jacket's collar and pulled him backwards. At the same instant, I swept his left foot from out beneath him. With his other leg in the vehicle, Berrazino had nowhere to go but down. The amount of force that I used to pull him off his feet caused him to land directly on the frozen black top of the parking lot, slamming the back of his head. His head cracked open on the frozen concrete; I could hear the ice melting from the loss of his 98.6 degree blood flowing freely out onto the ground.

I bent over him and checked for a pulse. I did not find one. Had I found one, I would have then suffocated Berrazino where he had fallen. I knew I was supposed to make him disappear, but that wasn't going to work. I was too short on time and didn't have the resources I needed. So I did the next best thing. I made Berrazino's death look like an accident.

When someone found his body, they would see that he was getting into his vehicle with his hands full of his keys and a cell phone and he slipped on the ice and cracked his head.

With a little luck, it would be ruled an accidental death and Berrazino's widow would eat well for the rest of her life, probably making a little money from suing Denny's for their negligence. I thought of this as I quickly covered up any tracks I left, glad the snow was coming down in buckets to help my trail disappear.

I got in my truck and started the long, treacherous drive back to Buffalo. Mazzio is a suspicious guy by nature and it would be better if I could take him out before he found out about his pal Berrazino. On my way back to Buffalo, I stopped at a pay phone and left a message for Sal.

"This message is for Mr. Boston. Mr. Boston, this is Mike from Fed Ex. There has been an accident with your package. Your package fell off one of our trucks and is damaged beyond repair. I know we were supposed to complete the delivery on this, but because of circumstances beyond our control we are not going to be able to. The damaged package will be left at our offices until we hear from you ready for pick up and inspection. I apologize again. Thank you."

I don't know why Sal liked me to leave him all the cryptic messages. Maybe it reminded him of the old days when wise guys couldn't talk freely on the telephones because of wire taps. Imagine what organizations like Sal's could have done if they had a guy like Geoff working for them back then? Maybe Sal just didn't completely trust technology either. In any event, it was one enjoyable part of my job when I left him the message his dentist appointment had changed or the florist needed to deliver his cookie bouquet.

CHAPTER #25

By the time I got back to Buffalo, it was close to six o'clock in the morning. I was supposed to meet Sal in his suite at the casino for brunch at 10:30 am. I made sure I wasn't being followed and I went back to my house. I showered, shaved and changed there.

I now had the complete version of the puzzle that I had been working on. Everything had slipped and fallen into place thanks to Bear. Once I met with Sal, I would have the green light to eliminate Mazzio. To me, killing people is just a job. It is never personal and I don't feel anything about it, one way or another. This time though, I was feeling some excitement. I would actually be killing someone I despised.

At 9:00 am, I left my house and headed to Niagara Falls. I hopped on the 190 and drove across Grand Island. I stayed on the 190 until I made the switch to the Robert Moses Parkway. This would take me along the upper Niagara River into downtown Niagara Falls. I made great time since the streets were newly plowed and traffic was non-existent. I was turning my car over to the valet by 10:00 am. I went into the casino and stopped in at the front desk. I had them buzz Sal's suite to let him know I had arrived. I was told to go right up.

Sal's suite was on the top floor at the end of the hallway. In addition to Carlo Bianchi, there was also one of the casino's armed security guards standing guard outside the suite's doors. I was instructed by Carlo to go right in, as if he would stop me.

I greeted Sal in the dining room area of the suite. After we exchanged pleasantries we got right down to business. He had a glass of fresh squeezed, ice cold orange juice waiting for me.

Sal said "After receiving your call last night, I waited until the body was discovered in Rochester. Once it was, I called Augostino. I told him he was a rat and I thought we had a deal. He didn't know what I was talking about. I told him about the police finding Berrazino in the Denny's parking lot. He swore to me he had nothing to do with it. He said he would call a captain in the Rochester Police Department and get back to me. When he got back to me, he said by all accounts, Berrazino's death was ruled accidental. Case closed. Augostino swears he had nothing to do with Berrazino dyeing. I told him I didn't like it because we didn't have a chance to question him. He apologized. We're in the clear. He doesn't suspect us one bit." With that he raised his glass in a solute and drank up.

"Very good. This works out better for us. I was able to get Berrazino to talk before his 'unfortunate accident'."

"I knew you would. However, I also have some news. This morning, I had a meeting with Mazzio." I nearly choked on my juice and slammed my glass down on the table next to me with a little more force than I had at first intended. "Don't look at me like that. I had him send Ragulli back to Buffalo and I had Carlo pat him down before I met with him. It was a safe meeting. Anyway, he tells me he knows who wants me dead. He tells me it's Jack Carlotti. I know I know, just as we first suggested, but Dom even has a tape recording of Carlotti saying he wishes I was dead and it won't be long until I am dead."

"Be that as it may Sal, according to Berrazino, Mazzio is the guy behind the hit on you and I."

"Really?" Sal didn't look or sound shocked.

"Come on Sal, are you surprised or did you just hope it wasn't true?"

"I guess I hoped not. The tape recording was good though. I did feel it was more convenient than convincing. Mazzio was trying to frame Carlotti. It would be easy to do with Carlotti being angry about my decision regarding the casinos." He set his glass down, pinched his eyes tight, frowned, and rubbed his hand back and forth across his forehead.

I explained to the top of Sal's head from where I sat everything I learned from Berrazino. How they wanted to eliminate me first and then him. How Mazzio was paying Berrazino a lot of money to make me disappear. How Mazzio was going to make it look like I killed Sal and then disappeared. He even said Mazzio was going to offer a two million dollar reward for my capture.

I could tell the things I was telling to Sal were upsetting him. It's hard to be in business with someone, especially the business they were in, without being friends with them. Especially if that friendship lasted close to twenty years.

Silence fell between us, Sal got up, went into his bathroom. I heard him start a shower that lasted a good thirty minutes before he finally came back, red crushed velvet robe and gold piped slippers to match meant he was done with this day, this event, this moment. I broke the silence after he got situated in his chair, gold Rolex watch peeking out over the arm of his robe, "So what do you want me to do?"

Immediate silence cut off only by the sound of the remaining ice cubes in his glass spinning in a circle around the square shaped vodka receptacle,

"Finish this. Go back to Buffalo. Eliminate Mazzio, Ragulli, Parrione, and De Luca."

"Carlotti?"

"Don't worry about Carlotti. I need to figure out who I want to put in place of Carlotti to run the Falls for me. Once I do that, I'll make a move against him. Carlotti is more talk than action, more brawn then brains. I have time until I need to take care of him."

"I will do it for you."

"I know you would, but no thank you. I sent you to Dallas to kill one person and it spiraled out of control. How many people have you killed from this one job?"

"A lot. I don't keep count. Either way, one more isn't a big deal."

"I know. After Mazzio and his people are gone, my main concern will be finding a replacement for them."

"You know Sal, I stay out of the operations part of your business, but, in this case, may I make a suggestion?"

"Please. I always respect the input of a friend."

"Have you ever considered Bramwell? He really went out of his way to help me in Dallas. If it weren't for him, I don't know what might have happened."

"Interesting choice. You know, I originally sent him out there to handle some real estate dealings I was having an issue with. He liked the area so much, he decided to stay. Then there was that problem with his business partner that you helped out with. Since then, he has gone pretty much legit. He owns several businesses and he is a good earner. His payments to me are always on time. Let me think about that. Thank you."

"No, thank you. Any ideas on how you want me to end this?"

"I don't care, just do what you do. We are running out of time. Even though Augostino wasn't suspicious of Berrazino's death, Mazzio will be. I think in this case, the direct approach is best. He will be at my house this evening. If he is there, you know Ragulli will be there as well. You know the compound better than anyone. Go there, tonight, and kill them. I will have a number for you to dial when it is over. When the person answers, tell them it is done. Then get out. A professional cleaner will come in after you and clean. After you have called the number, call me, directly. Will this work for you?"

"Yes."

"Godspeed my son."

"God has nothing to do with this. I'll call when it's done."

CHAPTER #26

I approached DiFlippo's compound on foot. I gained access to the grounds by climbing over the wall in the back half of his garden. I knew about the intricate alarm system and all of the sensors. Right before I climbed the wall, I remotely reset the system. The system would be temporarily taken off line as all the sensors and cameras reset. It is very similar to rebooting a computer. It takes about the same amount of time as well which for me was just enough time to get in, set up, and lie in wait.

While the system was resetting itself, I was up and over the wall. I planned on the system reset causing suspicion amongst Mazzio and his men. They could be suspicious all they wanted, the damage was done, I was inside and on the grounds. I knew where the motion sensors and cameras were set up and I easily avoided them as I approached the main house.

As far as plans go, it was a great one. I knew the area, I knew the people I would be facing, their strengths and weaknesses, and I knew where the sensors were that would set off an alarm and give them my location. I had alarm codes and keys to access every area I needed to.

So imagine my surprise as I was creeping through the garden towards the guest house when the roar of a shot gun blast ripped through the deep quiet night. I believe the shooter was De Luca. He was shooting at me from a considerable distance and he was using bird shot in a .20 gauge shot gun. Most of the searing hot pellets missed me, but several of them hit me on my left side and shoulder.

Through all my life, I had never been shot. I think about all of the missions I was a part of as a Ranger with the Army and all of the jobs I have completed over the years for different criminal organizations and it is shocking that I have never been shot. That fact changed tonight. After I was hit, I dropped to the ground and rolled a few times and came up in a military crouch next to a marble bench. I was in a lot of pain, I was having trouble breathing, and I couldn't find where the guy was that just shot me. For the first time in a lot of years, I, Rick Stevens, was afraid.

Was this the end?

What would it be like to move from this place to the next?

When I finally closed my eyes for good, would all of the people I killed be waiting to greet me?

Would my beautiful wife turn her head toward me in anger, sadness, joy, or indifference?

I shook my head a few times to clear those thoughts away. De Luca approached me from where he originally fired his weapon. At first I thought he was talking to himself, but then I noticed the blink of his blue-tooth ear piece. He was whispering that he shot me and saw me go down. He actually knelt on the ground where I originally fell. He was feeling the ground and looking for blood.

The last words De Luca said in this world were "I fucking hit him! I found blood!" After that, the .40 caliber slug from my H&K Pistol ripped through his head. I don't know who he was talking to, but I assumed it was Mazzio or Ragulli. Either way, they would now know I was injured and that made things a bit more complicated.

I left the area of the garden I was in and retreated to an old gardeners shed in the back near the fence line. I did a quick damage assessment of myself. My shoulder felt like it was on fire and I was bleeding from at least two holes that I could find. I was having trouble breathing and my ribs on my left side felt like they were broken. I could feel dampness on my shirt and I assumed it was blood.

I reached into the side pocket of my pack and I pulled out a package of quick-clot. I had at least four bullet holes and only three packages of quick-clot. I packed my wounds as best I could. I have never experienced pain like shoving an expandable sponge into a bullet hole on my own body. I almost passed out from the pain that seared through my shoulder as if someone was holding it to a patio grill. This was supposed to slow and/or stop the flow of blood from bullet wounds. I remembered when I purchased it hoping I would never have to use this. I took a few deep breaths and prepared myself to move. Not only was I having trouble breathing, but I was also sweating profusely. I took a few more deep breaths and calmed my mind down. It wasn't time to think or plan. It was time to rely on my training and experience. It was now a game of cat & mouse. Mazzio and his people knew I was here to kill them and I knew they were waiting for me.

■ ■

"Hey Dom, Sonny hit him with the shot gun!"

"Is he dead?"

"Not sure yet. Sonny is going to check it out. He said he saw him creeping by and he fired on him. He said he saw him fall. He is checking it out right now. What have you got Sonny?"

It had been a long few days for Mazzio. Everything he had worked for his entire life was falling down around him. After his am meeting with DiFlippo, Mazzio felt better. He felt like he had gained the old man's trust back and everything would return back to normal. He knew the old man believed him and his frame up job on Carlotti.

It had been a great day until he found out that Berrazino had slipped on some ice and broke his neck. Slipped on some ice my big white suburban ass, he thought. That was just how Steven's operated. He could murder just about anyone and make it look like it was a natural event. Maybe the police had been fooled but he hadn't. He knew Stevens would come for him tonight. So he was lying in wait, totally prepared.

He had Ragulli, Parrione and Carlotti in the house with him. He had De Luca and two other guys from Carlotti's crew outside the house. He told everyone, if they lived through the night, they would be promoted and given a huge bonus. It was winner take all and it appeared that they had scored the first by hitting Stevens. Mazzio was starting to feel confident until he heard Ragulli say "Aww shit."

"What-happened…Anthony? HEY! Answer me when I talk to you."

"Sorry boss, was talking to Sonny when I heard a gunshot. Now Sonny ain't answering me."

"He missed Stevens?"

"No, Sonny said he found blood on the ground, so Stevens is hit. He's injured. But it sounds like Steven's shot and killed Sonny. I got one of Carlotti's guys going over there to check it out. I'll know in a minute or so."

Well, Mazzio knew he was going to lose some people tonight. He was hoping the soldier's he had outside would be able to stop Stevens before he came inside. Mazzio would never admit it, but he was seriously afraid of Stevens. Even thinking that thought to him was enough to make him embarrassed and ashamed. At first he was happy that Stevens was wounded, but now, he wasn't so sure. The only thing in the world more dangerous than a grizzly bear protecting her young was an injured grizzly bear protecting her young. Mazzio was hoping the same wasn't true for Stevens, but suspected it was.

■ ■

I had to reevaluate my enemy. I hadn't given them enough credit, and they caught me by surprise.

I didn't want that to happen again. The throbbing screaming pain in my ribs and shoulder wouldn't let me forget my mistake.

I figured they would have two teams of people. One team would be outside the house and the other team would be inside the house. If I was in charge of protection, I would have two people patrolling the grounds and one person set up on the back of the house and one person set up on the front of the house. I would have the people set up on the house in sniper style blinds with high powered rifles. If anyone was able to get by the roving patrols, as soon as they got to the house, the snipers would be able to eliminate them.

So before I could approach the house, I had to identify and scout out what would be the best sniper locations, while I avoided the patrols. Even though I was injured and in pain, I still considered myself to have the advantage. The people I was facing didn't have the experience I did. They were men from the streets and lacked any experience in jungle warfare. I was in Ranger mode.

As I made my way cautiously towards the house, I came across another person. He was sitting on a bench in the garden, smoking. At first, I just observed the situation. I thought it was a trap. There was no way someone would be dumb enough to just sit, out in the open on a bench, and smoke. This wouldn't be effective against any adversary, especially me. Once I was fairly certain this was not some sort of set up, I quietly crept up behind him. I grabbed him from behind and drove the blade of my knife into his throat. He was dead before he hit the ground. He never got a chance to utter any meaningless last words. I moved on.

There were no snipers lying in wait. I was surprised and slightly disappointed. Mazzio knew what I was capable of and this was the best that he had to stop me? Just two guys outside? I knew he would have more people in the house, but I wasn't sure how many. It wouldn't matter. I had wanted to get at Mazzio for a long time now. I finally had the green light to do it. Nothing, not even being shot, was going to stop me.

■■■

"Hey. Anthony, you getting any responses from any of our guys outside?"

"Sorry Dom, no one is answering shit. Bones told me to hang on and I haven't heard back from him yet. I don't know what it could be. You think Stevens got them?"

"Yeah, he got them. Shit! I knew we shoulda' had more men."

Ragulli still didn't understand what he was seeing. He couldn't fathom why Mazzio was so afraid of Stevens. Sure he killed a lot of people, but so had Ragulli.

"Dom, we don't need more men. I told you, I can take care of him. You'll see."

"An-t-ony, shut the hell up! Is the alarm set? We have all the interior motion detectors set?"

"It's all set. I told you, I had a guy I know from North Tonawanda come in and set it up so it looks like the system is off line. When he gets in the house, he'll check the alarm panel or try to disable it. He'll see it isn't set and get confident. I have a wireless flat screen monitor here where I can track his movement through the house. We'll know exactly where he is. We'll know which way he is coming so Jack and I can set a trap to kill him. Have no fear Dom. I told you I could handle this."

For the first time all day, Mazzio felt a little better. He felt like they had finally outsmarted Stevens and had the upper hand. He started to feel his confidence returning. All was not lost. He could still eliminate Stevens and then send everything he had left to kill DiFlippo. With Stevens and DiFlippo out of the picture, he would be Don. Don Dominick Mazzio! He started to feel a small smile tug at the corner of his mouth. He kept his smile in full swing with arms reaching for a glass of whiskey when all of the lights on the entire estate went out.

■■

While I was planning my little trip this evening, I called Geoff and asked for help. I told him what I wanted to do. For the first time since I have met him, he told me it was impossible. I asked him if he could hack into Niagara Mohawks computer system to shut down the power on DiFlippo's estate. He said he couldn't specifically target one house or another. While I was shocked he couldn't help me, I thanked him anyway. Before I could hang up, he said "You know Rick, I can't target a specific house but I can target a specific grid."

"Geoff, I don't know what you mean by grid?"

"It's really very simple. The city is laid out in grids. A grid can be a block or a neighborhood. Are you with me so far?"

"I'm with you. Keep going"

"Say a transformer blows or a car drives into a power pole and cuts the line. The good folks at Mohawk will have to come out and repair the damage, right?"

"Right."

"They have to cut the power to the grid so they can repair the damage. You understand now?"

"Actually Geoff," I said now with condescension in my voice, "I don't. Forgive my irritation, but I am just about out of time here and frankly you are pissing me off."

"Wait, listen to me. Say you're going to repair an electrical outlet in your house. What is the first thing you do?"

"I go to the breaker box, kill the power."

"Exactly! If someone is going to repair a downed line or something, the first thing they do is cut power to the grid. Guess how all of the grids are controlled?"

"You're a genius. They're controlled with a computer, and if they're controlled with a computer, you can get into it."

"I will give you a phone number. When you want me to cut the power to the grid, send me a message. I will only be able to cut power for a few minutes, say, five or six minutes, max. By then, people in the neighborhood will be calling and complaining and people at Niagara Mohawk will take notice. They'll investigate why the grid is out and fix the problem. Once the problem is fixed, they will run a security scan to see what likely turned the grid off. They'll know right away it was a computer attack against them. They will essentially slam the back door closed I used to gain entrance into their system and change the pass code to get into their system. I can re-crack the code, but it will take time. It could be a few minutes, or it could be a few hours. All I can guarantee you is five or six minutes. Will that be enough time?"

"It will have to be. Thanks ."

So with the power off, I unlocked the back door and entered the house. I wasn't worried about the alarm system. Even though the system had a satellite back up battery, Geoff said he would make sure the company monitoring the house would never get an alarm signal. He would make sure of it.

The house was one big shadow. I had the advantage because I already had my night vision from being outside in the darkness. The people in the house would be temporarily blinded. I kept a silent count in my head. I had five minutes, just 300 seconds.

I moved as silently as a ghost. I knew my way around the house and could walk from end to end blind-folded and not run into anything. If I were in the house facing an adversary like me, I would have rearranged the furniture and left some empty cans or bottles in the middle of the walkways. But the people I was going against were not me, nor would they ever be me, and hopefully not kill me.

I was quickly clearing the first floor of the house when the beam of a flashlight cut through the darkness. Someone was walking down the stairs holding a flashlight and swinging the beam from side to side. Once again I thought that this was too easy. I waited in an alcove at the bottom of the stairs, my knife blade ready.

■■■

"What the hell happened to the lights Anthony?"

"I don't know Dom. They just went out all of a sudden."

"No shit! I am standing here in the same room! I can see that! Stevens cut the power. You still have him on your computer? You still able to see where he is?"

"Umm, no Dom. The power to the alarm system is dead. My screen is blank."

"Ok, he's obviously making his way here to kill us; Jack, head down stairs and see if you can find him. Anthony, wait at the top of the stairs and cover Jack. I'll wait here."

■■

I waited until the beam of the flashlight was facing away and I started to quietly stalk my target. Timing would be critical. I would need to remain silent. As long as the power stayed off, I could sneak in behind him and eliminate him.

As I was about to strike, I heard a noise from the top of the stairs. It sounded like someone stepped on a creaky floor board. Here I was, trapped in between two people that wanted to kill me. I stood still and put my knife away. I slipped out two pistols.

It was all about timing now. I raised both pistols at the same time. Using my right hand, my dominate hand; I aimed at the man that was a few feet away from me. I wanted to make sure I took him out because he was closer to me and more of an immediate threat. I raised my left hand towards the top of the stairs. I thought with a little luck I might be able to take both of my targets out at once.

I was wrong.

■■■

Dominick Mazzio waited patiently in the dark for his own death. He still had a few guys left but he was a realist; they were no match for Stevens. He had gambled and failed and now it was time to pay. He didn't want to die alone. He wanted to take Stevens with him.

So he continued to sit with his hands wrapped around his weapon in the darkness, waiting for the moment when air would exit his lungs and thought would leave his brain.

■■

I was truly passed the point of no return. I was committed to my actions. I couldn't stop what I was in the process of doing. Which was a shame, because a second after I started raising both of my arms to shoot my targets, I realized just how badly injured I really was.

My right arm did exactly what I wanted it to do: it rose to shoulder level and shot and killed my target. My left arm failed to make it farther than the middle of my chest. My shoulder and ribs were screaming in pain as I pulled the trigger. My timing was off, my aim was off, and I didn't even come close to hitting my target. All I did was give my location away to my enemy who had the higher ground.

Fortunately for me, his aim was about as good as mine was and when he fired off three rounds, I was already on the move and out of the way. I hit the ground and rolled back towards the stairs to cut off his angle. I came up in a crouch with my gun in front of me and fired my remaining rounds at where I thought my target was.

"Nice shooting Stevens. You hit the Picasso and ruined it." Ragulli taunted me. Then I heard him say, "Stevens in da house". He must have been telling Mazzio where I was. I didn't see Ragulli's hand extend over the railing until he started firing rounds down on me.

He missed, but it was a little too close for comfort. I retreated into the hallway and then further into the house. I had a decision to make. I could head towards the back of the house and attempt to get upstairs using the staff's staircase or I could wait and try to go up the stair case Ragulli was protecting.

While I was pondering my decision, the lights came back on. My time was up. I stopped in the back kitchen and got a drink of water. I was still bleeding from the left side of my body and knew I had to wrap this up quickly.

If I lost too much blood, I would be weak and possibly pass out. I started to head back towards the front staircase where I had last seen Ragulli.

■■

When the lights came back on, Ragulli made his way back to where Mazzio was hiding. He was on his hands-free device for his phone so Mazzio knew he was approaching. Once he was back in the room, Ragulli picked up the computer and restarted his program that was hooked into the houses alarm system. Using the motion detectors in the house, Ragulli was able to track Stevens' movements. He saw Stevens approach the staircase where they had their shoot out. Ragulli knew which way Stevens was coming. He also knew where he was going to set his trap.

■■

I hated the idea of walking up the staircase in the light. My plan had been to breech the second floor of the house while it was still covered in darkness. I thought about going through the house and shutting down all the circuits at the breaker box. The box was located in the basement and that was a far distance from where I was. If I made it to the basement and was able to once again shut the power down again, I wondered if I would have enough energy to finish my task. Would I lose too much blood and be too weak? I closed my eyes, took a deep breath and headed towards the stairs. It was time to finish this.

Going up stairs was harder than I expected. I was really losing a lot of blood and having issues breathing. I kept my right hand extended in front of me the entire time. If anything moved up there, I was going to shoot it. Since the railing was on the right hand side, I couldn't use it going up. I had to lean on the wall on my injured left side.

I made it to the top without incident. In front of me stood a small landing that lead into a loft area and a hallway that had three doors on each side. At the other end of the hallway was the back staircase.

I was kind of hoping someone would come out of one of those doors so I wouldn't have to check every room. I didn't have the luxury of being patient and waiting for them to come to me.

I was already starting to feel weak and a little light headed. I didn't think I could check all of the rooms. I would easily give my position away. If my enemies were in the third room, they would know when I was in the second room clearing it. They would have a chance to prepare for me. I had to make things happen. If I were to survive, I would need to surprise them.

I had a one in six chance of guessing correctly which room Mazzio was in calculating to roughly, a 16% chance of being right. Assuming of course, there weren't armed people in all of the rooms. At this point, I was betting Mazzio and Ragulli were holed up in one room waiting for me.

Which room to pick? Ok, first, the second room on the right is a bathroom. I eliminated that room. Who would want to wait in the bathroom to die? Down to five rooms, or a 20% chance of choosing correctly. One room was an exercise room. This contained a treadmill, an EFX Machine, a few weight benches and some free weights. It's a possibly hiding place, but not probable. I eliminated it. Down to four rooms, or a 25% chance of guessing right, assuming I wasn't already wrong. The last room on the left was Mazzio's office. He would be most comfortable in there, but that is where I would expect him to be and he would know this, so I didn't think he would hide in there. Down to three rooms now and up to a 33% chance of guessing right. Two rooms were spare bedrooms. One had a master bathroom attached and the other had a walk-in closet. The third and final room was used as a laundry room and storage area. DiFlippo's estate had several laundry rooms strategically placed so the staff wouldn't have to carry dirty laundry from one end of the house to the other. Any of these rooms could be Mazzio's hiding place.

If it were me, I would use the spare bedroom with the walk-in closet. My fallback position would be the closet. There would be no escape or surrender from that room or position. I eliminated that room. Mazzio was, at heart, a coward. He wouldn't put himself in a position where he wouldn't have a chance to retreat.

The laundry room and storage room was the first room on the right. I didn't think anyone would hide in the first room. They would give up their tactical advantage by hiding in the first room. By using another room, they would be able to gauge my progress of where I was in the hallway. Clearing a house is always done the same way: you clear each room as you come to it. They wouldn't hide in the first room I was supposed to clear. I eliminated the first room. That left the second spare bedroom with the master bathroom attached.

It was the last room on the right. It was the second closest room to the back staircase. This would give Mazzio a chance to retreat down the staircase if he had the opportunity. It would also be the second room I would go into, assuming I came up the back staircase and was clearing the rooms as I came to them. That was the room Mazzio was hiding in, I could feel it.

I quietly crept down the hall, trailing blood with every step I took. When I got to the door, I figured Mazzio would have a gun trained on it. I knelt down on the outside of the door frame and opened the door inward into the room.

Almost immediately shots rang out from the room and hit the door and forced it closed. Someone was in the room and by the sound of it, had a high powered shot gun with them. Because of this, the door was in shambles, and I could see into the room through the holes in the door.

As I was about to send some of my own rounds through the door, I heard a noise from the front staircase. With my attention temporarily distracted, whoever was in the room sent another shot through the door. I closed my eyes to protect them from the wood splinters that were soaring through the air. When I opened them, I saw Ragulli coming up the front staircase with a pistol in front of him. He must have went down the back staircase and came through the house so he could come up behind me. He was firing at me as he was running up the stairs so he missed me. If he was trained like me, he would have known that it was nearly impossible to hit a target with a pistol while you were running up the stairs. All he had to do was stop, aim, and shoot, and it would have been game over for me.

I was already crouched by the door so I fired a few rounds of my own at Ragulli. One of my rounds hit Ragulli in his shoulder and he dropped his gun and fell to the floor near the top of the stairs. He was down, but I knew he wasn't out.

Ragulli was slowly rolling around on the floor in pain. I hate to shoot a man when he is down, but I hate Ragulli more, so I took careful aim and fired two rounds into the top of his head. Now he was down and definitely out.

"Did you get him Anthony?" Mazzio said from inside the room.

"Nope he missed. Ragulli's dead. You're next."

"We'll see kid. Come through that door and we'll see. You're alone here and wounded. I have time on my side. I have a few people that are loyal to me coming as reinforcements. I can wait longer than you can kiddo. I can out last you."

Mazzio was right. He could out last me. Now that I was kneeling down, I thought it would be almost impossible to stand up again. My legs felt like led. I couldn't catch my breath and my vision was starting to blur. I had hoped he was lying about reinforcements coming.

"Come on kid, don't you have anything shitty to say"?

I looked through the bullet ridden door, but I couldn't see Mazzio. He was off to one side of the room guarding the door. The door wouldn't remain closed due to the damage it had from Mazzio's shots. I nudged the door open a few more inches and then I lay down on the floor and extended my gun. All I would need was Mazzio to show himself before I passed out. I concentrated on getting my breathing under control.

As I was lying there waiting for Mazzio to show himself, I heard someone walk up the back stairs behind me. Before I could react, I heard "Hey Dom, you got him? Holy shit, is he really dead"?

Before Mazzio could answer him, he stepped over my prone body and walked through the door into the room Mazzio was in. Using the last of my energy, I crawled in quietly behind him, using him as a shield.

"What do you mean dead Jimmy? SHIT!" Mazzio said with a surprised expression on his face. Then he saw me come in behind Jimmy "Bones" Scagliani but it was too late. The first three shots hit Mazzio in the center of his chest. He dropped the shot gun he was using as he fell back to the floor. As Bones was turning and trying to raise his weapon, I fired the rest of my ammo into him. He also fell to the floor dead.

I didn't know it at the time, but Bones was one of the guys that were on patrol outside the house. We must have missed each other while I was out there. That would explain why Ragulli announced that I was "in da house". He wasn't talking to Mazzio like I thought. He was on his phone with the wireless earpiece talking to Bones who was the only one left alive outside.

I wasn't sure if there was anyone else left. So I reloaded my gun and made my way out of the room. I was very weak and light headed. I concentrated on breathing. I went down the back staircase and out the backdoor. I was in the garden again. I made my way to the gardeners shed in the back. I went into the shed and lay down. I was really hurting at this point and was barely conscious.

I dialed the number DiFlippo gave me and told whomever answered the phone that it was done. I hung up and then dialed DiFlippo.

"Sal, Rick. It's. Done."

"Are you in trouble? You sound hurt."

"Weak. Was shot. Blood. Shed gardeners use."

"Hang on Rick, I am sending someone to help you"

Before I could answer.......darkness.

Epilogue

While bleeding to death in the gardener's shed, a very nondescript moving van arrived at DiFlippo's estate. After they entered the property, the gate was closed and locked. Four average looking men exited the vehicle and went inside the house. While the bodies were being removed, the bullet holes being repaired and the bloody carpets were being replaced, I stayed in a state of suspended animation. I wasn't completely passed out the entire time, but I wasn't awake either. I had visions or dreams. I saw things that weren't really there.

She walked around me with flowers woven into the pink satin ribbons that adorned her freshly painted toes and henna decorated feet. Designs inspired by another part of the world adorned her light skin and the scent of morning dew and lilac wafted to my nose. I saw her feet leap with every beat of my heart; I started to hear a giggle, then opened my eyes to the darkness that was the shed. In and out I would go never seeing the look, the face, or feeling closeness to death like that before. I had no idea if I was dreaming again, or having an out of body experience. I tried to bring her back, instead I saw Delilah with red fiery hair clawing her way toward me, fangs dripping with blood hearing the trademark laugh from Mazzio in the background....dark, cold, shed, I heard the sound of industrial truck brakes in the distance and a white light blew up from behind my eyelids.

A second nondescript moving van arrived with four more average looking people. They were there to assist the first crew. The second moving van wasn't alone. A truck with a box cap on the back also arrived. This truck drove through the property to the back yard nearly grinding the gears over the slippery recently frozen ground with little regard for the plants and shrubs it was destroying. It stopped outside the gardeners shed before me, headlights pointed directly at my face. Two people jumped out of the back of the truck and ran to me.

They half carried, half dragged me to the truck. The driver got out and helped the other two guys lift me into the back. Once I was in the back, my clothing was cut away from my body and I was placed on a gurney. Both guys immediately went to work on me. One of them focused on patching bullet holes and stopping the bleeding while the other one hooked me up to an IV.

The driver jumped immediately back into the front of the truck and left DiFlippo's estate as quickly as they had arrived. During all this, I was in that half-awake, half dream like state. Huge brilliant creatures hovered over me; they seemed to be talking either to me or about me. I couldn't hear them. I couldn't understand what they were saying. I thought maybe I saw my wife behind them but I wasn't sure, all I could hear was male voices and giggling.

■■■

I awoke to a white room, the sound of the Wheel of Fortune on in the background, and sitting next to my bed, reading a book, was Sal.

"Where, where am I?" I croaked out. My lips were cracked and my throat was dry. Sal held a glass of water with a straw in it so I could try to drink from it. Just the small movement it took me to lean forward to drink from the glass exhausted me.

"Rest. You're safe. You're in my house. I had you moved from the doctors' office to here. I always knew financing that kids business would pay off for me."

Over the next hour, as I came in and out of consciousness, Sal explained that the people that took me from the shed were licensed paramedics that in addition to working for an ambulance company, they also did 'favors' on the side for Sal.

After picking me up they transported me directly to the doctors' office that Sal paid for. The doctor was waiting there for me and performed surgery to remove the pellets from the shot gun. The doctor didn't have an operating room in his office, but he made due with what he had. After the surgery, they pumped me full of antibiotics and by the middle of the next day; I was transported to Sal's house. The room I was in looked like a room you would see at your local emergency room. It had a hospital bed, a bunch of medical machines and equipment. I was still attached to the IV. Sal said his private doctor was staying in the room right next to mine and he would personally monitor my progress.

A few days went by and the IV was removed. Eventually, all of the medical equipment disappeared and the doctor went along with it. I still felt weak and sore, but it was time for me to go as well. Sal knew I was getting restless, but ever the gracious host, he invited me to stay as long as I needed to.

"Thanks old friend, but I think it is time for me to be going."

"I can't thank you enough for all you have done for me."

"No need to thank me Sal. You're the one that saved my life."

"You saved mine as well. Are you sure you're able to leave? You still have some healing to do."

"I'm sure. I can heal myself just as well at home or at a five star hotel on the beach somewhere as I can here."

"What about mental healing? You have been through a lot in the last three weeks."

"I'm fine, or at least I will be once I feel sand beneath my feet. How is business Sal? Is it secure? Have the threats been eliminated?"

"My business is safe because of your help. There was only one other person left in Carlotti's crew that was loyal to him. However, he is no longer with us, so there is no need to worry. I took your advice and brought Bramwell in from Texas. He is proving to be a great asset. He has been running things lately and he is doing a great job. I am moving people around and promoting from within. The people I have left are still loyal to me."

"That's great news. What are you going to do about the Westsiders and the Camarillo's?"

"Right now there is an uneasy truce between the two sides. Neither one wants to go to war right now. Everyone is still making money and no one wants to risk that by going to war. Augostino met with Gillespie and made some sort of arrangement. The more time goes by, the less likely there will be a war."

"Are you comfortable with Augostino?"

"For now I am. I believe that Berrazino was running an operation behind his back and he had no knowledge of it. I'll keep a close eye on the situation and see if anything develops. If need be, I will go to the commission for advice or I can always set something in motion that will enrage the Westsiders enough to forget their truce with the Camarillo's and go to war."

"See Sal? You have everything locked down here. I am not needed. I'm going to go. We'll be in touch."

"Before you go, nobody knows you were injured. I kept it a secret. There are rumors out there that you eliminated Mazzio and 12-15 of his soldiers. Your reputation grows."

"Tis good, good for business. Potential clients will hear that and not want to negotiate my fees."

"Maybe, but maybe it's bad too."

"How could that be bad?"

"Maybe I should address the rumors as rubbish and say that even though you eliminated Mazzio, you yourself were also killed."

"How can that be good, for anyone? I would be out of business..."

"Exactly. You could go anywhere in the world you wanted and leave this behind. You could heal, mentally, physically, spiritually. This is your chance to walk away, to get out."

"Thanks, but no thanks. We've had this conversation before Sal. You know how I feel. I'll retire when you retire." With that, Sal gave me a small smile and we embraced with the half of my body I could still use.

■■■

After leaving Sal's estate, I went back to my house in Buffalo, showered, changed and packed a bag. This time, I disappeared for three weeks. I spent the entire time on a beach in South America.

During that time, I gained my strength back. I ate wonderful rich hearty meals, drank strong bourbon, and read several soul deepening books including the Bible. The day before I left, I checked my e-mail for the first time. I had two messages.

The first message was from Sal. He said Bramwell was asking about me. He said he had work for me in Texas when I was ready for it.

The second message was from my old friend in North Carolina, Bill Jenkins. Jenkins said he hadn't heard from me in a while and was wondering how I was doing. He said his offer still stood for me to come out to North Carolina to visit and stay with him.

Once again, I was at a crossroads in my life. It was almost like I was being given a second chance. There were too many questions surrounding it though.

Was it God giving me a second chance or was it just a coincidence?

Maybe it was a chance at redemption?

Maybe it was time to mend some old fences?

Was it finally time to forgive and move forward?

Was I holding onto my grudge because I was still angry and blamed God for taking my family?

Was it because I was afraid of God and ashamed of the actions I took?

Was it possible to go to confession and be absolved of all the evil, horrible things I have done?

Just how many Hail Mary's and Our Fathers would I have to say for my penance? Was I actually sorry for the things that I was responsible for?

It had been a long time since I felt like I was a part of the "normal" world and belonged in it...

Was that my fault or Gods?

Another crossroad....

Forget the past and attempt to find my final peace or continue down the road I was already so deeply vested? Maybe I would finally find the truth I created in the justice I served. I had to make a snap decision. Silence passed in the universe around me as if time had stopped. I nodded my head in acceptance of my choice knowing the consequences may never fully envelope me in this life time. I tapped out a quick e-mail, packed my bags and booked a flight. When the flight attendant announced prime boarding pass members, I walked solemnly and with courage to my assigned seat. I had boarded the flight to my next destination. For me it would always be a fight between what I know to be true and what I think really happens when justice is served. Taxiing down the runway to the rest of my days, I could see her dancing, silently smiling back at me in the shadow of what is my reality.

ACKNOWLEDGMENTS

I have to take a moment and thank the people that helped me take the idea of this book to a finished product. First, I have to thank my generous wife for allowing me the time and support while I chase down this dream. Thanks for reading the proof copy cover to cover and highlighting what needed to be fixed. Thanks for listening and not questioning my sanity when I was researching things like "The psychology behind human torture". I am very fortunate to have you in my corner.

I want to thank Dustin Elmore for all of his Saturday morning advice, encouragement and help during the crucial early stages of this book. I want to thank Acacia Stinnett for taking the time, while in the middle of starting her own law firm, to proof read and make corrections to the almost-final draft. I also have to say thank you to Tonya Holcomb for spending half a Saturday with me and taking numerous photos and for setting the shot that was used on the back cover of this book.

I also want to thank Danah Redmond for doing an excellent job of editing the final draft. Any mistakes and I am sure there are some, are mine and mine alone. I don't know how you found the time to edit my work, while starting a new job out of state, while raising a family and moving all at the same time. Saying 'thank you' to someone that has helped me fulfill a lifelong dream just doesn't seem adequate. I appreciate your help more than you will ever know. I couldn't have done this without you. Everyone, all of your help has meant more than words can express. Thank you.

Lastly, I have to thank you, the reader. I know how hard you work for your money and I know how fortunate I am that you decided to spend some of it on my first novel. I hope you enjoyed the story and my writing style. I know not everyone will, and that's okay. Maybe you'll enjoy the second one. From the bottom of my heart, I sincerely say THANK YOU!

ABOUT THE AUTHOR

Mark D. DiRienzo was born and raised in Niagara Falls, NY. Shortly after his 22nd birthday, he moved to Las Vegas, Nevada. During his eight years in Las Vegas, he embarked on many adventures and worked in many industries, specializing in security/law enforcement/investigations and corrections. He had the opportunity to travel the entire Western United States of America for work.

In his free time, he enjoys spending time with his family and friends, traveling, cooking and anything that has to do with being on or around the water or coast.

He now lives in Northwest Arkansas with his wife Jeanette and son Jackson. The three of them share a house with a very spoiled Pembroke Welsh Corgi named Columbo. He is currently working on his next novel.

If you would like to contact him please do. You can visit him on Facebook at Mark D. DiRienzo-Books. He maintains his own Facebook page and responds to all messages. If you want to e-mail him directly, please do so at: Markdirienzo@ymail.com. He can also be found on Amazon.com or his own e-store at: www.createspace.com/3626400